NEVER TEASE A SIAMESE

Also by Edie Claire
in Large Print:

Never Buried
Never Preach Past Noon

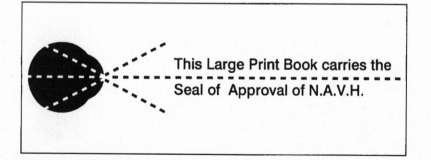

This Large Print Book carries the
Seal of Approval of N.A.V.H.

NEVER TEASE A SIAMESE

Edie Claire

Thorndike Press • Waterville, Maine

Published in 2003 by arrangement with NAL Signet, a member of Penguin Putnam Inc.

Thorndike Press Large Print Paperback Series.

The tree indicium is a trademark of Thorndike Press.

The text of this Large Print edition is unabridged. Other aspects of the book may vary from the original edition.

Set in 16 pt. Plantin by Al Chase.

Printed in the United States on permanent paper.

ISBN 0-7862-4980-3 (lg. print : sc : alk. paper)

For the people of the North Boros
— past and present.

(Note to longtime Avaloners:
Pay close attention,
and you might solve the mystery
before anyone else!)

ACKNOWLEDGMENTS

Special thanks go to John F. Waldron, whose knowledge of "Old Avalon" was indispensable in the plotting of this book. And as always, I thank those unfortunate individuals whom I routinely pester with police procedural and legal questions: Siri and Joe Jeffreys, Scott Robinette, and Gregg Otto. Lastly, I would like to thank any reader who has ever taken the time to send me an e-mail. Your encouragement means more than I can say.

Prologue

Bertha McClintock let out an exasperated groan as she sank her stout, sixty-three-year-old body into the generously padded, oversize plane seat she had lined up below her. "Thank *God* we're not flying commercial," she drawled, every syllable laden with practiced superiority. "If Richard's company didn't own its own jet, I don't know *how* I could stand it."

The slim, artificially blond woman of similar age who had slipped into the seat next to her offered a Mona Lisa smile and a nod. But Lilah Murchison only appeared to be listening. She had long since mastered the art of tuning out her old school chum — their historic biannual visits could not be conducted otherwise. And her friendship with Bertha, her most stimulating rival in the I'm-a-richer-widow-than-you-are game, had to be maintained. There simply wasn't anything, besides a good, down-and-dirty cat show, that gave Lilah more pleasure. Not to mention the fact that with Bertha came unlimited charter flights and free lodgings in New York City, perks like nectar to her miserly ways.

Still, Lilah did have her limits. Just a few moments before in the limousine, she had come dangerously close to smashing in her hostess's skull with a bottle of Merlot.

Bertha groaned again. "At least maybe we'll have a *quiet* flight this time. I can't believe that cat of yours is actually keeping her yap shut. What did you do? Give her some catnip or something? I used to give my Napoleon infant Benadryl — he slept like a lamb."

Lilah smirked, remembering the night she'd sat up until 2:00 a.m. with Bertha and her late pug in a smallish Las Vegas hotel suite, poking them alternately with a hairbrush until they rolled onto their stomachs.

"Did you say something, dear?" Bertha asked loudly.

Lilah didn't respond. She gazed worriedly into the cat carrier she had just placed at her feet and bent down to open it. "There, there, Mrs. Wiggs," she whispered softly, lifting out the gaunt Siamese and cradling it in her arms. The aging queen didn't seem herself today. "What's wrong? You always like to fly."

Bertha humphed. "She didn't like flying to San Juan."

Lilah's eyes narrowed. "We were flying over the ocean. You know cats don't like water. Besides, she's twenty-one years old. She's entitled to a few idiosyncrasies."

Bertha humphed again, one of her better ones. Bertha wasn't good at much, but she could humph with the best of them. She shifted her large frame restlessly in the seat. "Well, I certainly wish we'd get going. Where is that pilot? I've about had it with him. Always running late. The copilot is much more reliable, even if he is a foreigner. I shall have to speak with Richard."

Lilah held the unusually languid Siamese to her chest and watched as tiny beads of water began rolling furiously across the small plane window. She wished, for the hundredth time in the last thirty-six hours, that the unbelievably tedious Mr. Richard would make haste over the River Styx. Living husbands were such a trial, particularly when one had to hear about them. "There's a storm," she said quietly. "Mrs. Wiggs never has liked storms."

Bertha waved off the elements with a brush of her pudgy, jewel-laden hand. "I've flown in worse. We'll be above it all soon enough, provided that wretched pilot ever shows up . . ."

Ignoring her hostess once more, Lilah stroked the slender Siamese, and noted that her coat wasn't slipping over her prominent

9

bones quite as smoothly as it should. She pulled up a tiny lip to reveal dry, very pale pink gums.

A crack of thunder shook the air outside the plane, and Lilah's heart gave a thump.

Something was wrong.

Very wrong.

Three hundred miles to the west, a flash of lightning briefly illuminated a young woman rummaging through an antique jewelry box. Her eyes gleamed through two coats of glittery blue mascara as she brushed a strand of perm-it-yourself, fried hair behind a multipierced ear. "Aha!" she chortled, waving a shiny object under the nose of the handsome male Siamese who watched her from the dresser top.

"This has to be it!" She twirled the object around her finger for a moment, then let it slip to the polished mahogany surface below as something else stole her attention. "Could these be real?" she whispered, snatching a pair of teardrop emerald earrings from their satin-lined compartment. Hastily, she removed the Dale Earnhardt statuettes from her own lobes and replaced them with the green stones.

Her thin lips smiled into the mirror. "Hello, *dahling*. Yes, it is wonderful, isn't it?

Dean has finally come into his own, you know. Well, the old bat did *deserve* to die, didn't she?" Chuckling at her own wit, she removed the earrings and tried on another pair. She had made it halfway through the box when a loud whisper from her husband drifted up the stairwell.

"Rochelle, honey? There's no more time!"

Rochelle looked around the dresser top, and her heart stopped in horror.

1

"Yoo-hoo!" The frazzled voice drifted into the kitchen of Leigh Koslow's still-not-totally-moved-into suburban house, accompanied by a panicked rapping on the living room window. "Leigh, honey? You in there? Please, *please* be home!"

Leigh, who was sitting at her kitchen table wearing an oversized T-shirt, paused with her coffee cup en route to her mouth and listened thoughtfully. Mao Tse, her imperial black Persian, noted the interruption with the briefest flick of one ear, her full attention being required by the sparrow that was popping around on the other side of the sliding-glass patio doors. The voice was familiar, but Leigh had a hard time believing she was hearing it.

She rose from the table and took a quick jog up the stairs to grab a bathrobe. Hoping her husband hadn't packed his best one for his latest weekend political junket, she dove into their walk-in closet and looked around with uncertainty. Culture shock still had its grip on her — they might have been terribly cramped in the apartment, but at least she had known where her stuff was.

Most of it, anyway.

Not even bothering with the mangled heaps of clothing that lay strewn on her own side of the closet, she turned immediately to Warren's rack, where his second-best robe hung neatly in place. Making a mental note to ask her husband why he would need his best robe in a motel room, she threw on the remaining one. The rapping from below intensified, and she quickly sailed back down the stairs to see if her suspicions were correct.

They were. The ancient, boat-size sedan, parked half on and half off her rain-soaked driveway, was clearly visible through the dining room window. As was its frantic, polyester-clad driver, who stood pressed against the glass like a fly.

She rushed to open the door. "Mrs. Rhodis?" she asked in amazement, stepping back as the wet septuagenarian plowed past her. "What on earth are you doing here? Is everything OK?"

"Oh, honey!" the older woman said dramatically, her eyes brimming with tears. "Nothing's all right!"

Leigh looked at her friend with concern. Though Adith Rhodis was certainly not beyond a little melodrama here and there, her distress at the moment appeared genuine. Leigh took the woman by the arm and led her to the kitchen, since it was the only room that had something to sit on besides unpacked boxes. Mao Tse, who ordinarily could be counted on to greet visitors with a hiss, favored the older woman with no more than a sneer before returning to her sparrow-intimidating vigil.

"Coffee?"

Adith waved the offer away with an age-spotted hand, then smoothed her damp house dress tidily over her knees. "You must think I've lost my marbles," she began, "coming all the way out here like this. I would have been here sooner if I'd known where you lived."

Leigh winced slightly, afraid to think how many times Adith might have stopped to ask for directions. Though the woman was perfectly able to navigate in her own Pittsburgh neighborhood of Avalon, the quagmire of McCandless suburbs just a few miles north might as well have been a foreign country. But it was pointless to ask why she hadn't called first, just as it was pointless to ask why she'd rapped on the windows instead of using the doorbell. Adith Rhodis had her own way of doing things.

"I hate to bother you, honey, but I didn't know where else to turn."

Leigh took a sip of coffee and nodded encouragement.

Adith sighed. "It's my Ricky. He's in trouble. Bad trouble."

"Ricky?" Leigh's brow furrowed. The laconic husband, Bud, she knew about. And she'd certainly heard enough about Pansy, the Rhodises' allegedly psychic apricot poodle. But Ricky was a new one.

"My grandson," Adith explained. "Jimmy's boy." She shook her head worriedly and licked her lips. "He's a good boy, Leigh. A darling boy. Now, my Jimmy — I'll be honest with you. He's no good. Never has been. I'd all but given up on him ever marrying and settling down, but finally he did. The marriage didn't last, of course, but I did get me a grandchild. And my Ricky, he's different. He's got a heart of gold, and he's never been in trouble a day in his life."

Leigh was pretty sure she knew what words were coming next.

"Until now."

She smiled sympathetically, wondering how *she* fit into the picture. But Adith Rhodis was not easily rushed.

"He admits he shouldn't have been where he was," Adith continued. "But he wasn't there for what the police say he was. And he won't tell me why he was there, probably

15

because it's some sort of secret kid shenanigan, you know? But I've got to find out, or somebody has, because he might go to college someday, and he could too, and he could make something of himself, but he can't if this all goes on —" She broke off, her voice cracking. Then, just as suddenly, she collected herself, looking up at her hostess with fiery eyes. "And I just can't believe your daddy won't listen to me!"

Leigh's eyebrows rose. The light was dawning. Her father, Randall Koslow, owned the Koslow Animal Clinic in Avalon, and had long since been sainted by Adith for his unfaltering care of her paranormal poodle dynasty. Apparently, the halo had tarnished.

"Your grandson is in trouble with my father?"

"Terrible trouble," Adith said, chin lowered. "And you're the only one who can help him. Dr. Koslow's had him arrested for breaking into the clinic. They're saying he was stealing drugs!"

Leigh took in a breath. This *was* bad. As much as she would like to take Adith's word on her grandson's character, her father's judgment was a bit less biased. Might the teen be pulling the wool over his kindly granny's eyes?

"I know what you're thinking, and it ain't true!" Adith barked, defensive sparks flying from her own perpetually adolescent eyes. "My Ricky don't do drugs! And he certainly wouldn't steal any from your daddy!"

Leigh fingered the edges of her coffee cup hesitantly. The quest was almost certainly hopeless, not to mention the fact that she had been looking forward to an uncharacteristically domestic day of unpacking boxes, and that if she had to eat one more soggy bagel before finding the toaster, she would scream. But Adith Rhodis had been a lot of help to her and her cousin Cara during their brief stint as her next-door neighbors. And had Leigh ever showed up on *her* doorstep in the middle of a Saturday morning distraught over a family crisis, she had no doubt the older woman would drop everything to be of assistance.

She smiled with resignation. "I'll be happy to talk to my father for you," she offered. "But I can't make any promises. You know how stubborn he can be."

Adith Rhodis grinned, displaying a full complement of crooked, tea-stained teeth. "Not as stubborn as you, I'll wager."

Leigh grinned back.

For a Saturday morning, the Koslow

Animal Clinic wasn't terribly busy. The tiny parking lot was full to capacity as always, but Leigh had managed to find on-street parking only half a block away, which was a real coup. Planning to steal a word with her father over his theoretical lunch hour, she trooped down the steep, wet cobblestone street to the clinic, catching a glimpse of the muddy Ohio River as it churned far below at the base of the bluff. It was turning into a gorgeous spring day, but she couldn't shake a dull sense of foreboding. She had hoped that Adith Rhodis could further enlighten her as to her grandson's motives for breaking into the building, but the older woman didn't seem to have a clue, aside from the enigmatic "He said he was returning something that belonged to somebody else."

Randall Koslow, DVM, was a wise and tolerant soul in general, but he didn't take kindly to trespassers, and he had even less sympathy for drug traffickers, whatever their pedigree. Leigh knew well that if her father was convinced Ricky Rhodis had broken the law, he'd insist on the boy paying the price — for his own good, of course. And no tearful grandmother's pleas were likely to sway his opinion.

Unfortunately, neither were hers, unless

she could find another angle.

She opted to use the clinic's front door, it being closer than her usual back entrance, and was delighted to see the reception area temporarily client free. Nancy Johnson, her father's office manager and right hand, threw her a wave and a smile. Though Leigh hadn't actually worked at the clinic since she was a teenager, she still dropped by fairly often, and the staff knew her well.

"Your dad's got two more waiting on him in the exam rooms; then he'll have a minute," Nancy said pleasantly. Her attractive, cocoa-brown face was still smiling, but Leigh detected an unusual tightness to it, perhaps relating to the last night's events. Though being burglarized was never enjoyable, her father was at least used to it. The clinic had been broken into four other times that she could remember — not counting myriad less ambitious assaults on the Dumpster.

She smiled back encouragingly. Nancy was in her mid-twenties and had only been working for her father for a few years, but he already couldn't imagine life without her. Randall, who had both a generous spirit and a tendency to live in the present, was so poor with finances that if not for Leigh's budget-conscious mother, the business would probably be eligible for nonprofit status. But within a year of Nancy's rolling up her sleeves, the books had improved so much she looked like a reverse embezzler.

Leigh walked to the desk and leaned casually against the counter while the incurable workaholic pounded away at her keyboard. As business manager, Nancy wasn't even supposed to be at the clinic on Saturdays. But whenever the regular receptionist had car trouble (which seemed to happen exclusively on mornings after Pittsburgh Penguin games), Nancy would arrive with a smile on her face, ready to give flea lectures over the headset, run credit card authorizations, and make change simultaneously.

"I heard there was a little bit of trouble here last night," Leigh began conversationally. Multitasking Nancy, she realized, could be the perfect source of unbiased information regarding one Ricky Rhodis.

Nancy paused a moment from her keyboard and cast her dark eyes downward, her face now openly stressed. "Yes. I feel really bad about it."

"It wasn't your fault, I'm sure," Leigh said with empathy. The workaholism monkey had never cared for her back, but an overactive conscience she could relate to.

The younger woman shook her head uncertainly. "The boy came in late yesterday afternoon and sat down, and when I asked him if I could help him, he said he was waiting for somebody. We were very busy right up until closing time, and when he disappeared I didn't think anything about it."

"Why should you? He could have left with any of the clients."

"That's what I figured. But the police say he must have sneaked past me and hid somewhere. After we locked up he came out and tripped off the motion detectors. The police were here within minutes; they caught him red-handed."

Leigh considered. There were worse plans. It would be tough to break through the clinic's newest security system from the outside, but if one was already inside, there were plenty of places to hide. Going out later would spring the alarms, of course, but then the burglar would have a head start. Thank goodness for the motion detectors — even if they did annoy the Avalon police by going off every time a clever cat lifted up its cage latch with a paw.

"Did he take anything?"

Nancy shook her head. "Not that we know of. There was forty dollars in the petty-cash box — untouched. The police think he intended to steal drugs and syringes, but didn't get the chance."

Her voice held only the slightest hint of skepticism, but Leigh seized on it immediately. "And what do you think?"

Nancy looked surprised. "Oh, I don't know," she said guiltily. "I'm sure your father's right about him wanting the ketamine or the Valium. He just seemed like such a nice kid." She paused for a few seconds, nibbling unconsciously on the end of an already well-chewed pen. "He's been here before, you know."

"He has?"

She nodded. "I didn't recognize him yesterday, but I looked up his records this morning. He brought in a stray cat one time — a tom with a cat-bite abscess. He paid to have it fixed up and neutered and then gave it to a neighbor. Said he couldn't keep it himself. He was only fifteen then." She replaced the mangled pen behind an ear. "It's sad how drugs can mess up a teen, isn't it?"

Leigh looked at Nancy thoughtfully. Mrs. Rhodis had insisted that her grandson had a heart of gold. Could he actually have been telling his grandmother the truth?

Before she could get in another question, a stooped older man emerged from the first exam room, dragging an immense shaggy hound behind him. Nancy went back to work, and Leigh decided to try her luck with the rest of the staff.

She quickly ruled out Jeanine, Dr. Koslow's senior tech and self-proclaimed dental hygienist, who was busily working on an anesthetized greyhound in the treatment room. Jeanine was a devoted worker and a competent technician, but she was also a smug, brown-nosing snitch, and Leigh didn't care to have a transcript of their conversation relayed to Dr. Koslow later. When a quick search of the back revealed that the other veterinary assistants were all working in the exam rooms, Leigh headed down the narrow basement stairs.

Her arrival in the kennels was greeted by the broad smile of Jared Loomis, who spoke, as always, without a moment's interruption to his current task. "Hello, Leigh Koslow! How are you doing, Leigh Koslow? Did you hear about the guy who was arrested, Leigh Koslow?"

Leigh smiled back. She adored Jared, who, though he was born with Down's Syndrome, was nobody's charity case. At six-foot-three and two-hundred fifty pounds, his shuffling gait and odd speech patterns might have made another young man seem threatening. But with his amiable manner, fluffy head of pale blond hair, and immense blue eyes, Jared was more akin to a giant cherub. More important to Dr. Koslow, he had a wonderful way with animals and a work ethic second only to God.

"Hello, Jared," Leigh said pleasantly. "I'm doing fine. And yes, I did hear about the arrest. But I don't know much. What more can you tell me?" She took hold of the stainless-steel water dish Jared had removed from a cage and went to fill it up for him.

"Thank you, Leigh Koslow. A guy hid in here 'cause he was stealing drugs, Dr. Koslow says. A guy was stealing drugs and the alarm went off and the police came."

"Where do you think he hid?"

The big young man grinned at her as he took the full water pail and placed it in the cage he had just coated with fresh newspaper. "I think he hid in the paper cage. What do you think, Leigh Koslow?"

Leigh grinned back. Jared was modest, but not without insight. She walked over to the corner dog run, which had not been used for a dog in years, both because its chain-link gate was hopelessly off its hinges and because the floor drain had a tendency to back up in the spring. It had long since been designated the "paper cage," and was used to store the reams of used newspapers the staff collected for the cage bottoms.

"Papers were messed up, Leigh Koslow," Jared called to her as he looped a leash over the head of a dachshund and led it out for a few moments of freedom. She pressed farther into the run and could see that the wooden pallets on which the newspapers were stacked had been pushed askew, leaving a narrow crawl space behind that no casual glance would have noticed. She considered, then stepped out. "Did you see anything else unusual when you came in this morning?"

He nodded, then dropped to his hands and knees, pushing his head and massive shoulders into the dachshund's cage to wipe it clean. "There was stuff on the floor, Leigh Koslow," he said, his voice a tinny echo. "Cat carrier on the floor. Bag on the floor. I never leave stuff on the floor. Dr. Koslow says it's not safe to leave stuff on the floor."

She distracted the dachshund, who had begun to nip playfully at the young man's heels as he worked. "A cat carrier, you said?"

Jared's head emerged and he pointed to a spot near the large metal trash can in the middle of the room. "Cat carrier on the floor there." He then pointed to a spot by his feet. "Trash bag on the floor here. I cleaned them up. Dr. Koslow said to clean them up."

Leigh walked over to the stairs and sat down to think as Jared filled the dog's cage with clean paper, fresh dishes, and a bedraggled yellow towel. As soon as the dachshund's kibble was visible, it scooted back into its cage and dove in with relish. Jared was certainly a conscientious kennel cleaner, she mulled, so if he hadn't left the things out, who did?

Randall always kept a spare cardboard cat carrier sitting on top of the basement refrigerator, primarily to avoid puncture wounds on those naive new cat owners who thought they could hold Snowball in their lap while sitting next to a rottweiler. But why would Ricky Rhodis need one? A bulky cardboard box would hardly be Leigh's choice for carrying around a stash of drug bottles, needles, and syringes — particularly if one planned on making an inconspicuous getaway. *Point one: Ricky.*

"Jared," she began again, "that trash bag you said you found on the floor. Was it empty?"

"Cat poop, Leigh Koslow," he answered matter-of-factly. "Nothing but litter and cat poop. Isn't that funny, Leigh Koslow?"

She frowned. For a person who made

26

their living coming up with catchy ways to sell everything from baby food to industrial solvents, she was shamefully lacking in ideas as to why either the police or Ricky Rhodis would have deigned to empty the clinic's litter pans. Might her father have gotten bored while the police were investigating and picked up a scoop? Not likely. Even then, he would have thrown away the bag.

Heavy footsteps started down the stairs, and she looked around behind her. "Hello, Leigh," Jeanine greeted brusquely, her tight, patronizing smile in full form. "You heard about what happened last night, I guess. It was bound to happen, if you ask me, as crazy as that waiting room gets."

Leigh smiled tolerantly. It was no secret that Jeanine was more than a little jealous of Nancy's unparalleled rise through the staff hierarchy — never mind that one of the business manager's first actions had been to suggest offering the technicians full benefits. "Could you tell Jared to bring up Meno, the other greyhound? Briar's Joy will be ready to come down in five."

"I'll get her," Leigh offered, grabbing a spare lead from a hook on the wall and looking around at the cage tags. She noticed that there weren't many sick animals in the kennels — just a few boarders and the

27

dental patients who came in every Friday for a spot on Jeanine's Saturday-morning cleaning roster. Spying a red brindle greyhound, she checked the cage tag for any aspersions to its good nature and opened the door. As she was looping the lead over the dog's narrow snout, Mrs. Rhodis's words floated back to her.

He said he was returning something that belonged to someone else.

She led the willing greyhound up the stairs for the handoff, then pounded quickly back down. "Jared," she asked hopefully, "are these all the same animals that were here last night?"

"Doberman went home this morning, Leigh Koslow," he answered automatically, as if reciting from a roster. "Doberman went home this morning. He was here. Siamese and greyhounds here for Jeanine. Black cat sick, sick — he's been here. Dachshund, sheltie, they've been here."

She looked around at the assembled furry guests, her heartbeat quickening. A cat carrier, eh? Clearly, the Doberman and the greyhounds were off the hook. So was the sheltie, and the dachshund was on the large side, too. That left the cats.

She peered in for a closer look at the "sick, sick" black cat, which lay limply against the far wall of his cage, an IV line trailing from his forearm. His glittering green eyes watched Leigh with distrust, and his upper lip drew back over his teeth with a faint hiss. JONES, MIDNIGHT: KIDNEY FAILURE, the cage card read. She narrowed her eyes in concentration, trying to think up a good reason why Ricky Rhodis would steal an old, sick cat from a veterinary clinic.

She couldn't. Not aside from garden-variety insanity, which, prevalent as it was among the clinic's clientele, would be a tough line to sell her father. Her attention turned to the double-wide cage next door, which housed two silent Siamese. This she knew immediately to be unusual, since although the breed had many virtues, silence was not among them. Neither was healthy gums, which probably explained the silence.

Both lay sleeping soundly, their limbs splayed straight out in the distinctive position of those recovering from anesthesia. "You said the Siamese were here for dentals?" she asked Jared, who had moved on to mop the vacant greyhound run.

He looked up briefly, then answered while he worked the mop wringer. "The Siamese got dentals, Leigh Koslow."

Leigh took another look at the cats, both

29

of which were handsome seal points with bright, slick fur and angular lines. Her eyes drank in the cage card with a flicker of alarm. MURCHISON.

Lilah Murchison. The tiniest of shivers traveled down her spine, and she shrugged quickly to arrest it. She was thirty-one years old now, not six and a half. And it was clear to her rational, adult self that the incident that had given her years of nightmares was no more than a little girl's imagination gone amuck.

But still.

She had been an energetic child with a healthy amount of curiosity, and the gigantic purse that sat unattended in exam-room two had proved more temptation than she could take. It was a foot wide easily, both sides covered with sequined renditions of sapphire-eyed, seal point Siamese. She had run her fingers over the shiny designs, then popped open the top for a quick peek inside. Wallet, keys, makeup mirror — she sifted through each component, bringing it out into the light. She thought the squishy object in the plastic bag was probably a half-eaten sandwich. It was only after she held it inches from her face that she realized it was a mauled, bloody, and notably headless mouse.

She didn't scream then. She had simply frozen in horror. It was when two sets of extraordinarily long red fingernails clamped down on her shoulders and a husky woman's voice said "Boo!" that she had become slightly hysterical. She had whirled around to see a grown woman in a leopard-spotted minidress and thigh-high boots laughing at her wildly, and that had been all she could take.

It wasn't the sort of story a child confessed to a parent. She had, after all, been snooping in someone else's purse, which everyone knew could result in jail time. But the assessment of the first-graders at West View Elementary had been unanimous. This leopard woman clearly ate kittens for breakfast and mice for snacks.

After days of tortured nightmares, she had finally worked up the nerve to warn her father that Mrs. Murchison was raising cats for food. For unfathomable reasons, however, he had found this amusing, and the issue was never spoken of again. At least not until Leigh was twelve and learned that Lilah Murchison was so paranoid about rabies and parasites that she insisted every creature her pets dragged home be thoroughly tested for both.

Leigh's adult fingers clenched the cage

31

bars involuntarily as she remembered. Lilah Murchison might not have been a devil woman, then or now, but neither was she Mother Goose. Twenty-five years later, she and her prizewinning Siamese were still clients of the clinic, and she was a very wealthy widow. She was also rumored to be a black one.

Leigh straightened. Could Ricky Rhodis have intended to steal one of her Siamese from the clinic? If so, who did he plan to "return" it to?

"Leigh?" came a masculine voice from the stairs. She turned to see her father's gray, bespectacled head leaning down just below ceiling level. "Nancy told me you were here. Come on up."

She let go of the cat cage and took a deep, apprehensive breath. Randall was fair, but consummately practical, and her credibility with him was . . . well, somewhat limited.

Adith Rhodis was going to owe her.

2

"Preposterous." Randall Koslow removed the latest in a long line of cheap, dark plastic glasses, which, when observed in concert with his rail-thin frame and studious nature, made him look startlingly like the father of Dennis the Menace. He rubbed his eyes wearily and took another bite of his turkey on white — hold the mayo. "I feel very sorry for Mrs. Rhodis, but she's going to have to face facts. Better the boy get help now."

Leigh studied her father's determined face and wished she could think up another line of reasoning for why Ricky Rhodis should be let off the hook scot-free. Unfortunately, she couldn't. She tried again. "You don't think it's even a *remote* possibility that Ricky might have intended to snatch one of Mrs. Murchison's Siamese? Maybe for a rival breeder? Or wait — I've got it. The wife of her latest lover is out for revenge."

Randall lowered his eyebrows in a frown. In stark contrast to the women in his family, he was strictly a no-nonsense individual, and his daughter's attempts at levity were not scoring points.

"Okay, okay," she relented. "That's a little much, I grant you. I'm just trying to establish reasonable doubt here."

He smiled patiently, then let out a small sigh. "The female cat was a grand champion in her time, but she's well beyond breeding age, much less showing age. As for the male, you couldn't give him away. He's a medical nightmare. In fact —"

"Dr. Koslow?" An individual the size of a fifth-grader poked her head into the exam room where Randall and Leigh had paused for his stand-up lunch break. "Sorry to interrupt," she apologized brusquely, moving toward them.

Leigh stared at the stranger with undisguised curiosity. Any other female cursed with such a small frame would seem elfish, but this one's army-short hair, intense gray eyes, and unaccountable swagger somehow pulled off machismo. Her bulging muscles didn't hurt, either. "I need to talk to you," the woman ordered, holding Randall's gaze in a deadlock. "It's about Mrs. Murchison."

Leigh's eyes widened. Leopard woman was a popular topic today.

Randall took one look at his visitor's face, stuffed the remainder of his sandwich into the trash bin, and pointed to a chair. "Have a seat," he answered. "This is my daughter,

34

Leigh. Leigh, this is Nikki Loomis, Jared's sister. She works for Lilah Murchison. Her personal assistant now, I believe."

The two women nodded in greeting, though Nikki's nod was more of a sharp bob, and Leigh found herself fighting an urge to salute. She knew it wasn't charitable of her to besmirch the character of Jared's mother, but she had a hard time believing there was much shared gene pool between this woman and the gentle giant downstairs. She was further amazed that the clinic's own kennel worker had a sister who worked for Lilah Murchison. Nobody worked for Lilah Murchison. Getting on her staff was like applying for the secret service.

"Don't know how to say this," Nikki began with a clipped, militant tone. "But you may have heard on the news — a private plane went down yesterday over Lake Michigan."

Randall shook his head.

"Well, one did. And I got a call last night saying Mrs. Murchison was on it."

Leigh's stomach flip-flopped. News of plane crashes always did that to her, whether she knew anyone involved or not. And while she couldn't claim to have known Lilah Murchison well, she nevertheless felt a strong need for denial. Intimidating, savvy, arguably evil women like Lilah did *not* die without warning. They merely disappeared for a while and came back with different husbands.

The veterinarian cleared his throat. "You're certain?"

Nikki's head moved sharply from side to side. "Can't be, not yet. But she did call from New York yesterday morning. Said that she and her friend Bertha were going to take the McClintock company jet to Minneapolis. They were going to the Mall of America."

No one spoke for a moment, and Leigh let out a breath. Lilah Murchison — dead? She generally tried not to obsess over local gossip, but the yarns implanted during her formative years still held a certain power over her. And the web of this spider was large indeed.

Lilah Murchison's life was nothing short of legend — providing fifty years' worth of titillating conversation everywhere from happy hour at the Chuckwagon to luncheon with the North Boros Women's Club. Born to one of the poorest families in the working-class borough of Avalon, Lilah had spent the last thirty years in one of the finest old-money mansions in Ben Avon, the upscale community just down the river. And in getting there she hadn't just burned her bridges, she had pulverized them. Her path to wealth had been paved with the trampled torsos of virtually everyone she had grown up with — not to mention the bodies of three dead husbands — and her crimes against humanity and decency were known the length of the Ohio's north bank. Kitten eater or no, Lilah Murchison was one creepy dame.

Unless, of course, one took the opinion of Randall Koslow. "I'm very sorry to hear that," he said sincerely. "She was a good client and a fine woman. My sympathies to her son."

Nikki Loomis's eyes narrowed somewhat, their gray depths flashing. Leigh knew very little about Lilah's son, but she was guessing there were things to know. "Dean will get over it," the personal assistant snapped. "But there's nothing we can do now except wait. Bits of the plane have been found, but it went down in some pretty deep water, and they say they may never find the bodies."

Aha. Leigh tried to stop herself from spinning alternative scenarios in her head, but she knew resistance was pointless. Her brain minded her commands about as well as Mao Tse did. "Was there a passenger list?" she inquired innocently — or so she hoped.

Nikki turned on her with a frown, absently flexing an unnaturally thick bicep. "Not that I heard of. But two employees at the airport say they saw a thin blond woman in her sixties get on with Mrs. McClintock. And one mentioned that she was hauling a cat carrier." She turned back to Randall. "You know Ms. Lilah never went anywhere without Mrs. Wiggs."

The veterinarian nodded soberly. "True. She was devoted to all her pets." He paused thoughtfully. "Speaking of which — do you have any idea if she made arrangements for them?"

"No, and her estate's going to be a real mess because of the wait for a death certificate. But her son's been bugging the lawyer about reading her will, and it looks like the guy's agreed because Ms. Lilah's got so much stuff that has to be dealt with. Of course," she added heavily, "nothing's going to be changing hands until she's declared legally dead."

"Who will be taking care of the cats, then?" Randall asked.

"Me, unless the will says otherwise. I live in the house and watch them all the time anyway, so it makes sense. But Dean could make trouble. He tried to kick me out just this morning." She sniffed derisively. "The wuss."

Having suspicions about who might have actually kicked whom, Leigh made a mental note to avoid annoying Jared's sister.

"Do you need a place to live?" Randall asked with concern. "Or is your mother's house —"

"I'm *not* living with my doofus brothers!" she answered sharply. Then she moderated her tone. "Thanks for asking, Doc, but we'll be fine."

Leigh's mental notes had a tendency to get lost. "Jared has a brother, too?"

Nikki Loomis whirled around on her like a viper. "Jared is *not* a doofus," the little bodybuilder said icily, fists clenched. "Next to Bill and Red, he's a goddamned Einstein!"

Leigh took a quick step back, trying to figure out where her comment had gone wrong. "I didn't mean to imply —" Then she stopped backpedaling and smiled. Actually, she was glad to see that Jared had a bodyguard. "Take it easy," she said agreeably. "You're talking to one of his biggest fans here. I just didn't know he had any siblings."

Nikki's fists relaxed.

"Jared has been living in Mrs. Murchison's garage apartment for a while now," Randall explained. "He does her kennel cleaning in exchange."

Leigh looked from her father to Nikki and back again, gritting her teeth. *Jared* worked for Mrs. Murchison too? Her father never told her anything.

"I was concerned that he and Nikki have someplace to go if necessary," Randall continued evenly. Then he turned back to Nikki. "You'll let me know if you need help?"

She looked uncomfortable, but nodded. "So, anyway. Are the cats ready to go? Did Number One Son need any teeth pulled?"

Leigh startled at the segue. First, because Nikki seemed to be taking the sudden death of her employer quite in stride, and two, because Number One Son was an odd thing to name a cat when one already had the human version.

Randall shook his head. "No, they just got a cleaning. But I'd give them a couple more hours to get back on their feet."

Nancy Johnson popped her head in from the waiting room. "Dr. Koslow? I. J. Kloo's on line one. He says it's an emergency."

The veterinarian exited, leaving Leigh to stare awkwardly at Nikki, who stared unabashedly back at her. Luckily, Leigh soon

40

remembered her temporarily derailed mission to save Ricky Rhodis's questionable hide. "I hope you don't mind my asking," she began, watching the other woman's fists for signs of renewed tightening. "But as your brother might already have told you, someone tried to steal something from the clinic last night. Call me crazy, but I have this feeling that they wanted one of the Siamese. Do you have any idea why anyone might?"

Nikki's hands stayed relaxed. "One of those two?" she asked in a ho-hum fashion. "Seems unlikely. Miss Brooks is getting on in years, and you probably know about Number One Son's problems."

"Nikki?" Nancy poked her head back inside the room. "I'm sorry, but I couldn't help overhearing part of your conversation earlier. Is something wrong with Mrs. Murchison?"

Not anxious to hear the sobering news repeated, Leigh excused herself from the room and trooped sluggishly back down the stairs. If news of a plane crash — any plane crash — was depressing enough, the prospect of giving Adith Rhodis the bad news about her grandson — namely that she had failed to save him from one of those quaint cells with a twelve-by-twelve-inch view of the Monongahela River — weighed heavily on her spirits. She crossed over to the Siamese cats' cage and exhaled in frustration. The female was on her feet now, grooming her ruffled chest indignantly, but the still-recumbent male was only just paddling his legs.

Thinking that the bony felines must be uncomfortable lounging about on nothing but papers and the steel cage flooring, she turned to the stack of worn towels above the cages, collected a large green one, and opened the cage door.

"*No!*" The reaction of the kennel cleaner, who had been happily washing dishes in the sink, could not have been more dramatic if she had approached the patient with a straight razor. Jared whirled around, sending a stainless-steel bowl and dishwater flying across the floor, covered the distance to her in two paces, and blocked the cage opening with a meaty arm. "*No towels with Murchison cats*, Leigh Koslow!"

Despite his bluster, he didn't seem angry so much as scared. "Number One Son *eats* towels, Leigh Koslow!"

She stood like a statue for a moment, thinking, then calmly retracted the towel. *Wool sucking.* It was one of those weird feline psychiatric things she had heard her

42

dad talk about, along with Martian chasing (which affected her own dear Mao Tse) and excessive grooming (which thankfully did not). Wool suckers, which were very often Siamese, had a thing about cloth. They would chew on and sometimes even eat dish towels, carpeting, drapes. . . .

Jared pulled back his arm. She shut the cage door, then gazed through the bars at the groggy male, who had begun tossing his head in an effort to sit up. Could it be?

"Jared," she asked, trying to attract his attention as he began mopping up the water he had spilled. "What types of things has Number One Son eaten? Do you know?"

"Number One Son gets sick, Leigh Koslow," he answered, working feverishly. "Number One Son has to be operated on over and over. Dr. Koslow says he doesn't want to operate any more. No towels with Murchison cats, Leigh Koslow."

She stood thinking for another moment, then reopened the cage door. "I'm going to take him upstairs to my dad," she explained as she wrapped up the awkwardly thrashing cat in the towel she was holding. "I think maybe he needs an x-ray."

"Are you sure Dr. Koslow ordered this?" Jeanine asked skeptically, drawing herself up to full diva height. "I don't believe I heard anything about it."

Cradling the agitated cat on top of the hard x-ray table, Leigh fought back over a decade's worth of accumulated annoyance, and smiled. "Yes. Now, if you could just hang on to him for me for a moment, I'll gown up. The film's all loaded."

Jeanine pushed a strand of unruly, curly dark hair behind one ear with a scowl. "Just a minute," she said shortly, turning in the direction of the treatment room, where Randall was still on the phone.

Leigh let out an exasperated sigh. She supposed she *could* wait until her father was available, but she was perfectly capable of taking the x-ray herself, and frankly, she couldn't stand the suspense. What if she was right? Her idea was completely bizarre, but it made sense. Why else would someone want to steal both a worthless cat *and* the contents of its litter box?

Number One Son certainly had precedent. The file she had just read showed that he'd been operated on three times already for intestinal blockage: dish towel, oriental carpet tassel, and hair scrunchy, respectively. She couldn't imagine what clothlike item could possibly be valuable enough for someone to go to such lengths to retrieve it

— or even how the cat could have gotten hold of it in the first place — but she darn well wanted to find out.

"He's still on the phone," Jeanine reported sullenly, walking to the x-ray table and putting a hand on Number One Son. "But I suppose it's all right."

Leigh smiled and headed for the rack to slip on a lead gown and gloves. She hadn't gone three paces before she stopped cold.

"Oh, wait," she said to herself, out loud. "I can't."

She looked helplessly back at Jeanine, whose wide mouth broke into a devious grin. "Oh, no?"

Leigh's face reddened. "I mean, I might be able to, I just —"

Damn. She didn't know that she was pregnant. In fact, she probably wasn't. But she couldn't be sure she wasn't. And so she was stuck. Keeping a pregnancy secret at a vet clinic was like keeping a wig secret at a beauty salon. With Dr. Koslow's strict rules about x-ray and gas exposure, the staff knew about each other's babies before their husbands did.

And Jeanine would keep this little nugget to herself for all of about five seconds. "Say no more," the tech said smugly. "I'll gown up. You just hit the button."

Leigh bit her lip and held on to Number One Son while Jeanine got ready; then she stepped behind the lead shield and watched as the tech stretched the cat out on his side. She snapped the picture, unloaded the cassette, and headed for the processor.

Jeanine stayed at the x-ray table, smirking.

3

"*Now* do you believe me?" Leigh asked excitedly.

Randall removed his glasses and peered closely at the radiograph. It took a long time for him to answer. "Well, it seems to be moving along well enough. Not a lot of gas — none of the bowel loops are distended." He shook his head sadly. "Maybe it won't block him up this time. The cat's already got a bellyful of adhesions, and if I have to go back in again —"

"But what *is* this, Dad?" she asked emphatically, pointing. "It obviously isn't just cloth."

He took another look at the inch-long, roughly club-shaped white spot and shook his head. "No, it's metal. But this," he pointed to the fuzzy white area around it, "is probably the cloth that made him eat it."

Leigh stared. She wasn't great with x-rays, but she knew metal when she saw it. Being perfectly stark white on a field of black and gray, it was hard to miss. "It could be a ring, if you were looking at it straight on," she hypothesized. "Or some sort of broach."

"Maybe," he mumbled.

She pivoted him to face her. "You have to admit it, Dad. Ricky Rhodis could be telling the truth. Someone could have convinced him to snatch the cat before it was returned to Mrs. Murchison. Let's say they knew the cat had swallowed this — this whatever it is. That could be what Ricky meant when he told his grandmother he wasn't stealing . . . only returning."

Randall looked back at his only daughter skeptically. "This cat never leaves Mrs. Murchison's house, except to come here. How do you suppose it could swallow something that belonged to someone else?" He turned back to examine the film again, then shook his head. "It's probably no more than the pop-top from a can of tuna."

Leigh let out a breath. "However," her father continued, "your theory does explain the cat carrier and the bagged-up litter, though given the amount of time it takes for foodstuffs to pass completely through the system —"

"Dad," she interrupted, her hopes rising again, "we're not dealing with a Ph.D. in feline proctology, here, remember? They wouldn't know how long to wait. And as long as you admit it's a reasonable possibility that Ricky Rhodis wasn't stealing drugs, you really can't —"

Randall stopped his daughter's arguments with a raised hand, then shook his head with a smile. "Sometimes I think you should have gone to law school," he teased.

She grinned back. "Nah. I kind of like my soul."

He took the radiograph down from the viewer and turned around. "I'm going to take a few more views and make sure this cat's not in any immediate danger. Tell you what, you talk to the Rhodis boy and see if he'll give you a more reasonable explanation for his presence here than he gave the police last night. If so, perhaps we can drop the charges."

Leigh smiled broadly. She felt like jumping up and down, but her father never appreciated gush. "Thanks, Dad," she said. "I'll go visit him right after we're done. If we take a VD view right away, do you think —"

He interrupted her again. "You don't need to stay for the x-rays. Somebody else can help me."

"But —"

He waved off her protests, his standard matter-of-fact tone ever so slightly on the nervous side as he added, "We need to run an ethylene oxide sterilization anyway. That can be — well, hazardous."

Leigh took one look at his face and ceased her protests. He knew already.

Jeanine.

Imagining various ways of torturing the technician with her own dental equipment, she looked away.

"Fine, I'll go talk to Ricky," she answered. "He talks; he walks. How hard can that be?" She headed out into the hallway and turned toward the door, only to see the clinic's two joined-at-the-hip veterinary assistants, Marcia and Michelle, standing at the treatment-room door, grinning at her.

She made a quick turn for the exit and walked through it without looking back.

Jeanine was going to pay.

Trying not to think about her previous encounters with the facility, Leigh approached the Allegheny County Jail with confidence. She was going to get Ricky Rhodis off. Johnny Cochran had nothing on her — and she wasn't even an attorney.

Which turned out to be unfortunate. "It's not visiting hours," the graying desk attendant told her curtly, pointing one pudgy finger at a nearby sign. "Come back then. You on the list?"

Taken aback, but only momentarily, Leigh drew up her shoulders and tried her

50

best to look like she knew what she was doing. She ordinarily avoided lying, but a cause was a cause. "This isn't a social call," she said firmly.

"You a lawyer?" the man asked, eyeing her skeptically. "Or a spiritual advisor?"

Leigh smiled. *Eureka.* "The latter. I'm a personal evolution coach with the Church of the Blessed Redeemer. I've been engaged by Ricky Rhodis's grandmother to counsel the boy. She feels it's imperative that he get spiritual help immediately, and I agree."

The man's eyes narrowed. "Never heard of that church. Where is it?"

Leigh didn't hesitate. "North Hills — off of Babcock." She smiled with aplomb. Babcock Boulevard, like many Pittsburgh thoroughfares, snaked around the North Hills in about ten discontinuous segments, more if you counted all the "Old Babcocks" that kept it company. She had lived in the area her entire life and couldn't begin to recall all the road's convolutions — it was a reasonably safe bet this man couldn't either.

He watched her another moment, then shrugged. "Fine. You got ten minutes."

It took considerably more than ten minutes for Ricky Rhodis's bewildered face to appear on the other side of the glass panel.

He was a shrimpy kid, five-foot-six at the

most, skinny and pale with a thick crop of light brown hair. He could easily pass for fifteen or sixteen, although he had to be at least eighteen to land where he had landed. His pinched face looked both scared and tired, yet somehow resolute. He picked up the phone with question marks in his eyes, but he let her talk first.

"Nice to meet you," Leigh began cordially, looking around to see if their conversation was being monitored. There was a guard by the exit, but he didn't seem overly interested. "Leigh Koslow, here. Your grandmother sent me to help you out."

His soft brown eyes, which had the same mischievous sparkle as Adith's, flickered briefly with guilt. But he said nothing.

She cut to the chase. "You're here because my father, Randall Koslow, thought you must have been trying to steal drugs from the clinic. Your grandmother says that's not true. Is it?"

Ricky fidgeted in his hard plastic seat. It was several moments before he finally answered, his voice weak and tinny. "Can't say."

Leigh's brows arched. "Look," she said, lowering her voice, "I don't know why you think keeping quiet is in your best interests, but I'm telling you that my dad is willing to drop the charges — all of them — as long as he's convinced that you weren't stealing drugs. You convince me; I convince him; you're outta here. It's that simple."

She waited for the gist of her speech to sink in, but it seemed to be taking a long time. Ricky's eyes showed nothing.

"Did you hear me?" she asked, wondering if Mrs. Rhodis had left anything out of her grandson's story — like three years of inpatient treatment at Western Psych.

"Yeah, I heard you," he answered softly, scratching his fingernails idly on the countertop. "But I'm not saying anything else. I told them I wasn't stealing drugs and I wasn't. They can't prove I was."

"They don't have to prove you were stealing drugs to lock you up," she reasoned. "They've got you on breaking and entering."

"But I didn't break in," he protested mildly.

"Trespassing, then," Leigh said with irritation. "And enough with the technicalities. The point is, you're facing charges. Just tell me what you were really doing at the clinic. If you don't, I can't help you."

He started to answer, then paused in thought first. "How much time do you think I could get for — for what you said?"

She stared at him, dumbstruck. "More than you'd want to do, trust me." She couldn't imagine what was motivating the kid to keep mum, but it was clear she would have to motivate him otherwise. "And what about your grandmother? You think she wants to see her only grandson rot in jail? You'd break that poor woman's heart."

The guilty look returned in spades. "I told her not to worry about me," he said miserably. "I told her everything would be fine, and it will. You tell her that, OK?" He rose with a nervous jerk.

Leigh got up also. This kid was *not* going to walk out on her. She might have had men walk out on arguments before, but having one choose a prison cell over the pleasure of her company was downright embarrassing. "Ricky!" she spat into the phone. "I know about the cat."

Ricky had just pulled the receiver away from his head when his arm froze. He pulled the phone slowly back to his ear and opened his mouth to speak, but didn't.

"I thought that might get your attention," she said happily, plopping back down in her seat. "Now, can we talk? Please?"

Ricky remained standing, eyeing her with a strange mix of gratitude and resentment. He collected his thoughts, then spoke nervously. "I'm not saying nothing. You tell everybody that."

He slammed the phone in its cradle, whirled around, and made a beeline for the door.

Curse. Mutter. Curse. Mutter.

Leigh grumbled her way back to the clinic, stopping for a much-delayed fast-food lunch on the way. It was amazing she hadn't been hungry earlier, but then her appetite had been up and down ever since she had memorized the early symptoms of pregnancy. Naturally, they had all appeared immediately thereafter, twice. But much to her disappointment, both times were false alarms, and she now did her best to ignore anything out of the ordinary.

It had started raining again — a brisk April downpour. When she returned to the clinic there were only two cars left in the parking lot, which was good news, since yesterday she'd left her umbrella at Hook, Inc., the fledgling advertising agency at which she was a partner. She parked close and beat a hasty sprint to the back entrance. Her father was in the treatment room, gazing at a series of x-rays with Nikki Loomis at his side.

"Well," Leigh asked, almost breathless

from her jog. "Can you tell what it is?" Her eyes scoured the various x-ray views, trying to put the different shapes together like a three-dimensional puzzle. From side to side the white shape looked like a dagger symbol; from top to bottom it was only a thin line.

"I think it's some sort of key," Randall stated. "What I'm wondering is what it's attached to."

"One of those thin suitcase keys?" Leigh suggested. "Or a briefcase key, maybe?"

"Either way, I can't think of any he could get to," Nikki said with frustration. "He spends a lot of time in Ms. Lilah's room, and I really don't know what all's in there. But I know she keeps it safe."

Leigh's mind seized several possibilities. "Does Mrs. Murchison have a locked briefcase in her room? Or maybe a jewelry case of some sort?"

"What matters to the cat," Randall interrupted calmly, "is that the object passes without obstructing the bowel." He turned to Nikki. "We'll have to keep a close eye on him the next few days. I won't be back until tomorrow night, but I'll have Dr. McCoy come check on him if you'll leave him here at the clinic."

"No problem," Nikki answered. "But I

wish you'd come to the house for the will reading tonight. The lawyer said it was important you be there."

Leigh's eyebrows rose. She didn't consider herself particularly materialistic, but the words "will reading," when applied to a millionaire, were enough to get any normal person's blood pumping. Particularly when her father seemed to be the only person in Pittsburgh who actually liked the woman.

The veterinarian shook his head. "I'm sure it's just about making arrangements for the cats, and I can call her attorney Monday about that. But I've got to get my wife to Hershey ASAP, or I'll be sleeping on dog-food bags tonight."

Unfortunately, Leigh knew her father was only half joking. After twenty-odd years of planting tulips and pruning shrubs for various city beautification projects, her mother had finally won the coveted Garden Club Community Volunteer of the Year Award, entitling her to a plaque, a ribbon, and a free night's food and lodging at the Hershey Hotel. And if Randall didn't deliver her to that wondrous institution in plenty of time for a leisurely dinner, he would not only be sleeping on dog food — he would be eating it for breakfast besides.

Leigh, on the other hand, had nothing

whatsoever to do tonight. With her handsome husband still out of town, her Saturday night was looking like a frozen dinner, a few taped episodes of *That '70s Show*, and about five hundred boxes to unpack. All while a bunch of other people were gathering in Lilah Murchison's eerie old mansion, learning how much money they were in for when — or if — the mistress of the house was ever fished out of Lake Michigan. Might one of *them* be anxious to reacquire Number One Son's little snack?

"Dad," she began hopefully, "if the lawyer said it was really important, maybe I should go. As your proxy."

The veterinarian didn't look up, but Leigh could feel his eyes swiveling suspiciously in their sockets. She was surprised when he gave the desired answer. "Makes no difference to me. But you should check with the attorney."

His last words were only partly audible. A loud crash of shattering glass assaulted their ears, and she and her father both jumped in response. Nikki Loomis hit the deck. "What the hell was that?" the small woman boomed from the floor.

Randall answered calmly, but his eyes were wide. "I'll check it out." He strode off in the direction of the noise, and both Leigh and Nikki took off on his heels. At the threshold of the waiting room, they all stopped abruptly.

One of the colored glass windows that bordered the street was almost completely gone — its red shards scattered widely across the aged linoleum floor.

"Stay here," Randall ordered. He walked carefully around and through the broken glass to the front door, opened its three separate locks, and disappeared onto the front porch. Leigh stepped forward, her eye on a brown object that had slid under one of the chairs. Skirting the shards on the floor the best she could, she reached the chair and pulled it out.

It was a smooth rock, roughly the size of a grapefruit, and it was covered with printing from a red marker. "What is it?" Nikki asked, hustling over. "What does it say?"

Leigh looked up, her hands shaking slightly. It had been a strange day already; this was over the top.

"Nobody out there," Randall announced bitterly, coming back through the door. His blue scrub suit and sparse hair were completely soaked with rain, and his ordinarily unflappable face was now a pale shade of red, which Leigh knew to mean he was at his maximum anger point. He pounded across the reception area to the desk phone, this time crunching glass heedlessly beneath his feet. "Twice in one weekend!" he exclaimed while he dialed, his voice strained.

"What happened?" Nancy had come up from the basement office and stopped at the doorway, her eyes wide: Jared stood behind her, looking equally perplexed.

"It was a rock," Leigh responded. "Somebody threw a rock through the window."

The veterinarian's eyes fixed briefly on the object in his daughter's hands; then his call was answered. "Hello? Yes, this is Dr. Koslow at the animal clinic. We've been vandalized again —"

Nikki grabbed Leigh's wrist and took a look at the rock herself. "Jeez," she muttered. "What gives?"

Leigh wished she knew. Ricky Rhodis's little adventure might be explained away harmlessly enough, but hurtling a rock through a window was a prank of a different color; someone could have been hurt.

Was the message intended for her father? As the clinic owner he was the obvious target, but Dr. Koslow wasn't the type of person who liked keeping other people's secrets, much less harboring ones of his own. Belatedly worrying about covering up fingerprints, she leaned down and dropped the rock on top of the chair.

"Is that writing I saw on it?" Randall asked, hanging up the phone and crunching back across the room.

It was no accident that Leigh had dropped the rock print-side down. She faced her father and nodded grimly. "It says, *'If the truth comes out, I'll kill you.'*"

4

The rain had let up by evening, and as Leigh climbed out of the Cavalier in church dress number one, she was glad. She had no idea what type of apparel one wore to a will reading, particularly when nobody was completely sure the individual in question was dead. But she figured a nice blue, one-hundred-percent-cotton number could pass by in most crowds without drawing an eyebrow.

She paused a moment beside her car to ogle the Murchison mansion. By modern suburban standards, its square footage was nothing to brag about. But in aura, the house was huge. It was one of the oldest and stateliest mansions in the distinguished riverside borough of Ben Avon, and that was nothing to sneeze at. A dark, second-empire creation with three stories, a mansard roof, and ghoulish-looking bracketing around the large windows and under the eaves, it evoked images of everything from haunted wine cellars to dusty attics filled with dotty old uncles. Like most houses on the steep, populated river bluff, it had little yard to speak of, but every inch of what it did have

62

was ruthlessly hemmed in by dense, aging shrubbery. The main entrance was not even visible from the road, as the narrow brick walk zigzagged through a series of tall hedgerows. Even the entrance to the quaint two-story garage was concealed; the driveway pulled off from the side road at an acute angle and immediately disappeared behind a line of evergreens.

Lilah Murchison liked her privacy.

Leigh hadn't taken a step before a disturbingly familiar sedan rattled up behind her, rolled two wheels onto the grass, and stopped with a disturbing "whomp." Adith Rhodis popped out instantly. "Honey!" she began in a fluster. "I've been trailing you ever since your driveway. Didn't you see me? I was trying to get your attention. Danged horn's out."

Leigh imagined with horror the older woman swerving all over the road behind her. As preoccupied as her mind was, she hadn't seen a thing. "I'm glad you're OK," she said with relief. "What's up?"

Adith looked at her disbelievingly. "What's up? That's what I'd like to know! I haven't heard from you all day, and you know I hate those phone machines. Did you talk to your daddy? What did he say?"

Leigh sighed and dove into an explana-

tion that was complicated, and not neces-
sarily encouraging. Because although her
father had backed off his insistence that the
break-in was drug related, the rock incident
had made him considerably less inclined to
welcome Ricky Rhodis back onto the
streets. *Not just yet, anyway,* he had said
firmly as he scuttled off to Hershey. Ricky
couldn't have thrown the rock himself, but
why wouldn't he talk? Was he protecting
someone else? *There are too many unan-
swered questions.*

Which is why she had decided to push her
luck by showing up at the Murchison mansion a little early. She finished her explanation to Adith as gently, yet realistically, as
possible, and was surprised to see the older
woman's eyes light up with optimism.
"Told you my boy doesn't do drugs!" she
chortled. "Didn't I tell you? Everything will
be all right, then. Your daddy will come to
his senses soon."

Leigh smiled politely, then looked point-
edly at her watch, hoping the older woman
would take the hint. She should have known
better.

"Albert and Lilah Murchison's house,"
Adith murmured, looking it over with such
reverence that Leigh halfway expected her
to genuflect. Instead, she spat into a palm.

"Never thought I'd see the day." Rubbing her wetted hands together, she made a futile attempt to tame the white-gray hair that sprang straight out from her head. "Oh my. The girls will *love* this."

Leigh tried not to panic. "Mrs. Rhodis," she began carefully, "you can't go in with me. I'm only here as a proxy for my father."

The older woman waved away the concern as if shooing a gnat. "Oh, honey. Don't you worry about that. We'll just say I'm your aunt."

"But —"

"Now, look, child," Adith continued firmly, adjusting her polyester dress over her ample bosom. "I've lived in these boroughs for seventy-eight years now, and I haven't once been in one of these Ben Avon mansions, much less *the* mansion of *the* Lilah Murchison, who wouldn't let her best friend in on Christmas if she had one, which she never did. Now she's dead and doesn't care and I'm alive and do — and I'm going in that house with you and you aren't going to stop me." She paused, then donned her sweetest little-old-lady smile. "Now. Are you ready, hon?"

Leigh bit her lip. She could either risk a scene with Adith when the lawyer arrived, or have a public one on the street right now.

Procrastination ruled. "All right," she said with defeat, heading toward the house. "But behave yourself, please. Don't go snooping around or anything."

Adith nodded and fell in step. "Fine. I'll just distract the housekeeper for you."

Leigh reeled. "You'll do no such thing! I'm only here to find out about the will. For my father."

The older woman grinned. "Uh-huh. You want to know what it is that cat ate that's so danged important to somebody, and so do I. Now let's do it."

No response came to Leigh's mind as they followed the meandering walk up to the mansion's carved oak doors. She had to admit that getting Ricky Rhodis out of jail was no longer her only motivation. Someone was trying to intimidate her father — or someone else at the clinic — and though that whole situation could very well have nothing to do with Number One Son, the timing could not be overlooked. And Nikki Loomis, despite her insistence on not knowing what the cat might have swallowed, was clearly the person to talk to. Leigh pressed the doorbell.

"Yeah? Um, what time is it?" The startled personal assistant, wearing exactly the same jeans and T-shirt she had had on at the clinic earlier, greeted the odd twosome curtly.

"It's not time for me to be here yet, I know," Leigh explained quickly, cursing herself for being intimidated by a woman who weighed less than a Saint Bernard. "I'm sorry. But I didn't get a chance to talk to you again after the police came, and I need to. It's important."

Nikki looked up at her skeptically, but her gaze was not unfriendly, and Leigh found herself wondering just how old the woman was. She appeared to be somewhere in her mid-twenties, yet somehow she seemed wise beyond her years. "All right," she answered, swinging the large door wide. "But you'll have to talk while I get ready."

Adith grinned with delight, then brushed past Leigh's shoulder and scuttled inside.

Leigh threw her hostess an embarrassed smile. "Um, this is my friend Adith," she explained weakly as she followed. "I was — well — obliged to bring her." Perhaps the aunt story would have made more sense, but Leigh had enough batty aunts already. Nikki threw the older woman a brief but critical look, then, much to Leigh's relief, simply shrugged her shoulders.

The spacious tiled foyer, which was dominated by a splendidly carved wooden balustrade, looked elegant — and fairly normal. But when Leigh glanced at the library and parlor to either side, she couldn't help but feel as if she had walked into an industrial cleanroom. The hardwood furniture and flooring were rich and beautiful, but without a single rug on the floor or curtain on the windows, it all looked disturbingly stark.

Adding to the unusual milieu was the tremendous cacophony that rattled from every direction — a mixture of howls, mews, and cries that put one in mind of a medieval torture chamber. Leigh suppressed a shudder as she recalled the kitten-eating nightmares.

Nikki looked back at the other women's faces and laughed out loud. "Yeah, I know," she chuckled. "Weird, isn't it? They're not always this loud, but I had to shut up the free-rangers in the bedrooms. You should hear them when the exterminator comes and they all have to go in the kennels with the toms. That *really* ticks them off."

Leigh smiled self-consciously, aware that there was no good reason a big old house full of Siamese cats should cause the hair on the back of her neck to stand at attention. Nonetheless, Hitchcock could have made a fortune off the place.

Nikki pressed back toward the large kitchen where she began pulling glass tumblers out of a cabinet and onto the gleaming black marble countertop. The floor, too, was of marble tile, though its gleam was somewhat compromised by a thin coating of white fuzz. As Adith began buzzing about, peering into cabinets unabashedly, Leigh attempted to hold her hostess's attention.

"I need to talk to you about whatever it was that Number One Son swallowed," she began somewhat nervously. She had only met Nikki a few hours before and had no good reason to consider her an ally, but given that the woman already had access to Mrs. Murchison's cats 24/7, it hardly seemed likely she would involve herself in an elaborate plot to steal one from the vet clinic.

"OK," Nikki answered, struggling to flip open the safety latch on a large, shallow drawer of dish towels.

Leigh halted, impressed. "I can't believe how much trouble Mrs. Murchison has gone to to keep that cat away from cloth," she remarked.

"Oh, Number One Son's not the only one," Nikki responded. "Auntie Em has a taste for it too, though she hasn't swallowed anything so far. Ms. Murchison fixed up the house a long time ago for some cat named Abbott. He's dead now, but she always has at least one wool sucker to watch out for."

A light dawned. "They're named after characters from old movies," Leigh realized aloud.

"Yep," Nikki answered distractedly, "radio and television too. Ms. Murchison named a few that way when she first started out, and it bugged the other breeders, so she kept it up."

"So," Leigh mused, "Number One Son isn't a direct knock on this Dean guy."

Nikki's eyes narrowed. "No — it's from the Charlie Chan movies. But there is a kind of justice to it, if you ask me."

Anxious to strike before the mood soured further, Leigh pressed on. "There are some things I think you should know," she began lightly. "You said earlier that you couldn't think of a reason why anyone would want to steal one of Mrs. Murchison's cats, but I think I can. I think they wanted whatever it is that Number One Son swallowed."

Nikki showed no response. Leigh went on to explain about the cat carrier and litter bag Jared had found, and when she had finished, Nikki stood still for a moment and looked at her.

"Maybe," she said flatly. "But I still don't know what it could be."

"A broach?" Leigh suggested. "A key to a jewelry box or a safe?" She wasn't sure what she expected from Nikki, but a little enthusiasm would have been nice. Had their positions been reversed, Leigh would at this point have been scouring every inch of the mansion on her hands and knees, scouting for tiny keyholes. Perhaps having a pathological lack of curiosity was a prerequisite for Team Murchison.

"Look," Nikki said impatiently, cutting her off, "Ms. Lilah does have some valuable pieces of jewelry, but they pretty much stay in her bank vault. The stuff she keeps in her bedroom is only costume jewelry. So forget it."

A muffled crash made them both turn their heads toward the walk-in pantry, which Adith was exiting rapidly. "Cans came unstacked," she offered sweetly.

Leigh feared an explosion from Nikki, but none occurred. The personal assistant did look exasperated, but her focus was not on Adith so much as the glasses on the countertop. "I don't know anything about this entertaining crap," she snapped suddenly. "I just pay the bills, make appointments, and tell charities to go to hell. Do

71

either of you chicks know what to put out at a will reading?"

Since there was probably no one on the planet less qualified to answer that question, Leigh had to laugh. "If it were me, I'd break out pop and pass the cheese curls."

"White wine," Adith suggested eagerly. "With caviar."

Nikki looked from one to the other, then retrieved a couple of two-liters from the pantry and slammed them onto the counter next to the tumblers. "*Self-serve.* Now, come with me into the parlor," she ordered. "The others should be here any minute."

She walked ahead of them out of the kitchen, and Leigh caught Adith's eye and motioned for her to follow. She couldn't give up now; her time was limited. "Nikki," she called out as she walked, "could Number One Son have swallowed something that belonged to somebody else? A visitor in the house, perhaps?"

The younger woman reached the parlor, then turned. "Look, Koslow junior. In case you haven't noticed, Ms. Lilah wasn't the Avon Lady. Hardly anybody ever comes in this house except staff, and there aren't many of them. Nobody's going to want anything that cat ate, believe me." She stooped over to fluff a pillow, which in her case

72

meant beating it squarely with a fist. Her eyes turned suddenly hostile. "Nobody better smoke."

Leigh clenched her teeth, not the least bit swayed by her hostess's pragmatism. She was sure that Ricky Rhodis had been after the cat. "Are you sure that *no one* else has been here?"

The personal assistant's eyes widened, and she stopped in mid fluff, her face darkening. "Why, that —" The list of foul adjectives that followed was interrupted by the sound of a ringing doorbell, and Leigh, who had been standing by in rapt anticipation of an upcoming noun, let out an anguished groan as Nikki jumped up to answer it.

"Mr. Sheridan," Nikki said roughly, struggling to make her tone sound polite again. "I'm glad you're here first. Is there anything I'm supposed to do for this, other than point to chairs?"

William Sheridan, an impeccably groomed, dour man in his late forties, answered without a smile. "No, just a place to sit is fine, thank you. But I do need to talk to you privately for a moment." He turned to Leigh. "If you'll excuse us?"

"Oh," she replied awkwardly. "Of course. We'll just go" — she looked over her shoulder, but Adith was nowhere in sight —

"get a drink," she finished sheepishly, stepping backward.

"More news about the crash?" Nikki was asking the lawyer as Leigh retreated. She couldn't hear his answer, but she wanted to. She also wanted to know who Nikki had remembered had been in the house. But first she had to figure out where the heck Adith had gotten to.

She walked back through the hallway to the kitchen, and was disturbed to find it empty. She was even more disturbed to find the family room and the library empty as well, because Adith couldn't possibly have strolled anywhere else on the ground floor without running into Nikki and the lawyer. Leigh returned to the foyer and looked nervously up the stairs. Adith wouldn't just start prowling around the bedrooms, would she?

Her rhetorical question was answered by a small triangular head, which poked its way through the stair railing and peered at her with twinkling blue eyes. Another suddenly appeared on top of the newel post at the landing, its angular jaw dropping with a resentful cry. Leigh's spirits plummeted. Not only was Adith upstairs, she was accidentally letting out the cats.

The doorbell rang again, and Leigh

headed up the steps in haste. She certainly hoped there was a back way to the kitchen — or she and her accomplice were busted for sure. Scooping up one cat under each arm, she headed down the upstairs hallway. "Adith!" she whispered harshly, unable to hear herself over the loud mews of the remaining prisoners. "Where are you?"

She couldn't help noting the original works of art she was passing by on either side of the corridor — all of which were dark, dreary renditions of hunting expeditions. The late Albert's taste, she hoped. No self-respecting cat lover would approve of cruelty to foxes. Unless . . .

Stop that! She shook the hideous images from her head again and paused at each closed door to listen, but heard only mewling and a few ineffectual scratches. She was about to begin opening doors randomly — and taking chances on additional escapees — when Adith popped out of a second stairwell in front of her.

"Three floors!" the older woman announced proudly. "I found old Albert's office too. Did you know he met President Eisenhower?"

"We've got to get back to the kitchen. Now," Leigh ordered. She held up her arms to display her feline passengers, which were no longer enjoying the ride. "Where did these two come from? We've got to put them back."

Adith looked at the Siamese with a wrinkled nose. "Evil-looking things, if you ask me. Too skinny. Now, my Pansy —"

"Mrs. Rhodis," Leigh interrupted intently, "which door did they come out of? Quick!"

"Her bedroom," the older woman answered with a sly smile. "It's this way. Nice, but could use some curtains. Never been into mauve, myself."

After a complicated maneuver involving six human limbs and a pocketbook, the cats were finally returned to their prison, and Leigh and Adith were able to slip safely back into the kitchen through the rear staircase. They had not been there twenty seconds, however, when Nikki appeared.

"Welcome back," she said coarsely, picking up the two-liters. "Would you mind grabbing some glasses and bringing them into the dining room? Mr. Sheridan's getting ready to start."

5

Leigh and Adith were obliged to sit on a stiff-backed settee at the back of the parlor, which was fine by both. Not only did it offer an excellent view of the beneficiaries, but its proximity to Mrs. Murchison's antique rolltop desk allowed Adith to examine the latter's cubby-holes with impunity.

"I cannot state emphatically enough," the attorney began, casting a stern glance over the assembly, "that the will I am about to read is *not* yet being probated. No action will be taken with regard to the deceased's estate until a certificate of death has been issued. Is that clear?"

He looked directly at a young woman on the couch to his right, who had been twittering noisily into the ear of the young man beside her. She was wearing tight jeans and an even tighter Lynyrd Skynyrd tank top, but it was her algae-green lipstick that demanded the most attention. "Oh, right. Whatever," she said with a plastic smile.

The lawyer nodded slowly, not bothering to conceal his disdain. "I myself personally prepared this testament quite recently. I will admit that its terms are a bit unusual, but rest assured that Mrs. Murchison was in perfectly sound mind at the time, and that she followed all the necessary legal steps in altering her previous testament."

"Now, what do you mean by 'previous testament'?" the young man on the couch asked loudly, puffing out his chest with importance. This presented a challenge, since the severely wrinkled suit he was wearing was so small that it held his shoulders like a straitjacket. The suit's equally missized pantlegs ended somewhere in his mid-calf region, revealing worn tube socks and a heavily scuffed pair of loafers. But by far the most striking part of the ensemble was his belt — a wide plastic device laden with pounds of key rings, tools, and beeper-type appliances. "I know she had one with Lang and Madia a while back," he said authoritatively.

The attorney's voice was mild, but he looked down at the other man as if he were something on the bottom of a shoe. "As we have already discussed at length, Mr. Murchison, your mother was in the habit of updating her testament regularly. And though her business interests remain with Lang and Madia, she had chosen relatively recently to move her personal affairs to my firm."

Adith sniggered. "She wanted a little more action, that's why," she whispered hoarsely. "You think this guy's a dud. . . . Those other stiff-necks have all got one foot in the coffin."

Leigh threw her companion a doubtful look and tried not to smile.

"You don't believe me?" the older woman said with mock hurt. "She carried on with every one of her chauffeurs, didn't you know? My friend Virginia's brother-in-law Milton got a job doing her gardening and when he wouldn't play footsie with her she canned his behind, she did." Adith gave a wink and a knowing nod. "She *lived for it.*" She raised her chin superiorly. "That's what they say, anyway."

Struggling to maintain her composure, Leigh quietly shushed her companion, having the odd feeling that if she didn't, they were both going to wind up in detention. She tried hard to concentrate on the attorney's ramblings, but she had never had much patience with legalese, and Mr. Sheridan seemed consumed with pressing home the concept, particularly to the charming young couple on the couch, that nobody was getting *anything* yet.

By the time he cleared his throat and began reading the actual document in his hand, an elderly woman in an armchair at his left had dozed off.

" 'Firstly,' " the lawyer read, " 'I would like to reward my most trusted employees for their years of faithful service. To Peggy Linney, I leave —' " Mr. Sheridan paused, then bent down to nudge the sleeping woman awake. " 'To Peggy Linney,' " he repeated with irritation, " 'my most devoted housekeeper, I leave a trust, in addition to her existing pension, which will be used to provide her with room and board in a very comfortable independent-living facility for the rest of her days, with the proviso that none of her wretched, money-grubbing relatives be allowed to move in with her or mooch off of her in any way.' "

Leigh had to snigger a little herself, not at the words, but at the lawyer's efforts to pronounce them with dignity. Peggy Linney smiled broadly for a moment, then closed her eyes again.

" 'And to my most faithful chauffeurs —' "

Adith gave Leigh a giant wink and delivered a sharp elbow jab to her ribs. "Told you so!"

The lawyer read off a long list of personal items and nest eggs to be split among a half-dozen men, then bequeathed smaller parcels of money to several other employees, including Nikki. Leigh noted that of the dozen or so people in the room, only the young couple had not yet been mentioned. Were Lilah's son and daughter-in-law her only relatives?

" 'As for the Murchison residence —' " The lawyer raised his voice, and several attendees, most notably Adith Rhodis and the girl with the green lips, sat up at attention. " 'It is my desire that the house be used to maintain my precious cats in the level of comfort to which they have been accustomed. Toward this end, I would ask that Nikki Loomis continue to reside in the house and care for my pets as long as she so desires, knowing that doing so will earn her her current salary, with regular increases, until such time as all the cats have passed on. I do not wish that anyone else be allowed to reside in my house; however, Jared Loomis may continue to occupy the garage apartment as long as his sister remains in my employ. Should —' "

The lawyer was interrupted by the green-lipped girl, who bounced off the couch spewing a steady stream of vulgarity. "The *cats*. The *cats?* This is *my* house!" she screamed at the attorney. "I want it. I've always wanted it. Dean said I could have it!"

Dean Murchison rose slowly, the seams

in his pants visibly straining. "Now, look, dude," he said calmly, more as if addressing an errant child than an attorney, "that's just wrong. This house belonged to my old man. When my mother died it was supposed to come to me."

The lawyer, who had faced the woman's onslaught without visible reaction, adjusted his tie. "If you would allow me to finish, Mr. Murchison?" he said coolly.

Nikki Loomis cleared her throat, shifting in her own seat just enough to flex a bicep in Dean's direction. He looked at her with contempt, but nonetheless took hold of his wife's arm and pulled her back down to the couch. "Let's hear the rest of it, honey," he soothed, loud enough for the cats upstairs to hear.

The lawyer continued. "As I was reading, Mrs. Murchison states: 'Should Ms. Loomis choose to leave my employ, or should she not abide by the terms I have set forth, she will be replaced by a like employee, to be hired by Randall Koslow, DVM.' "

Leigh's ears perked.

" 'Inasmuch as Randall Koslow has provided my pets with top-notch health care for over thirty years now, and given that he is undoubtedly the only truly honest and dedicated man that I know, I ask that he oversee the care of my pets indefinitely, on the terms of a generous retainer as outlined below.' "

The lawyer paused, explaining to Leigh that the will then went on at great length about the disposition of each and every cat, and that he would share the details with her father at a later date. The gist of it, she gathered, was that in exchange for a handsome but not excessive amount of money, her father was now the godfather of twenty-three Siamese. " 'In addition,' " Mr. Sheridan continued, " 'I am bequeathing a total of five hundred thousand dollars to the feline charity or charities of Dr. Koslow's choice.' "

The younger Mrs. Murchison exploded for a second time. She maligned the good name of the Murchison Siamese — and cats in general — for several ear-shattering moments before her husband finally clapped a hand over her mouth. "Half a *million*," he bellowed, struggling to keep her down, "to *cat* charities?"

The lawyer puffed up his own chest. "Mr. Murchison, sir, I ask that you and your wife please restrain yourselves. If you cannot, I'm afraid we will have to end the reading."

"Ouch! Dang it, Rochelle!" Dean screamed in pain as his wife bit his hand, but he nonetheless managed to pull her into his lap and hold her with a wrestler's grip. He wasn't a big guy, but weighing in at about a hundred pounds, his female opponent was mostly fingernails. Once her arms were safely pinned, he slapped a conciliatory kiss on the back of her neck and glared at the attorney. "We're fine. Now tell us about the rest of the money," he ordered.

The lawyer eyed Rochelle warily, as if judging the distance between her thick heels and his kneecap. She sat quietly now, green lips pouting, but her eyes still flashed fire. The attorney took a step backward, then cleared his throat and launched into a long laundry list of holdings and securities. As soon as things got boring, Adith leaned into Leigh's side. "Whoowie!" she whispered heavily. "Half a million clams. Do you suppose he could send some of that to *dog* charities?"

" 'All of the aforementioned assets,' " the lawyer said meaningfully, waking everyone up again, " 'I leave to my one and only blood heir.' "

The words had barely left the attorney's mouth before Dean and Rochelle Murchison ejected themselves from the couch, hugging each other in mid air. "Damn that old witch!" the young man

84

yelled. "I knew she wouldn't do it!"

"Oh, baby!" Rochelle screeched. Her frizzy hair bobbed a good foot as she jumped, and her heels clanked like boulders on the hardwood floor. "We'll buy another house. A bigger house!"

Mr. Sheridan watched them for a moment before interrupting, his dour expression turning even more grim. "Excuse me," he said firmly, "but I am afraid you have misinterpreted the testament. Would you sit again, please?"

The couple stopped bouncing, but made no move to sit. The attorney continued reading anyway.

" 'Unfortunately, it so happens that my true heir is not the boy I raised as my son, Dean Murchison. To that ungrateful little leech, I leave an annual stipend of twenty-five thousand dollars, with regular increases, which, when combined with a decent salary, should leave him reasonably comfortable. He should be glad he lived the life of luxury as long as he did, and take to heart the fact that if he'd been a little more appreciative, I might have overlooked his lack of my own genes.'

" 'As it stands, my blood heir will inherit the lion's share without qualification, provided that proper identification is presented as described herein within five years of the date of my demise.' "

The room was deathly quiet, other than the slight wheezing sound of Adith's breathing. Dean and Rochelle had both turned white. The lawyer's face, in contrast, was quite red, and he eyed them both with a healthy dose of apprehension. Nikki stood up.

"I don't believe it," Peggy Linney said quietly.

"True heir?" one of the ex-cooks piped up. "I don't get it. What does she mean?"

The lawyer's face got redder, and he stroked his beard nervously. "It appears that Mrs. Murchison gave birth to a child who was not Dean Murchison, and that she wishes her blood relative to inherit. I'm afraid the will does not go into particulars about how or why this is the case."

"Who's the real father, then?" demanded a husky, gray-haired ex-chauffeur. "Does he get anything?"

"Yeah, how old is the kid?" demanded another, younger one.

"Gentlemen, please," the attorney pleaded. "I'm afraid I simply don't have the answers you're looking for. I was Mrs. Murchison's attorney, not her personal confidant. Besides which, I must strongly caution you that until we have a legal certificate of death —"

His last words were drowned out in the clatter as nearly everyone present jumped up and began chattering. Dean and Rochelle, still on their feet, remained standing like statues.

"Do you have any idea what this means?" Adith twittered, her eyes blazing. "Lilah Murchison has another child out there — a very rich child. Who could it be? Oh my, and when could she have had him? She was so very thin. . . ." She rose and took a step toward the door, turning when she realized Leigh wasn't following. "Well, come on, honey! I need to get to a phone. The girls are going to *die*. This'll even shake up Bud. Did you know Lilah winked at him once?"

Leigh took her companion by the arm and sat the older woman back down. The uncomfortable feeling that had been brewing in her stomach ever since she read the message on the rock had just graduated into an ulcer. *If the truth comes out, I'll kill you.* Maybe the two acts of vandalism weren't related, but she couldn't help wondering if "the truth" wasn't at that moment traveling somewhere in Number One Son's intestines. "Mrs. Rhodis," she asked intently, "how well did you know Lilah Murchison?"

"Oh, honey," Adith said with a chuckle, "that woman hasn't talked to the likes of me since the moon landing. But I used to know her. Back when she was Lilah Beemish — Avalon's own town tramp. My little cousin Laverne and her used to hang out some, but my aunt put a stop to that. 'Them Beemishes are nothing but trash,' she'd say."

A trashy woman with at least one big secret, Leigh thought. She knew the black-widow stories as well as anybody — three husbands, three suspicious deaths. The first one Lilah had married quite young, and supposedly just to get out of town. But the marriage had ended prematurely in a car crash, and she had limped back into town a penniless widow. The second husband and source of her current wealth she had pursued quite shamelessly — much to the chagrin of his well-connected wife, whom he had coldly cast aside. That husband had died of a heart attack, which to the locals meant poisoning. The last marriage was to Albert Murchison, Dean's presumed father, who had died in his sleep — i.e., a well-placed pillow.

Leigh had never really believed that any of the men were murdered. "Adith," she asked, "Mrs. Murchison was no spring chicken when Dean was born, was she?"

"Lord, no, honey," Adith answered gaily. "She was forty if she was a day. But Albert desperately wanted a son, and time was running out."

"How old was he?"

She whistled. "Oh, almost seventy, I'd say. It was a miracle they ever conceived."

"Well, apparently *they* didn't," Leigh answered dryly. She looked up to see if the lawyer planned on continuing, but found him hemmed in by a pack of agitated beneficiaries.

She thought for a moment. "Was Lilah the maternal type?"

Adith raised an eyebrow, then burst out laughing.

"I'll take that as a no," Leigh continued. "So if Lilah married Albert for his money, why would she even want a child? A son or daughter would just take away half her inheritance. Unless she was worried that if she didn't produce an heir, he would dump her for an even younger wife. . . ."

The older woman shook her head. "I can see Albert divorcing her if she couldn't have a kid. But she didn't marry him for his money. He didn't have a dime."

Leigh's eyes widened. "But this house was his!"

"Sure, the family mansion, the respectability. But Albert Murchison was a dud with money. Lost most everything his family gave him. It was Lilah's second husband who had the cash — and the clout. But that money was new money, if you know what I mean, and that fellow was an upstart — an outsider." Adith raised her chin. "Albert Murchison was genuine *class,* and that's what Lilah wanted next. A husband who could bring her up in the world."

And, Leigh thought uncharitably, who wasn't likely to live very long. "So, she faked a pregnancy and tricked him into thinking that Dean was their baby. And she probably had a prenup so that the money she brought to the marriage was safe from the child anyway. Amazing."

"Cold," Adith said wickedly. "She was vicious cold. Stole a baby to keep Albert Murchison happy after she'd given one of her own away. Now, that's the part I wonder about. Why would she give up a baby of her own?" Her lips pursed in thought. "Maybe it was during marriage number two — and her husband knew it wasn't his."

Leigh didn't answer. Her thoughts were back on the clinic, and how much Lilah Murchison had appeared to trust Randall Koslow. Enough to share personal secrets?

If someone was threatening Randall not to expose the contents of Number One Son's jejunum, that was bad enough. But what if "the truth" referred to something else — something her father already knew?

"But then," Adith continued to prattle, "how could she have been in the family way without anybody knowing? I suppose she did keep out of sight a lot. And some women just don't show, you know. Now, when I was carrying my Jimmy —"

Leigh's mind wandered as she scanned the room. Most of those present were on their way out now, but Dean and Rochelle didn't appear to be going anywhere. They had backed the poor attorney into a corner, literally, and the only thing standing between them and him was a particularly belligerent-looking Nikki.

Leigh put a finger to her lips and rose. "I'm going to move a little closer and see if I can hear what they're saying." Adith's eyes gleamed and she started to rise as well, but Leigh put a hand on her shoulder. "We can't be too obvious. I'll report everything later. I promise."

The other woman sat back down with a resentful look, and Leigh worked her way inconspicuously forward until she could make out the lawyer's words. Understanding what Dean and Rochelle were saying was not a problem.

"But why *doesn't* it say who this heir is?" the young man bellowed. "It has to!"

"I believe," the attorney answered, "that Mrs. Murchison wished to allow the individual the option of remaining anonymous. The choice of whether to come forward and claim the inheritance is his — or hers."

"Well, what if they *don't* come forward?" screeched Rochelle. "Who gets the money then?"

"As I stated earlier," the lawyer continued with admirable poise, "the blood heir is given five years to come forward. If he or she does not present suitable evidence of his or her parentage within that time, the inheritance is to be divided equally between Dean Murchison and Dr. Koslow's choice of feline charities."

The couple fell silent a moment. Then Dean rolled his eyes. "I have to share millions with a bunch of mangy cats?" he whined.

"It's still millions," Rochelle answered stiffly. "Right?"

The lawyer cleared his throat again. "Almost certainly. Although I must caution you both again that —"

"Let's get out of here," Rochelle said

loudly, grabbing her husband's arm. "We've heard all we need to hear."

Dean cast a goofy, conciliatory glance back at the lawyer and Nikki as he allowed his wife to turn him around. "Yeah, OK." The two stomped through the parlor back to the foyer and let themselves out with a bang.

Nikki exhaled loudly and plopped down on the arm of the couch. "Sorry about that, Mr. Sheridan," she said. "I'm surprised you don't bring security with you for these things."

The lawyer smiled unconvincingly. "All in a day's work, I assure you. Now, if you'll excuse me . . ."

Leigh backed up again, hoping neither Nikki nor the lawyer had been paying any attention to her. As the two of them walked to the front door, she crept back to the settee and scanned its empty cushions with a sigh.

Adith was gone again.

6

"Mrs. Rhodis!" Leigh hissed desperately up the back stairway. "Come down here! We're the only people left." There was no response, except for the eerie howling and mewling that had been echoing down from the bedrooms for almost an hour now.

"Mrs. Rhodis, eh?" Nikki's drill-sergeant voice, coming from a few inches below Leigh's ear, made her jump with a screech.

"I'm sorry," she said quickly, whirling around. "I know this is incredibly rude, but Adith —"

"I know who she is," Nikki said evenly, her gray eyes locking on Leigh's flustered brown ones. "I went through her purse after she disappeared the first time. You want to tell me why you brought a relative of the kid who broke into your dad's clinic into this house?"

Leigh reddened. "Um, well, yes." *Ouch.* This looked bad. She hadn't thought about how bad until now. "Adith is Ricky's grandmother. She asked me to try to find out what he was really up to, because she doesn't believe he broke into the clinic to steal drugs. But that's not why she's here.

She just happened to follow my car over here, and —"

Nikki's hard eyes showed a flicker of perception, then softened ever so slightly. "Don't tell me. She just *had* to see the house where Lilah Murchison lived."

Leigh nodded.

Nikki snorted. "Her and half of the North Boros."

"Look, I'm really sorry —"

"Save it. I don't care. As long as she doesn't mess with the cats or steal anything."

Surprised by the gruff woman's unexpected generosity, Leigh faltered a moment. "Oh! I'm sure she would never —"

"You've *got* to see this, honey!" Adith popped gleefully out of the stairwell, her arms extending an onyx statuette of two humans in an indisputably compromising position. "It's Mexican!"

Leigh's face drained of color as she shifted her gaze toward Nikki. Adith's eyes followed, then widened. "I've always appreciated fine art, you know," the older woman said smoothly, pulling the piece back and cradling it protectively with an arm. "I'll just put this right back . . ."

Adith did a jerky about-face and disappeared from sight, and Leigh apologized for a third time. "I'm sorry. We'll be going now. I'll give my dad the news as soon as he gets back. It was — um, very generous of Mrs. Murchison to think of him."

Nikki looked back at her strangely. "Whatever. I just work for the woman."

An awkward moment passed as they waited for Adith to reappear. Not one to endure nervous silences, Leigh decided to press her luck. Nikki had been about to say something before the lawyer had arrived — something about a person who had been in the house before Number One Son discovered lunch.

"You know," she began as evenly as possible, "I can't help wondering if the incident with Number One Son — and maybe even that rock being thrown — has something to do with Mrs. Murchison's will."

The smaller woman stared hard at her for a moment, her pale eyes difficult to read.

Leigh continued. "When I asked you earlier if you remembered anyone who might have been in the house —"

"Dean," she answered flatly. "Dean and Rochelle were here yesterday morning, hassling me." Her expression darkened. "Dean thinks he's God's gift to the human race — always has. Ms. Lilah spoiled him rotten when he was a kid. Anyway, they were over here with some lame story about how Ms. Lilah had called and told them she wanted to see them at the house right away — that she was coming home from New York early. I let them in, and Rochelle slipped right off — said she had to use the bathroom. I tried to follow her, but Dean hung me up. God only knows what she was doing."

"Ten bucks says dropping something the cat found," Leigh answered. "Something Rochelle might have wanted back?"

Nikki looked thoughtful. "Maybe," she admitted reluctantly. "Dean and Ms. Lilah had a huge blowup a few days ago. I'm thinking maybe she told him he was out of her will."

Leigh's pulse quickened. "Had she done that before?"

"Threatened, sure. They were always at each other's throats about something." Nikki hesitated, as if she wasn't sure whether to say more. Then she looked at Leigh purposefully. "I've got no clue what Number One Son could have swallowed that was so important, but if Dean really wanted it back, I guess I wouldn't put it past him to try to steal the cat out of the clinic. He could have been watching me when I dropped the two cats off over there Friday afternoon — maybe he was afraid Number

One Son would throw it up. Either way, if he didn't want Ms. Lilah to find out what the cat had eaten, he'd have to do something fast."

"Do you know if Dean or Rochelle were friends with Ricky Rhodis?" Leigh asked eagerly.

Nikki scoffed. "The less I know about Dean Murchison's personal life, the better. That guy comes closer to getting my fist in his face every time I see him."

"Thank you, anyway," Leigh said with a smile. "I think you've just helped get Mrs. Rhodis's gullible grandson out of jail." *Now — the message on that rock.* "Do you have any idea who this mysterious heir might be?"

To her surprise, Nikki rolled her eyes. "Oh, forget about that."

Leigh's brow wrinkled. "Forget about it?"

Nikki gave her head a shake and waved one hand dismissively in the air. "I suppose Ms. Lilah could have another kid out there, but if you ask me, it's just a scam. Ms. Lilah was a big one for pulling hoaxes, and she loved to dangle her money in front of Dean and make him jump through hoops for it. She'd think it was hilarious to make him sweat for five years, not knowing if he was getting the money or not. I can just see her laughing."

"But to tell everyone he wasn't really her son!" Leigh said with disbelief. Adith had said the woman was cold, but . . .

"He might be adopted," Nikki said casually. "He doesn't look a thing like his parents. But what difference would that make? I'm telling you, all he cares about is the money, anyway."

Adith had appeared at the bottom of the stairs again, this time looking quite proper. "Thank you so much for your hospitality, Ms. — er . . ."

"Just call me Nikki," the younger woman said tonelessly. "And tell that grandson of yours that if he knows what's good for him, he'll stay the hell away from Dean Murchison."

Adith looked questioningly at Leigh.

"I'll explain everything later," Leigh replied, and she pulled her companion forcibly toward the door.

Leigh stopped pacing across her parents' small living room and paused to look out their window for the fortieth time. They were not home from Hershey yet. They had not been home any of the twelve times she had called the house earlier, and they had not come home in the last half hour she had been staked out at their house. Pretty soon, she was going to explode.

She began the pacing again, wishing for anything to burn off the nervous energy that had kept her up most of the night.

If the truth comes out, I'll kill you.

Was the threat from Dean and Rochelle Murchison? If the mystery heir really did exist, they would be the only ones who stood to gain from that person failing to come forward. Except, of course, for a few choice cat charities. And she doubted that many nonprofit veterinary organizations secured their funding with drive-by rock throwings.

Maybe, incredible as it sounded, Number One Son had swallowed something that pointed to the identity of the real heir. Or maybe Number One Son was only part of the picture. What if, on one of her father's emergency house calls to the mansion, he had wittingly or unwittingly stumbled across something he shouldn't have? What if he already knew who the real heir was?

The questions spun maddeningly in her head, as they had since yesterday evening. She wished again that her husband were home, or that their mutual college friend, Detective Maura Polanski, had not been working all night. Both could be counted on to help her make sense out of nonsense, and either would be more effective than she at making Randall take the threat on the rock seriously.

The grating sound of car wheels on a gravel driveway met her eager ears, and she flew to the window. Her parents' Taurus was pulling into the garage behind the house.

She went immediately to stand outside the back door, not wishing to give her mother a stroke by appearing in the kitchen like a burglar. Characteristically, however, her mother chose to have a stroke anyway.

"For heaven's sake, dear!" Frances crooned, her eyes wide as she hurried up the walkway. "Whatever are you doing here? Is Warren all right?"

Leigh forced a smile. Frances Koslow's lifelong fear of her daughter's accidental and/or foolish demise was topped only by her concern for her sainted son-in-law.

"Warren's fine, Mom," she assured. "He'll be back from Philly tomorrow night. I just need to talk to Dad."

Frances eyed her daughter skeptically, then turned her penetrating gaze back on her husband. "What's going on? Is something up at the clinic?"

"Everything's fine, dear," Randall said mechanically, making his way into the house with a suitcase in each hand and another one under his arm. "Number One Son doesn't need surgery again, does he?" he asked Leigh as he passed her.

"No," she answered. "I mean, not as far as I know. I haven't heard."

Randall nodded and disappeared into the house.

"Exactly what do you need to talk to your father about?" Frances questioned, carrying two shopping bags into the kitchen and depositing them on the table. "And why don't you try parting your hair on the other side for a change?"

Leigh chose to ignore the second question. As for the first, her father had obviously not found his mention in the will of a millionaire to be sufficiently interesting to tell his wife about. Typical. "It has to do with Lilah Murchison," she admitted.

"Your father told me about the plane crash," Frances said heavily. "Tragic. But what does that have to do with you?"

Out of the corner of her eye, Leigh caught her father escaping into the basement. She couldn't really blame him for avoiding her. The taciturn veterinarian had, after all, just completed a four-hour car ride with her mother. But talk he would, and now, or the impending explosion of her brain would realize Frances's every fear.

"Later, Mom," she answered over her shoulder, taking off toward the basement door. She caught up with Randall at his tiny workshop, where he was busily engaged at screwing something into something else. "Dad," she began almost breathlessly, "you've got to hear what happened last night."

She first related his role in the will, and was gratified to find him pleasantly surprised about the money earmarked for feline causes. He was less enthused about the Siamese guardian role, though it did not seem to surprise him. What did surprise him was what wasn't supposed to.

"How could you think I would know something like *that*?" he asked her in amazement. "In thirty years I never said a word to that woman about anything besides her cats. Why would I?"

She looked back at him with confusion. "But you have to know *something* about the heir, Dad. Maybe you just don't realize it. Why else would someone be threatening you to keep quiet?"

Randall finished whatever he was doing with the screwdriver and started sanding instead. "I don't believe anyone is," he said calmly. "It was just a prank."

Leigh launched into a quick explanation of everything she had learned about Mrs. Murchison's son and his likely role in the foiled kidnapping of the Siamese, but it did not make much of an impression. "I assure you that whatever is going on with the woman's heirs," he said finally, "it has nothing to do with me." He took a breath and put down the sandpaper for a moment. "But I do believe now that Ricky Rhodis was probably after Mrs. Murchison's cat, and it sounds like there's a good chance he was doing it for her son. So, no harm done. His grandmother can deal with the moral issue; as for the criminal charges, I'll drop them first thing tomorrow."

He cleared his throat and turned to face her. "Now. No offense, but —"

"I know, I know," Leigh interrupted with frustration. "Introvert attack. I'm gone. But you should know that I'm going to run all this by Maura, and see if she thinks you're in any real danger from that rock thrower." She paused. "OK? You'll listen to her opinion, won't you?"

Randall offered a perfunctory wave as he took out his electric sander and flipped it on to high speed.

Leigh took the hint.

★ ★ ★

She knew perfectly well that, with boxes still piled to the ceiling in her toasterless new house, she had absolutely no business going to visit an old woman she barely knew in a shabby boarding house in Avalon's neighboring borough of Bellevue. But here she was. Her father might be determined not to take recent events seriously, but someone had to.

Randall wouldn't lie to her about not knowing the identity of Lilah Murchison's heir; she was certain about that. But it was not improbable that he had information he didn't know he had. She knew her father's work habits well enough to know that Lilah could have confessed serial murder to him, and if he was in the middle of administering ear mite medication, he wouldn't remember a word of it. Furthermore, three decades of living with her mother had given the man a nearly infallible female chatter detector, and when the alarm went on, his brain shut off.

But she was determined to get some questions answered or bust, and first on her list was whether Dean Murchison, or his equally charming wife, was indeed responsible for the threat on the rock. She wanted to think so, primarily because she suspected that the duo's bark was worse than its bite, but it bothered her that the rock had been thrown before the will reading. Had Dean and Rochelle had an inside scoop? If so, they had done a darn good job of acting surprised in front of the lawyer.

She knocked on the flimsy wooden rim of the boardinghouse's screen door, but in looking through it, realized no one was likely to answer. The door opened into a bare corridor, off of which came a staircase and four other doors, each marked with a number on a cheap square decal. She entered tentatively, having no idea which room belonged to Peggy Linney, the woman Lilah's will had identified as her "most devoted" housekeeper. She was lucky the woman's name and address were even listed in the phone book. But given Mrs. Linney's age, it seemed a good bet that she might have worked in the mansion around the time Dean was born. And given the woman's comment of the night before, Leigh couldn't shake the feeling that this was one employee Ms. Lilah had kept in the loop.

Things had happened pretty fast after the lawyer had dropped the mystery-heir bombshell, but Leigh did remember that it was the otherwise-somnolent Peggy Linney who had been the first to speak. "I don't believe it," the elderly woman had said. And they were reasonable words to say. But the phrase had hit Leigh, even at the time, as having an unexpected tone. One that implied it wasn't Dean's parentage she questioned — so much as the fact that Lilah was admitting it.

Maybe Leigh had been the only one to pick up on that, and maybe she hadn't. But she was certain it had not been her imagination.

She cast her eyes around the inside of the front door, but there were no mailboxes or buzzers to help her identify the right room. Having no better idea, she stepped up to door number one, ready to knock. But before her knuckles had struck the thin wood, an elderly man with a brace of salt-and-pepper schnauzers began descending the stairs.

Leigh stepped over. "Hello," she greeted politely. "I'm looking for Peggy Linney. Could you tell me which apartment is hers, please?"

The man threw her a long, critical glance, leaving his schnauzers ample leeway to sniff her shoes. The dogs must have had little interest in cats, because once their examination was complete they dismissed her entirely and pulled hard for the front door. "Number two," the man said gruffly as the leashes pitched him forward.

Leigh knocked on the door at the end of the hallway, and a gravelly voice answered immediately. "Who is it?"

She cleared her throat. "It's Leigh Koslow, Dr. Koslow's daughter from the vet clinic. I was at Mrs. Murchison's will reading last night; I wondered if I could talk to you for a minute."

"About what?" The grating voice didn't miss a beat.

"About my father," Leigh said, thinking quickly. "I'm afraid he might be in danger, and I think you might be able to help me figure out why." There was no response for a moment, and she bit her lip anxiously. The poor woman had no good reason to talk to her, and Leigh knew it. Still, her gut instincts said that the best way to get the truth out of Peggy Linney would be to tell it herself.

After a long pause and some shuffling noises, she heard a latch click, and the door swung slowly open. The woman who had fallen asleep at the will reading stood with one hand on the doorknob and the other on a tattered walker. She surveyed her visitor critically from head to toe, her nose squinched up slightly as though smelling something unpleasant.

"Come on in," she said gruffly.

7

Leigh shifted slightly in the lumpy armchair, trying not to let on how uncomfortable it was, even for an individual with ample padding over the relevant bones. "I won't bother you for long," she said, trying not to stare at the rather large mole that dominated Peggy Linney's Roman nose. "But I got the idea from the will reading that you had been with Mrs. Murchison for a very long time."

The older woman nodded proudly. "Been on there since seventy-four. Ms. Lilah hired me herself, just after she married Mr. Murchison."

"So you were there when Dean was born. I mean" — Leigh corrected awkwardly — "when Lilah and Albert adopted him."

Peggy's eyes turned hard. "Bullcookies, missy! I don't care what Ms. Lilah said in that crackerbrained will of hers. That boy's hers and I'll swear it to my grave. He was born on March fourth, nineteen seventy-seven. I was there every minute of it."

Leigh swallowed. "You were?"

"I delivered him!" the older woman barked. "He was purple as an eggplant — came out mewling and never stopped since." Her thin lips parted in a smile. "He's a fine boy, Dean. His mum should have been prouder of him. Ms. Lilah was no youngster then, you know. And when he came, he came fast — no time for any hospital. I delivered him right there on the bedroom floor."

"*You* delivered him?" Leigh repeated, incredulous. "Then why would Mrs. Murchison say in her will that he wasn't her biological son? I mean, she had to know that you were a witness."

"Don't bother making sense of Ms. Lilah," Peggy said simply.

Leigh sat quietly for a moment, attempting to regroup her thoughts. "Do you think she has another child somewhere, then? I mean, is it possible —"

Peggy waved her off brusquely. "Ms. Lilah's just tormenting the poor boy." She sighed deeply. "He had a happy enough childhood, but when he turned into a teenager something just went wrong. Ms. Lilah didn't have any patience with him. She was way too hard on him if you ask me, but she never did. When he married that Rochelle girl it was like the last straw — Ms. Lilah all but disowned him. That crazy will of hers was just one last dig. She'll give him his inheritance all right, but she'll take her time.

Some people can be more ornery dead than alive."

The speech seemed to take a lot out of the woman, and she slouched farther down in her chair. "Still can't get over her dying like that," she said soberly. "Here I am with arthritis, diabetes, and bad kidneys, and she's the one that's dead."

Leigh felt a wave of guilt at pestering the woman, but there were still some things she wanted to know. She took a deep breath and attempted to explain the threat on the rock, and why she believed that it somehow involved Mrs. Murchison's will. "So I guess what I'm really asking is," she concluded somewhat hesitantly, "do you think that with all that money at stake, Dean could be — well, dangerous?"

Peggy's beaklike nose wrinkled disdainfully. "Of course not! Dean's got a temper, but he's not a bad young man. He's just not what Ms. Lilah seemed to want." Her voice turned even more sour. "Whatever the hell that was."

"What about Dean's father?" Leigh asked quickly. "Did he have a good relationship with his son?"

Peggy shook her head slowly. "They never had much of a chance. Mr. Murchison wasn't the nurturing type, and the boy was only five when he passed on. But the man was pleased as punch to see that baby, let me tell you." She smiled to herself. "He was sixty-nine, and finally had a son. You never saw a prouder papa."

The older woman seemed to sink into some kind of reverie, and her eyes closed. Leigh took the opportunity to squirm into a more comfortable position in the wretched chair. "But besides Dean," she persisted, "are you absolutely sure that Mrs. Murchison couldn't have had another child?"

Peggy's lids flew open, her increasingly impatient-looking eyes boring into Leigh's. "Have *you* ever had a baby, young lady?"

The question was a no-brainer, but for some reason it took Leigh a moment to answer it. "No," she mumbled. Realizing that her hand had just reflexively gone to her waistline, she quickly pulled it back to her side.

Stop thinking about it. "No," she repeated. "No, I haven't. Why?"

If Peggy's glare could dig holes, her visitor's pupils would be long gone. "Because if you had," the woman continued icily, "you'd know that it's not the kind of thing a woman forgets."

Leigh managed to keep a reasonably

pleasant look on her face as she stole a deep breath. She hadn't suggested that Lilah had forgotten anything, but pointing that out didn't seem wise. She had clearly struck the wrong cord with Peggy Linney, and it was too early in the game to strike out.

"Well," she said brightly, "it's nice that Mrs. Murchison was able to have such a fine son so late in life. I'm sure the inheritance will all work out, then." She rose. "Thank you for your help, Mrs. Linney. I suppose my father might be right, and the message on the rock was just a prank. Or at least it doesn't sound like it has to do with the Murchisons." She motioned for the woman to stay seated and walked past her toward the door.

"At any rate," she said en route, trying not to trip on the myriad waves in the worn carpet and wondering how the older woman could manage them, "at least Mrs. Murchison thought to provide you with a nice place to live someday." She meant only to offer some light chitchat for her exit, but once the words were out of her mouth, she realized how asinine they were. Not only had she insulted the woman's house, but if the divers didn't find Ms. Lilah's body, a death certificate might not be issued for years. Years that Peggy

114

Linney probably didn't have.

Before she could apologize, however, the older woman laughed. "Ms. Lilah's been after me to get out of this place forever. She never did understand I like it here. I got everything I need, and the kids and grandkids are right nearby. I wouldn't move into no swanky old folks' home whether it was free or not, and she knew it."

Leigh removed her foot from her mouth, said a courteous good-bye, and shut the door behind her.

"So, do you think I'm just being paranoid," she asked, snatching the piece of pepperoni that was attempting to escape from her pizza on a mozzarella rope, "or could my dad be in any real danger?"

Detective Maura Polanski wrinkled her wide brow in concentration for a moment, shoveling several large bites of sausage and mushroom into her mouth at the same time. "Hard to say," she announced finally, leaning back with satisfaction.

The cheap folding chair groaned under the husky policewoman's two-hundred-plus pounds, and Leigh wished she had bothered to unstack the real kitchen chairs from their heap in a corner of the dining room. But since she and Warren still hadn't had a real sit-down meal in the house, the demand had not been critical. "I suppose I should take Peggy Linney's and Nikki Loomis's word for it that the mystery heir is a hoax," she continued. "After all, they did know Lilah Murchison as well as anybody. But I have trouble accepting that the rock was just a coincidence."

Maura looked thoughtfully at her friend for another moment before answering. "Even if Mrs. Murchison did make up the other heir as a hoax, her son may not be sure of that. Maybe he even suspects someone in particular — someone at the clinic."

Leigh's eyes widened. She had been assuming that the message on the rock was meant for her father because he had the most obvious connection to Mrs. Murchison. But what about the other employees? There was Jared, of course, but several of the others were also locals; there could be any number of connections she didn't know about.

"If it is Dean behind the rock, I'll be relieved," she admitted. "I'm no psychologist, but he doesn't seem evil to me — just a little slimy. And far too dim not to get caught. But I still can't get around the fact that the rock was thrown before the will was read."

Maura shrugged as she poured an immense amount of Diet Coke out of a two-liter and into a plastic Pirates cup. "Money is power. And from everything I've ever heard about Lilah Murchison, she was the controlling type. She probably taunted him about the will on a regular basis. I'd be surprised if he had no clue. Real surprised."

The policewoman downed the Coke, then sat forward again, her voice turning official. "Here's what we'll do, Koslow. I'll give Chief Schofield a ring and let him know that you suspect Dean Murchison of throwing the rock, and why. He'll take it from there. If Dean's planning any other intimidation tactics, they'll probably be able to trip him up."

Leigh nodded in thanks. The Avalon police force was Maura's alma mater, and if she trusted the current police chief, he had to be trustworthy. Maura, only daughter of the late, great Avalon icon Chief Edward Polanksi, knew her stuff. If she hadn't, she never would have been promoted to the county's General Investigations squad.

On the other hand, she thought uncharitably, what could Schofield really do? He could keep an eye on Dean, sure, but unraveling the complexities of an eccentric socialite's psyche required a more feminine touch. And she was already halfway there.

"Knock it off, Koslow."

"Excuse me?" Leigh looked up into her friend's scowling face, which given its hopelessly adorable cherry cheeks never seemed as imposing as the detective might like. "I didn't say anything."

"You didn't have to," Maura answered, still scowling. "I can see the wheels turning in that devious little head of yours all the way over here. Now drop it. You can't know that this Dean guy isn't dangerous, and the police force needs your help about as much as it needs tea and crumpets. *Got it?*"

The policewoman leaned forward threateningly, but her six-foot-two-inch frame and dagger-shooting eyes had little effect on the woman she had known since she was a teenager.

"Sure," Leigh replied agreeably.

Maura rose to her feet with a groan. "Like I believe you. Besides, you're not my problem. When's the Future President of the United States getting back, anyway? He'll be thrilled to hear all this."

"Not till tomorrow night," Leigh answered glumly. They had coined the nicknames — Future President, WonderCop, and Creative Genius, back in their college days, when they had been the Three Musketeers. They still inhaled pizza together on a regular basis, though the presence of Maura's steady — a city homicide detective Leigh had good reason to resent — had complicated the tradition. It was nice to have a girl's night in for once. "And I'm afraid he's in for a bit of a shock, since I told him I'd be unpacking boxes all weekend."

Maura's eyes scanned the bare kitchen counters and box-cluttered floor, then landed on the trash can that sat beside the sink. She raised an arm and lofted her greasy napkins cleanly into it. "I'll take that as my cue to leave," she said mildly, walking toward the door. "Tell your better half that I said to put your leash back on. By the way, next time Frank's buying."

At the mention of the cop who had once invited her on an involuntary tour of the county jail, Leigh forced her lips into a smile. "Right," she offered as warmly as possible. "Can't wait."

Monday's eight hours in the office seemed to last seventeen, and by the time 5:00 p.m. rolled around, Leigh couldn't think up a single business tag line that didn't have the word "solutions" in it, and it was a cardinal rule that anyone at Hook, Inc. who resorted to the "S" word must both buy a week's supply of donuts and offer a public apology. Not yet ready to admit defeat, she closed the file and shut down her computer, resolving to be inspired tomorrow.

The rest of today, however, was devoted to closure on the Murchison fiasco. True to his word, her father had managed to spring Ricky Rhodis, and per her request the teen was waiting to see her at his grandmother's house.

She tooled up Ohio River Boulevard from her office on the North Side and swung into the driveway of the lovingly dilapidated Rhodis home, one of the few private dwellings still remaining on the bluff side of the road. It had a beautiful view of the Ohio River, or at least it would have, if the Ohio River were beautiful. Unfortunately for the Rhodises, this particular stretch of the Ohio was dominated by the smokestacks of Neville Island, and it took a good deal of imagination to omit them from the vista.

Her foot had barely touched the first crumbling porch step when Adith popped out, all smiles. "Careful, honey!" she begged in a singsong. "I don't know when Bud'll get around to fixing those danged steps. He's always says 'in the spring, Adie,' but I ask you, isn't it spring right now? Well, isn't it? Come on inside, child."

Leigh, who knew better than to interrupt her hostess by answering rhetorical questions, entered the clean but perpetually dank old house and paused to pet the obese apricot poodle gyrating at her feet.

"See there," Adith prattled on, "Pansy remembers you! I knew she would. . . ."

Leigh's attention was quickly drawn to the familiar slip of a teen who sat before her in the living room, slouched on a flowery couch covered with ancient yellow plastic. "Hello again, Ricky," she offered.

He acknowledged her with a nod.

"Now everybody have a seat," Adith ordered. "Bud went walking, but he'll be back."

Leigh had no sooner lowered herself into a plasticized armchair than Adith started in. "Now Ricky, honey, you go ahead. You tell Ms. Koslow everything you told me. And don't leave nothing out, either."

The boy looked up at her miserably, and sighed. "OK, Grandma. I told you I would." He then began muttering in a voice Leigh could barely understand. "Grandma told me about the will. About Dean and Rochelle not getting anything, and so I figured it didn't matter anymore."

Leigh's heart beat faster. So, he *was* working for the couple from hell. And he had been keeping his mouth shut in hopes of a payoff.

"Dean and me — well, we used to work together at the Ponderosa for a while. Dean didn't stay long. He was just broke for a while 'cause Rochelle got fired from the nail salon again. But he was a funny guy, and after he left, we kept up. Every once in a while he had money and then he'd hire me to deliver stuff an'at. Once he gave me fifty bucks just to pick up some stuff from his mom's house. He was always going off about what a witch she was, and how she had all this money but wouldn't give him any of it."

He paused to take a breath, and Leigh took one too. It was hard work trying to understand the kid's mumbling Pittsburgh drawl.

"Anyhow, last week he told me he had a real important job that needed done. He said his mom was mad at him and was trying to kill his cat."

Leigh's eyebrows rose, and she eyed the teen with disbelief.

"It was true!" he protested. "The cat was his like when he lived at home, you know, and she'd always hated it but wouldn't let him have it 'cause she hated Rochelle and 'cause Rochelle had dogs an'at. She was trying to poison it. But Dean knew that it was coming into the clinic, and so he figured out a way I could steal it out from there easier than from her house. I was just supposed to hide until everybody left, then put the cat in a box and run out with it." His eyes turned defensive. "I never did take anything from that place. Was just gonna take the cat, and it was Dean's."

"I see," Leigh said mildly, trying her best not to sound judgmental. The kid might not be brain surgeon material, but he didn't seem to mean any harm. On the other hand, he wasn't telling her the whole truth either. "What about the bag of cat litter on the floor?" she asked. "I don't see why you should have to clean out the cage. Was that Dean's idea, too?"

He blinked at her uncomprehendingly. "Well, sure. He was going to take the cat to another clinic and get it checked out. You know — for poison. He told me to make sure I got all the poop too, 'cause they might need to test it. They had to have proof of what the old lady was doing so they could press charges."

Leigh looked critically into Ricky's large brown eyes. Though spirited, they were remarkably ingenuous. He really believed what he was saying. "So why didn't you explain everything to the police when you got caught?" she asked, though she already knew the answer.

"He did it for me!" Adith broke in defensively. "Dean and Rochelle told him they were coming into major money real soon, and that he could have ten percent of it if he only kept his mouth shut, no matter what happened. He didn't really think he could be put away for stealing drugs he didn't steal, and he was willing to wait it out if it meant he'd have a fortune in the end. He was going to use part of the money to help Bud and me fix up this house." She sniffled ostentatiously. "Isn't that about the sweetest thing you ever heard?"

Leigh glanced back at Ricky, who looked thoroughly embarrassed but not at all guilty, and a wave of uneasiness swept over her. Any kid who believed an heir to millions would fork over ten percent to a gopher he found at the Ponderosa could never come up with a cover story as convincing as the poisoning yarn. No, that little gem must have come from Dean and Rochelle themselves, which meant somebody had a little more brainpower than she was comfortable thinking about. There was something else wrong with the picture that Ricky had painted too, but she couldn't quite put her finger on it.

She stood up. "Thanks for being so honest, Ricky," she said genuinely. "I'll explain things to my dad."

"He's going to apologize to Dr. Koslow in person, aren't you, hon?" Adith said firmly.

Ricky nodded stiffly, his face still down.

Mrs. Rhodis was right, Leigh thought to herself. *He's not a bad kid.*

"Sorry to run," she said as she headed for the door, "but I need to get to the clinic ASAP."

Adith sprung up behind her, narrowly avoiding tripping over her own poodle. "Have you got any more ideas on that mystery baby?" she asked, eyes sparkling. "The girls and I are stumped. We just can't figure a time she could have hid a pregnancy. Not as thin as she was. Unless it was when she ran off with that first husband. She was a little chubbier back when she married him, but still, they weren't out of town for more than a few months before he was killed in that accident. . . ."

Leigh held up a hand. "I really don't think there is a mystery baby," she confessed. "Both Nikki and Peggy Linney think Lilah Murchison contrived the whole thing just to rattle Dean's cage, and given what Ricky just told us about him, I can't say I blame her."

Adith's eyes widened. "When did you talk to Peggy Linney? At the will reading?"

"No, I went to see her yesterday afternoon," Leigh answered, disturbed by the look on the older woman's face. "Why?"

"I thought you might have already heard," Adith answered, her voice dropping to a conspiratorial whisper. "They found her dead in her bed this morning."

8

"I can't believe she's dead," Leigh repeated for the fourth time.

"Could you get a pulse for me?" Randall Koslow asked through his surgeon's mask.

Leigh slid her hand underneath the blue paper drape and felt for the inside of the cat's back leg. "About one fifty," she said, glancing at the wall clock. "And strong." She hadn't been able to stop thinking about Peggy Linney, even for a moment, since she had heard the news a half hour before. And while being startled at the sudden death of someone she had just visited might be expected, the sick feeling that had settled deep in her stomach seemed out of proportion.

"Mrs. Rhodis said she died in her sleep," she mumbled.

Randall did not look up from his task. "It happens," he commented soberly. "Check his color, would you?"

She pulled back the part of the drape that covered the cat's head, and drew in a breath. At first she had thought her dad was doing a simple spay — but now that she thought about it, he rarely did anything but emergencies this late in the day. And the abdominal incision he was working through was unusually long.

"This is Number One Son!" she exclaimed. "He did get obstructed. Is he going to be OK?"

Randall didn't answer, and she realized he was waiting for information from her. She touched the Siamese's gums with a fingertip, pressing until the area went white. When she pulled back, the gums quickly turned pink again. "CRT's good," she answered, then lightly touched the corner of the cat's eye. He blinked. "Palpebral's fine. Have you found the metal piece?"

She watched as her father's gloved fingers gingerly handled a solid mass of twisted intestine. "Adhesions?" she asked anxiously.

Randall nodded, his head still down. "The blockage doesn't seem to be in the worst of it, though. I think I can get it."

Leigh was silent as her father concentrated. They would soon find out what it was that Dean and Rochelle had wanted back so badly. Or, what it was they *didn't* want Lilah Murchison to see. Her thoughts returned automatically to Peggy Linney.

It can't be a coincidence.

Could Peggy Linney have been murdered? Her legs were starting to shake slightly beneath the surgery table. She checked the cat's color again, then pulled over a stool and sat down.

Perhaps someone else knew that Peggy Linney was an eyewitness to Dean's birth. Perhaps they wanted to silence her. Had they been watching Leigh as she visited? Was it her visit that made someone see the old woman as a threat? If she had never gone to see Peggy, would —

"Here it is," her father announced, holding up a gnarled mass of green cloth with a hemostat. Leigh held out a paper towel, and Randall dropped the hemostat and all onto the middle of it. She sat down with the soggy paper towel in her lap and probed the tangled threads with the tip of the hemostat. In a few moments, she had managed a semireconstruction. "It *is* a little key," she announced. "On some type of cloth key chain. Woven threads of different colors, maybe — I'll have to wash it up."

Randall merely grunted as he bent studiously over his patient, sewing carefully. "I'm just glad it didn't perforate."

"Does it mean anything to you?" she asked hopefully. "I mean, did any bells go off when you saw it?"

He didn't answer, which she took as a rather disappointing "no." She stared hard at the tiny key, which was paper thin and shaped like a footnote symbol. She had similar keys that opened luggage padlocks, but this one was a little more ornate, with a three-dimensional design at its base.

Perhaps Rochelle had simply been attempting to steal something of Ms. Murchison's, she reasoned. Rochelle had found the key and opened whatever it was, but when she cast the key aside, there was Number One Son, licking his lips. When the thief realized what had happened, she would have had to try to hide it from her mother-in-law, particularly if Dean was on thin ice as far as his inheritance was concerned.

Mrs. Rhodis's troublesome words came back to Leigh in a flash. Ricky had told his grandmother that Dean and Rochelle claimed to be "coming into major money *real soon.*" Why should they think that before the plane had even crashed? And why, she realized suddenly, feeling foolish for not wondering before, would Lilah, a woman in her sixties, put provisions for Peggy Linney in her will to begin with? Why would she expect her much older, frailer housekeeper to outlive her?

"Help me rinse and reglove, would you?" Randall asked, the stitching on the bowel completed. Pushing her new and disturbing thoughts to the side, Leigh rose and helped him prepare a new sterile field. They had just finished when the A-team checked in.

"Doc? I haven't heard you call. Are you ready for —" Jeanine eyed her substitute with the merest hint of jealousy, but quickly replaced it with a knowing smirk. "Oh. Hello, Leigh. I didn't realize it was you in here. How are you feeling?"

"Fine," she returned tersely, trying — a little — to disguise her current animosity. It was too early to even take a pregnancy test, but ever since Leigh's slip at the x-ray table, the snooty tech had insisted on eyeing her like they shared some colossal secret. God forbid the woman should run into Warren in the next few days — she'd probably tell him everything herself.

"So, how's the patient, Doc?" the tech said loudly, leaning over the surgery table as if to inspect Randall's work. "Oh, yes. Adhesions. I *told* Nikki Loomis last time not to let that cat get near anything cloth, *ever*. He's lucky to be alive. What did he eat this time?"

Randall continued sewing. He respected Jeanine's work as a tech, but that didn't mean he listened to everything she said. "It's a key," Leigh answered, holding out the paper towel. She couldn't think of anything to link Jeanine to the Murchisons, but she resolved to try. If the key didn't mean anything to her father, it had to mean something to somebody else at the clinic. And if anyone else was to be incriminated, it was only fair that the most obnoxious went first. "Look familiar?" she asked, pushing the smelly mess closer to Jeanine and watching her expression.

The tech reached out a bony hand and pulled the towel closer still, her nose practically touching the mass of threads. "Cloth key chain," she said with authority. "That'll get 'em. Not to speak ill of the dead or anything, but that woman should have known better by now. I say — if you can't keep the cat safe, then maybe you shouldn't have it at all."

Leigh swallowed the unkind retort brewing in the back of her mind. Jeanine clearly had no idea what lengths Lilah Murchison had actually gone to protect Number One Son. Which also meant it was very unlikely she'd ever set foot in the mansion.

"Did you ever meet Mrs. Murchison?" she asked in her most innocent voice.

A look of annoyance flashed across the technician's face. "She never came to the clinic, or I would have given her a piece of my mind. I offered to do her vaccinations for her at the house one time, but she only wanted Dr. Koslow." She glanced up at Randall, who was otherwise absorbed, then tossed her head in his direction as she threw Leigh an arching eyebrow. "And I mean *wanted* him," she mouthed silently.

Not sure whether to laugh or be nauseous, Leigh changed the subject. "Did you hear that Peggy Linney died?"

Jeanine's face was perfectly blank. "Who?"

"Oh," Leigh backpedaled. "I thought you might know Mrs. Murchison's old housekeeper, but I guess she never came to the clinic either."

Jeanine shrugged, and Leigh reluctantly crossed her name off the suspect list. The tech lived in Moon Township anyway; she wouldn't be familiar with the Avalon-Bellevue-Ben Avon set unless they had pets.

"If the inquisition is over," Randall broke in suddenly, his gloved hands in the air, "could I get some help here? I need a status check."

Leigh started to step over, but Jeanine was at the table in a flash. The tech stood by until the stitching was completed, all the while prattling to Dr. Koslow about how his newest associate insisted on using a ridiculously expensive suture material on spays, and why it was Nancy's fault for ordering the stuff in the first place. Leigh was about to consider strangulation with the same when Jeanine mercifully remembered something else she had to do.

"By the way," Randall began as she turned to leave, "did those new recirculating blankets come in yet?"

Jeanine shook her head. "Not unless they're in one of the packages that just came. But I'll check."

She was off like a shot, and Leigh pulled out a towel to cover Number One Son, whose bare abdomen was wet and sticky-orange from the Betadine scrub. She stayed by the cat while Randall tidied up, her mind once again deep in thought. Since Dean Murchison was clearly behind the catnapping, which was more than likely tied up with the belief that his mother's death was imminent, then he was almost certainly behind the rock throwing as well. In which case, she thought with relief, Peggy Linney's death must have been a coincidence. Because the elderly woman had offered no threat whatsoever to Dean's inheritance; in fact, she had appeared to be one of his biggest fans.

"I'll tell you what I think, Dad," she said

with optimism, and more to herself than to him. "I can't believe that the plane crash was anything but an accident, but I do think that Mrs. Murchison had some reason to believe she was going to die soon. Maybe she had just been diagnosed with cancer, or heart disease. In any event, I think she was miffed at Dean when she wrote that crazy will, and I think she let on something about it to him. That's why he and Rochelle were desperate to keep her from finding out they'd been snooping in her house. They wanted to get back in her good graces before she really did die. Of course, I still don't know why they were snooping. Maybe they were in a tight spot and planned to steal money or jewelry. Maybe they'd done it before."

"Makes sense," Randall responded, much to her surprise.

"The only thing I still don't get is why Dean is afraid that someone at the clinic can mess things up for him. You say you don't know anything, neither Nikki nor Peggy Linney believed that Mrs. Murchison ever had another child, and besides Jared being Nikki's brother, I can't find a link between the Murchisons and anyone else here."

Her father's raised eyebrows indicated that she had lost him. "You still think that rock had something to do with Lilah Murchison's death?"

Leigh took a deep breath. Her father's ability to focus might make him a brilliant scientist, but the flipside — blindness to the obvious — could be a real hindrance. "Maura seemed to think it was a possibility," she said reasonably, "because whether or not the mystery heir is real, and whether or not Dean is Lilah Murchison's biological son, he might *think* someone here knows something that could cause him trouble."

Randall humphed. It was as good as a concession.

"So who here would know about Mrs. Murchison's private life?" she questioned eagerly, lowering her voice. "I've ruled out Jeanine already. And as for Jared, even if he did know anything, I don't think anyone would threaten him with a written note."

Randall thought for a moment. "Marcia and Michelle are both Avalon girls. Nancy lives in an apartment in Bellevue and Nora lives in the Rocks, but I don't know where they grew up." He shook his head. "I'd forget the rest. The part-timers are all too young to know anything about the seventies."

Leigh considered hopefully. Marcia,

Michelle, Nancy, and Nora. One of them had to know something that Dean and Rochelle Murchison wanted kept quiet.

Jeanine reappeared at the doorway, a small rectangular box in hand.

"There weren't any packages from VetCount," she explained regretfully, setting the box down on the extra surgery table and slitting the tape with her fingernails. "But this one lost its label, so we'll check it out."

"The blankets should be in by now," Randall grumbled, adjusting the towels carefully over the unconscious cat. "I ordered them weeks ago."

With a cry that startled them both, Jeanine suddenly recoiled. "Oh no, not again!" she screeched.

Randall and Leigh both charged the box, but Leigh got there first. Nestled in among a slew of Styrofoam peanuts, dirt, and grass was a cheap, hard-plastic baby doll, its blue eyes and frizzy yellow hair caked with mud. Wrapped around its middle was a piece of plain paper bearing a message in handwritten, red-block letters. *Let the past stay buried, or everyone there will be.*

9

"Where did it come from?" Randall asked tensely, examining the loose cardboard flaps. The box was addressed to the clinic on a plain white, computer-generated label. Otherwise it was blank. "It didn't come with the rest of the mail; there's not even a postmark."

"I didn't bring it in," Jeanine said quickly. "Nora got the mail."

"What's all the yelling about?" asked the chubby brunette in the doorway. "And what did I do?"

Leigh looked at the amiable thirty-something technician, the clinic's best cat holder and would-be stand-up comedian. Leigh had always liked Nora. She was smart, even-tempered, and didn't care for Jeanine.

"Was this box with the rest of the mail this morning?" Jeanine snapped.

Nora's brow wrinkled, and she stepped closer. As her gaze rested on the box's contents, her pupils widened, but only slightly. " 'Let the past stay buried, or everyone there will be'?" she read curiously. "Damn. And I wanted my ashes scattered over Graceland."

"Did it come with the mail or not?" Jeanine hissed.

Nora shrugged. "I don't know. I don't think so. I took in three or four boxes and dumped them in the office. I wasn't really paying attention."

The door frame was suddenly filled with two more bodies. Marcia and Michelle appeared with jackets on and purses in hand, evidently on their way out for the day. "What's going on?" Marcia asked, stepping forward.

Leigh cringed in anticipation of the forthcoming blast, and she noticed that her father did also. Marcia and Michelle were nice enough, but they weren't the brightest bulbs in the factory and were drama queens besides. Lifelong friends who did everything together, they giggled at every puppy, gushed over every spay, and blubbered like banshees during euthanasias.

Their screams nearly brought down the ceiling.

"Oh my God!" Michelle wailed when she had caught her breath. "Is that what was in that box? It could have been a bomb or something!"

"A bomb!" Marcia squealed. "Did anybody check for wires?"

"Calm down, please." Randall said quietly. His voice was perfectly controlled, but there was no missing his simmering annoyance. "Michelle, you've seen this box before?"

The young woman nodded, her face pale. "It was on the back doorstep when we came in this morning. I thought it came UPS or something."

"Does it *have* a UPS label?" Jeanine sniped. "Does it *have* any label at all?"

"Sorry." Michelle gulped.

"Who is it supposed to be for?" Marcia asked, her voice shaking. "What does it mean?"

Leigh seized her opportunity. "We think maybe a guy named Dean sent it. You know anybody named Dean?" She watched the three suspects' faces carefully.

Nora's registered a blank, but Marcia and Michelle nodded in unison. "There's two in Avalon," Marcia said quickly. "Dean Hamly and Dean Murchison."

"Dean Hamly's a sweetheart," Michelle chimed in. "He's got three kids. We used to baby-sit for him."

"Dean Murchison's an asshole," Marcia added unapologetically. "My sister dated him once, and she said —" The assistant broke off when she glanced up at her boss. "Well, anyway. He's a goof, and he's, like, weird too. I can see him doing something like this."

"But why would he?" Michelle asked no one in particular. "You think he could be, like, a psychopath or something?" They both looked fearfully at Randall.

"We don't know who sent it," he said simply.

"It's just like the rock," Jeanine said dramatically. "This makes two threats, plus the break-in. And whoever is behind it, now they're threatening *all* of us."

Leigh cringed again, but not fast enough, as Marcia's and Michelle's renewed screams rattled the lightbulbs in the surgical lamps.

"Stop that!" Nancy Johnson cried harshly. The normally serene business manager's face was angry as she forced her way into the surgery. Leigh had never seen her miffed before, but dealing with Marcia and Michelle all day could fray anyone's nerves. "We've got clients out front who are convinced some poor animal is being tortured back here. What's going on?"

All the principals in one room, Leigh thought to herself. Excellent. "We've gotten another anonymous threat," she answered, motioning toward the box.

Nancy stepped closer and looked into it,

then backed up, obviously daunted. She said nothing.

"I'm going to call the police and let them handle it," Randall said firmly. "Nobody else touch the thing. Marcia and Michelle — go home. Nancy — tell the people the girls saw a mouse. Nora — go back to whatever you were doing. And Jeanine — take Number One Son to a cage and keep a close eye on him till he's awake. *Now.*"

Reluctantly, the staff scuttled, and Leigh wished that her father had waited a few moments longer. The staff's reactions were giving her valuable information. She would bet money that Nora had nothing to do with the threats. On the other hand, Marcia and Michelle's personal knowledge of Dean made them very likely to know something, whether they were aware of it or not. And Nancy had been visibly disturbed by the box, which deserved further questioning.

As her father headed off to call the police, she peered again into the nest of dirt and Styrofoam. It was undeniably creepy, even if the sender hadn't been so macabre as to injure the doll itself, which, other than being muddy and having no clothes on, was fine. But what did it mean? Did the fact that it was a baby doll have something to do with the mystery heir that no one — with the apparent exception of Dean — believed existed?

She let out a breath and shuddered a little. Marcia and Michelle knew Dean, and they had even wondered if he was a psychopath. Having had some acquaintance with a psychopath in the past, she didn't think so. She didn't even think Dean was a violent person. But then, she had never really talked to him one-on-one.

Perhaps it was time.

"You want to meet for lunch today?" Warren J. Harmon III, District 2 County Councilman, was dressed in his standard business suit and looked divine. He generally did, a fact that Leigh had foolishly overlooked during the first twelve years of their acquaintance. It had taken her a long time to see past the skinny, acne-scarred teenager she had met as a University of Pittsburgh freshman, but when her eyes had finally opened, she had been instantly hooked. Her good-hearted geek of a buddy had morphed into a savvy and successful local politician, with his integrity still amazingly intact. Along with — conveniently enough — his weakness for her.

"I can't," she said, her voice full of genuine regret. "I have . . . other plans."

He looked at her thoughtfully. "Like what?"

When she didn't answer, he pulled over a rickety chair and sat down next to her at the breakfast table. "All right. Enough. Tell me what you've been doing all weekend. And don't say unpacking, because I'm not blind."

Leigh's eyes scanned the cluttered room. "I found the toaster," she offered weakly.

Her husband just looked at her. He had always had the unnerving ability to read her mind, and since their marriage a year earlier, he had only gotten better at it. "Perhaps I should ask, 'which relative is it?' Has your Aunt Bess gotten into trouble again? Or is it Cara?"

Leigh smiled. "The women of the Morton clan are all fine, thank you. I'm merely helping my father with a little melodrama at the clinic. We'll talk about it tonight. Promise." She finished her java and rose, hoping she had sounded sincere. She did intend to tell him everything eventually; his opinion could be valuable. But this morning, there simply wasn't time. Besides, if he knew what her immediate plans were, he wouldn't like them. Neither would Maura, but she could deal with that later.

"And why didn't you mention this last

night?" he asked, still eyeing her suspiciously.

An evil smile spread across her face. "We were preoccupied."

Warren hid a grin behind his coffee cup. "That's no excuse."

Leigh planted a kiss on his cheek. "Gotta go."

Avalon's Chuckwagon Café was short on ambience and long on grease, but it was easy on the budget, and Leigh came from a long line of cheapskates. She glanced over the stained plastic menu toward the dark wooden doors, which swung open to the sound of a clanging dinner bell. Dean and Rochelle Murchison entered, he dressed in jeans, a black T-shirt, and dirty sandals; she in a midriff-baring top and spandex. They scanned the dingy room with sunglasses on.

"Over here." Leigh waved, plastering a smile on her face. It didn't really matter if she was noticed, since no one she had any respect for could possibly be eating there also. "Have a seat."

The couple slid into the booth opposite her, the adornments on Dean's massive belt clanking as they settled themselves on brown vinyl cushions patched liberally with duct tape. Dean wrapped an arm around his wife, removed his sunglasses, and eyed his hostess with amusement. "I still don't know what you want to talk to us about," he said in the same, overloud, self-important voice that had bugged her at the will reading. "Your dad want more of Lilah's money?"

With great effort, she returned a smile. Dean Murchison was the kind of sleazeball who looked at every woman as though confident she wanted him. "Of course not," she said pleasantly, teeth gritted. "Your mother has already been extremely generous with her cats."

"Tell us about it!" Rochelle sniffed, her sunglasses still on. Leigh tried to read the other woman's expression, but the dime-store mirrored lenses showed only her own reflection. It was a good trick. She would have to remember it.

"I asked you here because I need your help figuring out something." *And also because it's a public place, and as pathetic as you look, you may still be dangerous.* "Ever since your mother's plane went down, my father has been receiving threats at the clinic. We wondered if the two things might be related, and we figured you were the best one to ask. What do you think?"

Dean didn't answer immediately, and Leigh squirmed in her seat. Perhaps con-

146

fronting the couple head-on had been a bad idea, but she didn't think so. Despite Maura's rather forceful insistence to the contrary, she *did* know the difference between police business and a little harmless fact-finding. Namely, that only one of the above ever happened fast enough. She wanted to know if Dean Murchison was behind the threats at the clinic, and she wanted to know now. Sure, if he was guilty, the Avalon PD would eventually catch him in the act, or come up with some physical evidence tying him to the rock or the doll. But why wait for the wheels of the justice when, for the cost of a few burgers, a clever story, and a ditz act, she might very well settle the whole mess over her lunch hour?

"I'm sorry," she apologized as a waitress appeared. "I'm picking your brains and I haven't even fed you yet. Please, order whatever you want. It's the least I can do."

She selected the grilled cheese and bacon combo on page three; her guests mumbled off their orders without looking at the menu. It figured.

As soon as the waitress had departed, she dove in. "I have this theory, you see, but nobody can really help me with it except you guys." She lowered her voice for effect, and was gratified to see both members of her audience leaning in. Rochelle even took off her sunglasses. "I think that somebody is planning to try and pass themselves off as your mother's real heir. Now, you and I know that your mother doesn't really have another heir — that she just made that up."

"We do?" Dean said.

Rochelle poked her husband in the ribs, and Leigh tried hard not to notice. "But I think that somebody's planning to fake some evidence, like a birth certificate, to try to get your inheritance. Only someone at the clinic knows that this person can't be Lilah Murchison's child. And that knowledge is getting them threatened."

"Yeah," Dean bellowed, leaning back again. "We know all about the messages and stuff. The fuzz think *we* did it." He chuckled.

Leigh feigned innocence. "They do? Why would they think that?"

Dean shrugged. "Like because I'm the one with the most to gain, I guess. But they got it figured different from you. They think somebody at the clinic knows who the real heir is."

"But there is no real heir."

"Course not," Rochelle answered smoothly, her voice pitched low. "But the police don't know that."

"They don't know anything," Dean agreed, projecting an idiotic grin. "They have no clue what a witch Mummy dearest was, either. She never gave me squat, did you know that? All those millions, and she let Rochelle and me live like pond scum."

Rochelle nodded enthusiastically, the spikes of hair on her head lagging a little behind the bobbing of her chin. Her voice was screechy again. "He's had to *work* for a living!"

Leigh made a mental note of the tone switch, then turned back to Dean, trying hard to look sympathetic. "That's awful. Did you have a rough childhood?"

Dean shrugged again. "Eh. It was OK."

"Lilah was never around," Rochelle piped up bitterly. "He was, like, raised by the maids, you know? Servants and cats. That's what he grew up with. Skinny, cross-eyed cats."

"I see," Leigh answered, a better picture of the Murchison household beginning to form. "I was sorry to hear about Peggy. Are you going to her funeral tomorrow?"

The waitress arrived with drinks, and Dean squinted at her over his Rolling Rock. "Who?"

Rochelle appeared equally perplexed, and Leigh paused a moment, surprised. "Peggy

Linney, the housekeeper. She was at the will reading. I thought maybe she was one of the staff who raised you."

Dean snorted. "Linney the Ninny? That woman made my life more miserable than my own mother did. 'Eat your peas! Wipe your feet! Stand up straight!' " He shook his head. "Damn, what a battle-ax. She just died, huh? Hell, I thought she croaked years ago. Couldn't believe it when she showed up at the will reading. Gave me the creeps."

He took a long swig of beer, and Leigh watched him curiously. Peggy Linney had spoken so positively of him; in fact, she was the only one Leigh had yet heard of who did. But the feeling was clearly not mutual. He had appeared not even to recognize the woman's first name. Was he acting?

She studied his dark brown eyes, but she wasn't sure. Both these two could not be as neuron deficient as they appeared, not if one of them had managed to come up with the cat-poisoning story that had so successfully manipulated Ricky Rhodis. If she had to guess now, she would say that it was psychotic-in-training Rochelle, and not her inflated husband, who was hiding half a brain up her sleeve. But she needed more to go on. "Wasn't there anyone at the house that you were close to?" she continued with concern.

Dean started to speak, but his wife cut him off. "All the servants were mean to Dean except one," she remarked, her tone now slightly bored.

Dean nodded. "Yeah, Hetta was cool." Then he looked up at Leigh suspiciously, his face breaking into another too-wide, disturbing grin. "What do you care, anyway? I thought you wanted to know who was messing with your dad."

Leigh did a quick regroup. She had never been much good at keeping her deceptions straight. "It could be important," she answered, thinking quickly. "If someone's planning on claiming to be Mrs. Murchison's child, it's likely to be someone who knew her well. Someone who had an inkling what would be in her will."

His face darkened. "Yeah, I guess."

"Are we ever going to eat?" Rochelle complained. She stood up and faced the door to the kitchen, cupping both hands around her mouth. *What're you doing back there? Killing cows?*"

Leigh shrank in her seat as Dean grabbed his wife by her spandex and pulled her back down into the booth. "They could at least bring the fries out," Rochelle responded, pouting.

Leigh stole a surreptitious glance at her watch and began to plan a premature exit. Fact-finding was one thing, but these two were Loony Toons. She had to get what she needed quick. "Anyway," she began, "do you have any idea who might want to claim to be your mother's heir?"

"Lots of people," Dean said mildly, grinning again. Leigh pulled her eyes away from his with frustration. To his credit, he was smart enough to notice she was looking at him closely. Unfortunately, he seemed to be chalking it up to his sex appeal. As his wife continued to scowl in the direction of the kitchen, he offered Leigh a wink and a leer.

She tried not to shudder. "Do you know any of the staff at my father's clinic?"

He seemed confused. "I don't even know who works there. Except the retard."

Leigh's blood began to simmer. Fifteen seconds. She would give him fifteen seconds, and then she was out of there. Case closed or not. Otherwise she'd be in jail for assault with a ketchup bottle.

Rochelle had zoned back in. "Why don't you tell us who works there, and we'll tell you if we know them?" she suggested sweetly.

A little too sweetly. Especially considering the fact that her husband was, at that

152

moment, attempting to run a bare toe up and down Leigh's calf.

"Will you look at the time?" she announced loudly, bolting from her seat. "I'm so sorry. I forgot I had an important business meeting this afternoon. Advertising clients, you know, very demanding. Gotta run. But thanks for your help." She pulled a twenty from her wallet and slapped it on the greasy tabletop.

"But you haven't even got your food yet," Dean protested, looking disappointed.

"Don't worry about me; I'll grab a Snickers," she answered as pleasantly as possible. "Thanks again. Good-bye!"

Trying not to run out of the restaurant as fast as she wanted to, she forced herself to glance backward as she went out the door. The food had just arrived, and Dean was picking fries off his plate while it was still in mid air.

Rochelle was staring back at her.

10

Leigh nibbled on the emergency bag of pretzels she kept in her desk drawer. She was feeling a bit woozy. A perfectly good opportunity for a decent lunch with her husband wasted — and for what? Precious little information, along with the unwelcome knowledge that Dean Murchison's toenails needed a trim.

She gazed at the half-written e-business pamphlet sitting idly on her monitor and sighed. Getting paid to be creative was great — unless something else happened to be on her mind, in which case her efforts weren't worth squat.

Enough. She clicked on SHUT DOWN, switched off her monitor, and grabbed a handful of pretzels to go. She had gone into business for herself for several reasons, not the least of which was the ability to set her own hours. So what if she didn't sleep the rest of the week? She couldn't sleep as it was.

She had thought that talking to Dean and Rochelle Murchison face-to-face would somehow guide her instincts to an answer. Were they responsible for the threats at the clinic? And if so, were they actually dangerous? She still wasn't sure. Her knee-jerk reaction was that they were perfectly capable of delivering the threats, and that Rochelle — at least — was wily enough to be dangerous. But she had also gotten the strong impression that the gruesome twosome themselves didn't understand everything that was going on.

Whether they knew for a fact that another heir existed or whether they only suspected it, one thing was certain. If they were behind the threats, they must have a good reason to believe that someone at the clinic was involved. And that's what was driving her crazy.

That, and the gnawing fear of which she had been unable to rid herself since she learned of Peggy Linney's death. Peggy had been positive that there was no other heir; she even claimed to have delivered Dean herself. But what if that seemingly harmless old woman had been lying through her teeth? What if she *did* know something?

What if it had cost her her life?

"Working real hard, I see."

Leigh turned around from the black monitor she had been staring at to see over six feet of detective standing behind her. "Do you get paid more when the computer's on?" Maura asked with a grin.

"Time and a half," Leigh answered, offering her absent office mate's chair. "What brings you by?"

Maura sank heavily into the flimsy swivel seat. "Officially, a break-in at the State Store two blocks down. Unofficially, I wanted to let you know that I talked to Chief Schofield."

Leigh leaned forward. "Then you know about the doll that came yesterday?"

Maura nodded. "There's nothing to tie either threat to Dean Murchison yet, but they're keeping their eyes open." She paused a moment, looking at Leigh with the serious, concerned expression Leigh had come to know and fear. Maura Polanski took most anything from bad manners to felonies in stride. When she got concerned, it was no laughing matter.

"I didn't know about Peggy Linney's death until this morning," she began solemnly. "Schofield called me back to tell me about the doll, and he mentioned that the woman had died before he had a chance to question her." She eyed Leigh with a mixture of sympathy and annoyance. Ostensibly, she knew it wasn't Leigh's fault that her name seemed to turn up on an inordinate number of police reports. But that didn't mean she held her completely blameless. "Did you realize that you were the last person to see the woman alive?"

Leigh blinked. *Damnation.* Couldn't the woman have had a neighbor over for Sunday dinner? A pastoral call? A Jehovah's witness? "I didn't realize," she answered grimly. "Mrs. Rhodis said she died in her sleep. I was there midafternoon."

"Mrs. Rhodis was misinformed," Maura responded. "At least partly. Peggy Linney's body was found Monday morning by a home health aide. She was fully dressed, slumped over in her chair, and appeared to have been dead for some time."

Leigh swallowed uncomfortably. "And what did she die of?"

Maura's policewoman gaze was unfaltering. "Well, that's the problem. You see, Peggy Linney was seventy-nine years old and in very poor health. There was nothing particularly surprising about her death; in fact, both her doctor and her family were pretty much expecting it. So —"

"So there was no autopsy," Leigh finished.

The policewoman shook her head. "She was cremated at Fields Funeral Home last night. Service is this afternoon."

The two sat quietly for a moment while

Leigh's stomach flip-flopped. "You think she was murdered," she said finally, "don't you?"

The "m" word took a moment coming out of her mouth. Saying it out loud seemed to make it real, and she didn't want to deal with that. Pranks and intimidation were one thing; killing was another.

The detective drummed her pudgy fingers on the desktop. "No way to prove that now," she answered tightly. "And not enough good reasons to open an investigation. But just between you and me and your blank computer screen — I don't like it."

Leigh took a deep, but shaky, breath. "You know something I don't?"

Maura paused a moment before answering. "Schofield talked to her neighbors in the building this morning. Turns out she had two other visitors last Sunday before you. The home health aide, who comes every morning, and a man in his late forties or early fifties, dressed nice and carrying a briefcase, who the neighbors didn't recognize. The woman next door to Peggy said he was medium height, skinny, with a full gray beard, and that Peggy seemed to be expecting him. Any ideas?"

An image popped into Leigh's head. "Yes," she answered. "It sounds like Mrs.

Murchison's lawyer. Sheridan, I think his name was. I met him at the will reading."

Maura's pupils widened slightly. "Mrs. *Murchison's* lawyer?"

Leigh nodded mutely, disturbing thoughts crowding her brain. Peggy Linney had found out about her role in the will Saturday night and had seemed reasonably content. What did she have to see the attorney about that couldn't wait until Monday?

"Koslow," Maura said sharply, interrupting her thoughts, "I've got no good evidence of any foul play where Peggy Linney's concerned, but I don't like what I'm hearing. You and your dad both need to lay low until Schofield gets a handle on things. Capiche?"

Leigh didn't answer, instead choosing to throw away the sweat-sodden pretzels she had been absently smashing in her fist.

"Koslow."

"Right, right," she answered as sincerely as possible. "Are you going to find out what she wanted to see Sheridan about?"

The detective shook her head. "I can't overstep, Koslow. Unless the Avalon PD calls in the county, this is Schofield's case." She paused a moment, then looked at Leigh thoughtfully and went on. "I have learned a little more about Lilah Murchison's death, however."

Leigh nodded encouragement.

"The recovery team has found two bodies. Positively identified as the pilot and Bertha McClintock, whose husband's company owned the plane. They'll look for another day or so, and that's about it. If no more bodies are found, it could take years for Lilah Murchison and the copilot to be declared legally dead."

"Years," Leigh repeated. "Anybody know why the plane crashed?"

"Officially, it's still under investigation. Unofficially, the weather was rough, and both the pilot and copilot were seen drinking before they got on board."

Leigh grimaced. Evidently there were some benefits to flying commercial.

"And there's something else I wanted to tell you," Maura continued. "I went to see my mom last night."

Eyebrows lifted, Leigh braced herself. Maura going to see her mother was, in itself, not big news. She visited almost every day at the Alzheimer's care center where Mary Polanksi had been living for over a year now. But since Mary's condition had deteriorated considerably, Maura only rarely brought back reports.

Before Mary Polanksi's mind began to fail her, she had been one of the sharpest minds in Pittsburgh, and the undisputed genius behind the professional success of her husband, the late Avalon Chief of Police. Mary had had a photographic memory and near-perfect recollection of faces, times, and places of interest to her. But she was also both reticent and retiring, preferring to let her husband receive all the accolades.

"Mom said something that threw me a little," Maura began. "She doesn't always know who I am anymore, and when she does talk, she's usually somewhere in the past. Sometimes what she says makes sense to me, sometimes it doesn't.

"Last night, I was talking out loud about some things on my mind. I don't usually give details about cases, just in case someone's listening or Mom decides to start repeating things. But I did mention the name Lilah Murchison."

The detective threw up her hands. "I don't know why that name struck a chord with her, but it did. She hadn't said a word all evening, and all of a sudden she sat straight up in her chair and looked right at me."

Leigh leaned forward. It hadn't occurred to her that Mary Polanski, a working-class girl and lifelong Avaloner, would be all that familiar with the rich and notorious Lilah Murchison. But it should have. Lilah was an Avaloner by birth. Plus, she and Mary were about the same age.

"What did she say?"

"She said," Maura answered slowly, "and I quote: 'Lilah Beemish is a filthy, selfish slut, and I hate her.' "

Leigh's eyes widened. She had never heard Mary Polanski utter so much as an H-E-double-hockey-sticks, nor had she ever heard her malign anyone short of a convicted murderer.

"Beemish was Lilah's maiden name; I checked," Maura continued. "Alzheimer's can change a person's personality, I've heard that. And I've heard that victims can get more unpleasant or even violent. But so far Mom hasn't shown any signs of that. It seemed to me like the kind of thing that maybe before her illness, she would have just thought to herself. But now, she can't help saying it out loud."

"A slut?" Leigh repeated. It was a relatively tame word now, but she knew that to someone of her mother's generation, it was a strong condemnation. "Mrs. Rhodis said Lilah had a trashy reputation as a teenager," she added. "But —"

"But that doesn't explain why my mother

would have such strong feelings about her," Maura finished, reading her friend's mind.

"I know."

"Did she ever say anything about Lilah before?"

"Not a word. Her friends would all gossip about Lilah like everyone in town always did, but Mom would just listen politely."

Leigh thought a moment. It was tantalizing to think that Mary Polanski might have some long-buried resentment toward Lilah Murchison. What could the woman have done? Stolen one of Mary's boyfriends? It seemed unlikely, since the only boy Mary had been interested in post-adolescence was the man she had eventually married. But unfortunately, whatever Lilah had done to Mary seemed unlikely to shed any light on the problems at hand.

"It's probably neither here nor there," Maura offered, reading Leigh's mind again. "Just thought I'd mention it." She rose.

"If you or Schofield find out anything more, will you tell me?" Leigh asked.

Maura eyed her suspiciously. "If it affects the threats at the clinic, sure." Her voice turned gruff. "But I'm warning you, Koslow, this is police business, not *Encyclopedia Brown*. *Stay away* from Dean and Rochelle Murchison. No cute little spying missions. I mean it. Those two could be dangerous."

Leigh offered a salute and a smile. *Too late,* she thought thankfully.

The detective's eyes narrowed, but she held her tongue.

Leigh stepped tentatively into the parlor of Fields Funeral Home, marveling that its crimson-on-maroon color scheme had still not been reined in by female hands. The marriage of its aging proprietor had long since been given up as a lost cause, but Vestal Fields's inadvertent ability to hire equally color-blind employees was astounding.

She gave the suited gentlemen at the door a vague greeting and scooted quickly to the side, camouflaging her own maroon dress next to a heavy crushed-velvet drape. The wall board said that the Linney funeral was to begin at two o'clock, but she wasn't entirely sure she was in the right crowd. Only twenty or so people were present, and she didn't recognize any of them.

Then again, why would she? They were obviously family members. Kids in their fifties, grandkids in their thirties, great-grandkids. Only a few older people, the neighbor with the schnauzers not among them. No one from the will reading. She sidled around the walls of the parlor as inconspicuously as possible, attempting to get a good look at everyone. In a moment they would all be called into the chapel to sit, and then her vantage point would be poor.

She wasn't sure exactly what she was looking for. But her irrational guilt over Peggy's death was weighing even heavier since Maura's visit, and she figured that taking time to attend the woman's funeral couldn't hurt. Since there was no autopsy, no one would ever know if her innocent visit on Sunday had preceded a peaceful final slumber — or a vicious attack. But Leigh couldn't help wondering if someone at the funeral knew more than she did. If so, she hoped they would tip their hand just like in *Columbo*. If not, at least she would be another warm body in the sparse crowd.

"Well, well. If it isn't Leigh Koslow," a booming voice sounded behind her left ear. "I didn't know you knew the late Mrs. Linney — God rest her soul."

Leigh cringed. Vestal was a nice enough man, especially considering her less-than-completely-aboveboard dealings with him in the past. But when trying to be inconspicuous, Vestal was about as convenient to have around as a hot-pink feather boa.

"Hello, Mr. Fields," she returned politely, her own voice barely above a whisper. "I'm . . . um . . . trying not to disturb the family."

"Oh, of course not," the round little funeral director answered, lowering his own voice dramatically. "We all grieve in our own ways."

Leigh looked back at him out of the corner of her eye. It was an odd comment, even for a man as perpetually absorbed in the hereafter as Vestal was. He had inherited Avalon's premier funeral establishment at a young age, and though he could be accused of a little cost-cutting hanky-panky here and there, his prowess at his craft was unquestioned. A born schmoozer, the man knew everyone living, dead, and hovering in between for a borough in either direction, and if approached in the appropriate manner, would dish all their dirt for a song.

Or, preferably, your signature on a prepaid burial plan.

He cleared his throat and stood silently next to Leigh by the curtain, rocking back and forth on the heels of his shiny black shoes.

Perhaps she was being overly optimistic, but she swore there was something the man was dying to say. "I don't know the family at

166

all," she whispered, trying to encourage him. "I only met Peggy the day before she died. It seemed to happen so . . . suddenly."

"The end always seems sudden," Vestal said knowledgeably. "No matter how long you're expecting it. The time of a person's passing is always the most stressful time for a family to deal with details. That's why we believe so firmly in planning ahead, you know." He paused only a second, then leaned his mouth closer to Leigh's ear. "Although in Peggy Linney's case, I'd say it was a necessity — otherwise the poor woman would wind up in a particle-board crate."

There was no doubt remaining. Vestal had dirt.

"I've heard that Peggy's children were a bit opportunistic," Leigh said charitably, remembering Lilah Murchison's will. "But I'm sure they cared for her. You don't think they were" — she opened her eyes unnecessarily wide and batted her nearly nonexistent lashes. Vestal was of the old school; a demure woman in need was his call to action — "*unkind* to her. Do you?"

"No, no," the funeral director said comfortingly. Then he glanced furtively in either direction. "There was no evidence of physical abuse on the body, anyway. But they bled her dry, they did. She was Lilah

167

Murchison's right-hand woman, you know, for years and years. Only quit when she couldn't do stairs anymore. Now, say what you will about Lilah Murchison — God rest her soul, but when she liked her staff, she paid them well. Yet Peggy had nothing. She gave it all away or the kids took it, one or the other." His concave front puffed up high. "I knew her kids wouldn't pay for a funeral, so I pitched her on a pre-paid. Peggy would have none of it. Said it was wasted money. But when I sold Lilah Murchison her package I pled Peggy's case, and darned if the woman didn't set up her housekeeper with the Bronze Elite II package. *Cash.*"

Leigh couldn't help but be impressed. First by the generosity of a woman so widely touted as a miser, and second by Vestal's uncanny sales ability. "That was certainly charitable of Mrs. Murchison," she responded. "How long ago did she buy the plans?"

She had no conceivable business knowing that information, but as she had correctly guessed, Vestal did not care. "Oh, years ago," he said proudly. "We started Bronze Elite in eighty-nine; Bronze Elite II came along in ninety-one. I thought more of the women would want perpetual upkeep on graveside florals, and I was right." He looked at her with a lifted eyebrow. "We don't have Bronze Elite anymore, but we do have a new package I put together just for young people concerned about their parents. It's called —"

"Oh, my," Leigh interrupted. "That woman in the green looks so much like Peggy. She must be her daughter."

Successfully, if temporarily, derailed, Vestal cast a knowing eye. "Yes, that's Carol Ann. Her brothers are over by the potted palm: Dick and Robby." He lowered his voice to where it was barely audible. "Those boys took their mother for every dime she had. Peggy wasn't the type who could say no to her own flesh and blood — God rest her soul."

Leigh's gaze shifted from the two over-weight, underdressed men smoking cigarettes by the potted palm to a woman in a cheap purple cocktail dress who had stepped out from behind them. Leigh took one look at her heavily made-up face, and swallowed. "Who is that woman?" she asked hastily, pointing.

"*Oh,* her," Vestal answered, poorly disguising a measure of delight in the topic. "She's the granddaughter from Cleveland. Carol Ann's girl Becky. Several of the older kids here are hers, I believe." He paused for

169

another short throat clearing. "Of course, it's my understanding that she's never been married."

He uttered a loud "tsk tsk" to which Leigh did not respond. She didn't give a hoot about the woman's marital status. Nor did she give a hoot that the provocative dress and gaudy makeup Becky was wearing were glaringly inappropriate for a grand-mother's funeral. What Leigh was fixated on was the woman's thick dark eyebrows, her narrow, close-set brown eyes, and the way her cleft chin tapered down to a near-perfect point.

It seemed an uncanny coincidence, and she knew in her gut that it was not a coincidence at all.

The woman was the spitting image of Dean Murchison.

11

"How old is she?" Leigh asked in a whisper.

If Vestal thought this an odd question, he didn't show it. "Oh, about forty I'd say. Very — um, *well preserved.*"

The pun was far too bad to acknowledge. Even if it weren't, Leigh's mind was otherwise occupied. The math made sense; Peggy's granddaughter would have been a teenager when Dean was born. A young, unwed mother looking for an out — an older, possibly infertile one desperate for an heir.

The pieces fit perfectly. Peggy Linney might very well have delivered Dean Murchison. She just hadn't delivered him from Lilah. And with her own progeny set to inherit the Murchison millions, she certainly wouldn't want anyone to know it.

So Peggy had been hiding something. Did it get her killed?

Leigh's head swam. It would make no sense at all for Dean to want Peggy dead, since they wanted the same thing. In any event, she would bet a week's pay that Dean had no idea the crabby old housekeeper who was always telling him to wipe his feet was actually his great-grandmother.

Vestal was talking again, but Leigh wasn't listening. If the will had been correct about Dean not being Lilah Murchison's biological child, was it correct about her having a real blood heir, too?

She felt like she needed to sit down. The room was blisteringly hot all of a sudden, and the maroon curtains appeared to be doing the wave. She half felt Vestal take her by the arm and lead her into the chapel, and she willingly settled into a pew, automatically muttering some assurances that she felt just fine. By the time Vestal had reappeared with a Dixie cup full of water, she did feel fine. But she couldn't even begin to concentrate on the service.

She watched the back of Becky's head, platinum blond with a good two inches of dark brown roots, bob around irreverently as the pastor spoke of Peggy's devotion to her family. An adolescent boy on one side of her played obliviously on his Game Boy, while an older teenaged girl popped her gum and examined her nails.

A mother of two, Leigh thought to herself, *at least.* Did she know about Dean? Did she know who he was, where he was?

She straightened as a grim thought struck her. If Peggy Linney was killed because of what she knew — could her granddaughter be in danger also?

By the end of the service the Dixie cup in her hand had been kneaded into a gritty lump of mush. Becky and the children rose quickly, and Leigh didn't hesitate in standing up to follow them. The woman might end up thinking she was completely crazy, but she could deal with that. What she couldn't deal with was another member of the Linney household dropping dead while she stood idly by.

"Feeling better?" Vestal had reappeared at her side — inconveniently blocking her path. "You look like a young woman who shouldn't have skipped lunch," he said cheerfully, extending a packet of cheese crackers.

Leigh looked helplessly over his shoulder as Becky and her children pushed their way out of the chapel. "Thanks so much," she responded with a smile, tucking the crackers into a dress pocket. "I guess my blood sugar is running a little low today."

Vestal's eyes practically brimmed over with glee. "How long you been married?"

Oh, great. "I didn't mean —" She broke off the non-explanation. She was *not* discussing anything personal with the loose-lipped funeral director, no matter how helpful he might have been. "I'm sorry," she continued, pushing past him as politely as possible, "but I really need to talk to Peggy's granddaughter. It's important." Thanking him again for the crackers, she exited the chapel as rapidly as was seemly and rushed out into the lobby.

Gone. She skirted the rest of Peggy's family and headed out onto the front walk, where she could see the woman in question and her children heading for a rusted, peanut-butter-colored hatchback parked crooked on the street. "Becky!" she called out. "Wait!"

The woman turned and looked at her pursuer blandly, as though being chased on the street by a stranger was not a particularly unusual event. Leigh sprinted to her side and stopped abruptly, almost too breathless to speak. She simply *had* to get a treadmill.

"I'm sorry to be yelling at you," she apologized, "but I needed to talk to you and I was afraid you were leaving." She extended a hand. "I'm Leigh Koslow. I knew your grandmother."

The kids, who had halted only to watch the strange woman running, now proceeded to get into the car. Becky didn't move, but her hands-on-hips posture made her lack of interest clear. "Oh?"

"Do you think," Leigh began, planning her next moves quickly, "that we could talk privately somewhere? It won't take long, but it's very important, I promise you. It's about . . . an adoption."

Becky's sparkling purple eyelids flickered. She said nothing for a moment, then tossed her car keys through the car window to the teenaged girl in the passenger seat. "Heather, take your brother and go to Wendy's. Pick me up here in ten minutes. And I mean *ten* minutes, not fifteen!"

The girl scooted eagerly to the driver's side and revved up the engine with a roar. Her brother was vaulting into the front seat as she pulled away from the curb and sped off down the street.

Becky seemed unconcerned. "Now who are you again?" she asked irritably.

"Leigh Koslow," she repeated, realizing the name was meaningless. She gestured to a set of concrete steps in front of the house they were passing, and the woman reluctantly sat down next to her. "I'll be honest with you," she continued. "I didn't know your grandmother very well; I only met her a few days ago. But I do know that she once helped you out with a problem. And I could be totally wrong, but I'm afraid that that *favor* might have gotten her into trouble.

And you need to know — because for all anyone knows right now, it could get you into trouble too."

Becky bit a purple-and-orange-striped fingernail. "How do you know all this?"

Lucky guess? The honesty, such as it was, had to stop here. There was a chance that this woman didn't even know what had happened to her baby. And while Leigh didn't want Becky or anyone else in Peggy's family to come to any unwitting harm, she also didn't want to be single-handedly responsible for shaking up the family tree — particularly if fruits like Dean were going to fall off of it.

"Peggy told me some things," she hedged. "But not much. Just enough for me to worry that something she knew was scaring somebody. I'm looking into it because someone has been threatening my father, and I think it may have something to do with Peggy and the baby. Can you tell me more? Please?"

She held her breath. Her story was lame and full of holes, but she didn't want to tell Becky much more until she knew more herself. With any luck, Becky would be the talkative type.

As it turned out, she was. "I'm surprised Grandma talked about it," the woman began with a mumble, still biting the nail. "She told me never to tell anyone. Not even my mum knew what happened to the baby."

"What did happen to your baby?"

Becky shrugged. "Don't know. Never did. Grandma took it and said she had found a wonderful home for it with some family in West Virginia. All I knew was that Grandma gave me a place to live after my mum threw me out of our place in Brentwood. And after the baby came, she smoothed things over so I could go back home. Course I didn't stay long. Once I hit seventeen I was out of there; Grandma was always good about giving me money and stuff."

She paused long enough to give Leigh a searching look. "What's all that got to do with your dad? I don't get it. Nobody's talked about that baby in years. Hell, I got four more where he came from, so what does it matter now? I was just a kid."

Leigh felt like biting her own nails, but refrained. "It probably doesn't matter. It was just a long shot." She jumped up off the steps. "So, are you headed back to Cleveland?"

"Yeah," the woman answered suspiciously. "Look, should I be worried, or what? I mean, are these people who adopted

177

the baby going to sue me or something? It's not like I've got any money."

"No," Leigh assured, "it's nothing like that." Her conscience was feeling better now. Becky clearly knew nothing in particular, and in any event would soon be back out of state. She wouldn't be in any danger; and neither, it sounded, would her mother. Peggy and Lilah had had the good sense to keep them out of it. Unfortunately, Leigh had now opened a rather large can of worms.

She thought fast. "You see, there was an illegal baby-selling ring going on around the same time your baby was adopted, and my father —" This whopper of a lie would take some serious penance, she thought miserably. "My father is a journalist and he was writing this story about private adoption in the seventies, and one of the people who had been involved in the ring way back started threatening him if he brought up anything that would get them into trouble. Peggy wasn't mixed up in anything illegal herself, of course, but when she died so suddenly after he interviewed her . . . it just looked a little suspicious, that's all. But I'm sure now it was all really nothing."

She did some quick fact-checking in her head. Did that make sense? Barely. She

178

hadn't explained how her father would know to interview Peggy in the first place, and there was probably a statute of limitations snag, but she was counting on Becky to overlook all that.

She did. "I don't think Grandma would have done anything illegal," Becky said thoughtfully. "It's not like she stole the baby, because I was going to give it up for adoption anyway." She paused, her purple eyelids flickering again. "But she may have gotten paid for it."

Leigh sat back down with a thump. "I thought the baby went to a couple in West Virginia," she whispered.

"Yeah," Becky began slowly, "that's what Grandma said. But I don't think that's what she did."

Leigh waited. Becky said nothing. Leigh waited some more.

"See, Grandma set me up in a boarding-house a couple months before the baby came," Becky explained finally. "But she didn't talk about any couple in West Virginia then. She said that maybe she could help me raise the baby. But I was too scared — and I was just a kid, you know. I had stuff I still wanted to do. We used to argue about it. Then just a week before I had it, she suddenly started talking about how maybe

179

giving it up *would* be the best thing. And then she told me she knew the perfect family, and that they would raise him as their own. When I went into labor we didn't go to the hospital — she had this doctor come over, and they delivered him right there and took him off. I didn't think about it then, but you know, now it seems kind of funny."

Leigh cursed her overactive imagination. This was a new low, even for her. Never before had she accosted a perfect stranger at a funeral and unwittingly convinced her that her dear departed granny was a black-market kingpin.

"And there was something else, too," Becky continued. "I overheard her talking on the phone one night after she thought I was asleep. I wouldn't have paid attention except it was so strange. She was saying something like 'Everybody feels like that after they've had a baby. It's just your hormones.' And I wondered who she knew that had just had a baby. Then she said 'Once you get this little one in your arms, everything will be fine.'

"I could tell she was talking about my baby, so I asked her about it the next day. She got really nervous. She told me that the woman she was giving the baby to had just had a stillborn. I thought that was pretty neat — I mean, that my baby would make this other woman happy again. Only I couldn't figure out why Grandma was so jumpy about my knowing that. But now — well, I don't know what to think."

Leigh sat on the hard steps with her tongue stuck somewhere deep down in her throat. She didn't know what to think either.

She walked in the back door of the Koslow Animal Clinic in a daze. Perhaps it was just the low blood sugar talking, but her conversation with Becky seemed to have brought up more questions about Dean's birth than answers. She shuffled down the basement stairs and opened the freezer outside her father's office. Deftly avoiding the pathology specimens, she selected one of the single-serving casseroles her mother had stocked and popped it into the microwave around the corner. She did not feel well.

"You don't look like you feel well," Nancy observed from her business manager's desk, the one tidy spot in the veritable sea of dog food, extra gas canisters, and stacked veterinary journals that passed for Randall's office. "Are you all right?"

Leigh sank down on a pile of dog food

181

bags and waited for the ding. "I'll be fine once I get some food in me," she said dully.

Nancy watched her with concern. "Did something happen? Do you want me to get your dad?"

Leigh shook her head. "I'll talk to him after I eat. I just skipped lunch, that's all. It couldn't be helped." The memory of Dean Murchison's roving toes reared its ugly head again, and she shivered involuntarily.

Nancy noticed. "Really, Leigh. You look awful. Where have you been?"

"At Peggy Linney's funeral," she answered matter-of-factly. Much to her surprise, Nancy visibly recoiled at the name. Leigh stared at her. "You knew Peggy Linney?"

Nancy didn't answer for a moment. The microwave dinged, but Leigh ignored it.

"My mother worked with her a long time ago," Nancy answered quietly. "Let's just say Peggy wasn't very nice to her."

Not speaking ill of the dead was all well and good, but it hardly served Leigh's purposes at the moment. Leaving Nancy to ruminate further, she retrieved her lukewarm casserole and began to attack it with a plastic fork. "What type of work did your mother do?" she probed after a few mouthfuls.

Nancy ceased looking uncomfortable and smiled a little. "My mother was a housekeeper — the best in the business. She simply *loved* cleaning things. She said it purified the soul." She paused a moment, looking wistful. "Momma should have had her own business; she would have been wonderfully successful. She always said she couldn't handle the business side of things, though — that she just wanted to clean. She told me I should work hard at school so I could handle the money when I grew up." She extended the pile of checks in her hand with a sad smile. "And voilà."

The implication hit Leigh like a ton of bricks, and she cursed herself for not getting around to questioning the staff sooner. "Your mother worked for Lilah Murchison, didn't she?"

The wistful look left Nancy's face, and she exhaled loudly. "Yes, she worked with Peggy Linney at the Murchison house for years. She enjoyed the work, but Peggy was —" She seemed to be debating whether or not to be rude, and Leigh rooted heavily for her catty side. "I shouldn't say it now, but Peggy was a bitter, narrow-minded racist, and she made my mother's life miserable."

"I'm sorry," Leigh responded sincerely, feeling ever-so-slightly less of the irrational guilt she had been shouldering. "How long did your mother work at the mansion?"

"A long time," Nancy answered sadly. "Too long. She worked there right up until I went to college, and then she got too sick to work. She died of breast cancer."

As Leigh offered her sympathy yet again, Jared bustled into the office with a whisk broom. "Is it OK if I sweep now, Nancy Johnson?" he asked loudly. "Doctor Koslow says not to sweep if it bothers you, Nancy Johnson."

Nancy offered a smile. "That's fine, Jared. Go ahead. You won't bother me at all."

"Thank you, Nancy Johnson."

Leigh watched the young man's powerful arms move the broom in great arcs across the floor. "Speaking of being a wonderful cleaner," she quipped, shoveling the last bites of casserole eagerly into her mouth, "Jared's a natural. I need him at my house."

"I work for Doctor Koslow and Lilah Murchison, Leigh Koslow," Jared answered immediately. "They say I do a good job, Leigh Koslow."

She couldn't help but grin. "You do a fabulous job. A heck of a lot better than I would do, I promise you that." She shifted on the dog food bags and realized that the package

184

of cheese crackers Vestal had given her was still in her dress pocket. She ripped it open hungrily.

"Mrs. Murchison says she wants me to work for her forever and ever, as long as I want, Leigh Koslow." Jared continued, his broom in constant motion. She had no doubt that what he said was true; it couldn't be easy to find an honest, dependable person willing to work after hours cleaning out the litter pans of twenty-three cats — garage apartment or no.

"I'm glad Mrs. Murchison isn't dead, Leigh Koslow."

12

Leigh stopped in mid chew. She glanced quickly at Nancy, wondering if there was a news flash she had missed. Surely not — no one survives four days of floating around Lake Michigan in April, do they? Nancy's equally puzzled expression seemed to concur.

"What do you mean by that, Jared?" Nancy asked patiently. "You know that your sister told you Mrs. Murchison was dead."

Jared continued sweeping, and did not look up. "Mrs. Murchison isn't dead, Nancy Johnson."

Leigh and the business manager exchanged confused glances. Perhaps Jared was in denial, but if so, the reaction was delayed. Nancy scribbled quickly on a piece of paper, then showed it to Leigh with a shrug. *Memory problem? Nikki said he wasn't that upset — he hardly ever saw L.M.*

"Jared," Leigh asked slowly, "we think Mrs. Murchison is dead. Why don't you think she's dead?"

Jared didn't answer for so long that Leigh was almost ready to repeat herself, thinking he hadn't heard her. But finally he turned and started sweeping the same section of floor for a second time. "Nikki said Mrs. Wiggs was dead, Leigh Koslow," he said evenly. "Mrs. Wiggs came home. Mrs. Murchison has to come home. Mrs. Murchison never goes anywhere without Mrs. Wiggs. That's what Nikki says, Leigh Koslow."

Both women sat stupidly for a moment, watching Jared sweep as if hypnotized. "That's the oldest cat," Nancy said quietly to Leigh. "She was traveling with Mrs. Murchison when the plane crashed."

Leigh finished off the last bite of cheese cracker. This business of being constantly blindsided by unwanted information was taxing, and if her mental faculties were going to be put through any more paces, she had to have some carbs. So, she tried to think logically. Jared thought he had seen a particular cat, and that's why he thought Mrs. Murchison was alive. No problem. Either that cat never went on the trip, or Jared had seen the wrong one.

"Jared," she began conversationally, "when did you see Mrs. Wiggs?"

His answer was downright chipper. "Last night, Leigh Koslow. Third floor litter pans. Mrs. Wiggs sleeps on the windowsill, Leigh Koslow."

She swallowed. It would be perfectly logical to assume that Jared had mistaken one cat for another. It would also be extremely unlikely. Because although there were whole categories of information that totally bypassed the young man's comprehension, what he knew, he clung to. It was his whole world. If her father's claims of Jared's ability to remember clients' pets were even half true, Leigh had no doubt that he could recognize any of the twenty-three Murchison Siamese — probably with a blindfold on.

"Did Nikki see her too?" she asked softly.

He shook his head. "Nikki goes out skating on Monday nights, Leigh Koslow. Every Monday night Nikki goes out skating."

Skating? No time to ponder that. "Did you tell her this morning, then?"

"Tell her what, Leigh Koslow?"

"Did you tell Nikki that you saw Mrs. Wiggs?"

"Nikki isn't here, Leigh Koslow."

She took a deep breath. Nancy caught her eye with a concerned look.

Leigh decided to try one more angle. She refused, in the absence of hard evidence, to let herself revisit her original inkling that Lilah Murchison had somehow cheated the grim reaper. With no death there would be no will to probate, no millions waiting to be fought over, and — ostensibly — no more threats to the clinic. It would be entirely too fortuitous.

She rose and followed Jared into the back storeroom. His head was still down as he conscientiously swept up piles of hair and the occasional piece of stale kibble. "Jared," she said, trying to keep her voice light, "has Mrs. Wiggs been home all week?"

He shook his head firmly, making his blond curls gyrate. "Mrs. Murchison never goes anywhere without Mrs. Wiggs. Mrs. Murchison went out of town. Mrs. Wiggs went out of town. Mrs. Wiggs came back. Mrs. Murchison came back."

"Have you seen Mrs. Murchison?"

The curls shook again. "I don't disturb Mrs. Murchison, Leigh Koslow."

Leigh felt Nancy's presence behind her. "We'll have to talk to Nikki," the other woman said quietly. "Jared," she asked, "is Mrs. Wiggs still at home?"

"Mrs. Wiggs gone this morning, Nancy Johnson," he answered. "Mrs. Murchison gone this morning. I have to sweep."

And with that summary dismissal, he ambled off toward the bathroom.

"So what do you think, Dad?" Leigh

189

asked, more than a little annoyed at their sudden audience. She had relayed Jared's story while Randall was scanning a fecal slide at the microscope, and instantly Jeanine, Marcia, and Michelle had materialized in the vicinity.

"I think," he said finally, rolling back his stool and pitching the slide into the sink, "that I'm about to be late for an appointment." He rose, maneuvered through the throng of women, and made haste for the basement stairs.

"Do you think Mrs. Murchison's been hiding out?" Marcia asked when Randall had gone, her eyes wide. "Because I can see her doing that. You know, just to see how everybody reacted."

"That's sick," Jeanine the all-knowing offered.

"She is sick!" Marcia's hip-twin, Michelle, chimed in. "Everyone knows that. I'll bet she's not dead after all. Nobody that evil ever dies."

"That's ridiculous," Jeanine snapped. Her hand suddenly flew to her mouth. "Oh, my God! I bet *she's* the one who's been threatening everybody."

The short silence that followed was ended by a chuckle from Nora, the only one of the staff who still seemed to find humor in the situation. "Yeah, I think she and Freddie Krueger are setting us up," she said lightly, dropping two capillary tubes into the centrifuge. "I wondered what the hell that chainsaw was doing in the autoclave."

"She's kidding!" Jeanine said quickly, forestalling imminent screams from Marcia and Michelle. She then turned back on Nora with venom. "Will you be serious, please?"

"I'm the only one who is," Nora protested. "I heard what Leigh just said, but none of us had any reason to think Mrs. Murchison was alive until today. Why would she threaten us to keep quiet about something we didn't even know yet?"

"She could have guessed we would find out," Marcia squealed, "because of Jared!"

"Or what if," Michelle squealed, "Doctor Koslow has known *all along?* What if they were in this *together?*"

All heads turned toward the basement doorway, and the inevitable screams erupted.

"Stop it!" Leigh broke in this time, her hands over her ears. She'd been trying to sit back and studiously listen to her suspects babble, but enough was enough. "You're being completely ridiculous. You've all worked with my dad for years. Does he

191

seem like a criminal mastermind? Does he seem like the sort of person who would waste valuable clinic time helping some crackpot socialite torture her relatives for kicks? Does he?"

There was no answer.

"Of course not," she said emphatically. "But he *is* the kind of person who would fire his employees for standing around screaming instead of taking care of the animals."

On that rather unkind note, she stomped off to the basement herself, muttering uncharitable comments with every step. Her dad in cahoots with Lilah Murchison to fake her death. *Please.* The man couldn't sit through a complete episode of *Quincy*.

"Dad?" she exclaimed, surprised to find his white lab coat replaced with a sport jacket. "Where are you going?"

"The attorney's." His tone indicated clearly that he saw the errand as a drudgery. "I've got to get the details about Mrs. Murchison's cats."

Her eyebrows arched. "I'm coming with you, then."

He threw her a tired look. "That's hardly necessary. This meeting is simply about the cats." He cleared his throat. "Frankly, I'm a little concerned about your level of involvement in all this. Vandalism and threats are police business." He paused ever so slightly. "Isn't Warren home yet?"

Leigh couldn't help but smile. He and her mother had both thought that marrying a man as responsible and mild-mannered as Warren would somehow magically convince her that cross-stitching and Tupperware parties were primo entertainment. They had been sorely disappointed. Not that she had anything against Tupperware. Some of the best meals she had ever eaten had come in Tupperware. But she hadn't *cooked* them.

"He came home last night," she answered. "And I'm not just amusing myself by asking all these questions. I'm looking out for the clinic and I'm looking out for you. Whether you like it or not, Lilah Murchison has dragged you into her affairs up to your eyeballs. And ignoring all the warning signs won't make them go away." She grinned. "That's a quote from you, by the way: Cancer Lecture number thirty-six."

Randall's brow wrinkled. "I repeat: this is a police matter."

Her expression turned serious. "Dad, I happen to know a little about how the police work, OK? The Avalon PD are good people, but they're plenty busy with actual crimes

193

that have already been committed. They don't have time to chase down leads on a bunch of strange things about Lilah Murchison's will that don't add up. As far as they're concerned, that's soap opera stuff.

"But I have this feeling," she began tentatively, "that Peggy Linney didn't die of natural causes. Don't ask me for proof because there isn't any. But if I'm right, it means that someone out there wants Mrs. Murchison's money badly enough to kill for it."

She took a deep breath. She hadn't told him half of what she had learned since waking up that morning, and it had been a very long day. She hadn't told anybody everything — but she would tell Warren and Maura tonight. Between the three of them, she was confident they could make sense of it. Particularly if they had just a few more pieces of the puzzle — several of which she felt sure she could wrangle out of Mrs. Murchison's lawyer.

"I just need to go with you to see Sheridan," she pleaded. "I need to ask him a few things, and then I'm going to run it all by Maura. I believe there's a real possibility that Lilah Murchison was *not* on that plane. And if she's alive, it will nip all these threats right in the bud. Wouldn't that be worth the effort?"

Randall threw her a long, hard look. When he spoke, his voice was sober. "Jared is certain he's seen Mrs. Wiggs since the plane crash?"

She nodded briskly.

"Jared knows those Siamese," he commented, almost too low to be heard. "Nikki Loomis said that a witness watched Mrs. Murchison get on that plane with a cat, but I suppose she could have gotten off at the last minute."

Leigh smiled broadly. "My thoughts exactly."

"Just let Sheridan do his spiel with me first," Randall had instructed. "Then you can pester the man."

Leigh had readily agreed, although now she was regretting her acquiescence. Not only was the list of specific instructions for the Murchison cats endless, but the chairs in the attorney's stark office were distinctly uncomfortable. She supposed they were artistic, given their curving chrome side arms and solid black sling seats. But she had never been one to suffer for the sake of art, and her spine felt ready to snap.

The lawyer droned on and on, evidently

believing that pronouncing words like "part" and "presume" with extra syllables would increase his billable hours. Leigh picked up bits and pieces of Mrs. Murchison's instructions, such as the fact that some of the younger cats were to be offered for sale. But the majority appeared to be set for life in the otherwise lifeless Ben Avon mansion. She also picked up on the fact that Lilah seemed to have no qualms about saddling Randall with an unreasonable number of pesky duties — assuming that his "generous retainer" would make all well.

The woman was a real piece of work.

By the time Sheridan had finished his drawling explanation of her father's obligations, Leigh had almost dozed off. It was the words "Is there anything else I can do for you?" that roused her.

"As a matter of fact, yes," she answered, attempting to uncoil her damaged spine. She had planned the order of her questions from most to least pressing, certain that the by-the-book counselor would clam up on her eventually. "I suppose you've heard by now of Peggy Linney's unfortunate passing?"

Sheridan nodded expressionlessly.

"I visited her the afternoon before she died," Leigh began. "She told me you had

196

been there earlier."

"Oh?" Sheridan's voice could not have sounded more disinterested as he restacked the huge sheaf of papers on his desk.

Leigh soothed the qualm of conscience she always got when lying to decent people (Dean and Rochelle notwithstanding) by reminding herself of the beauty of vague pronouns. Peggy Linney had not said squat about Sheridan, but Maura had, and Maura was female.

The next moves would be a bit trickier. "She seemed healthy enough when I saw her. I just wondered if she had seemed all right to you."

Sheridan's brow creased a bit. "I noticed nothing out of the ordinary in regard to her appearance, Ms. Koslow. If you're wondering about the nature of my business with her, however, I'm afraid I'm not at liberty to discuss it."

Yikes. This would be harder than she thought. She supposed that if she could fool the man into thinking that Peggy Linney had already told her the reason for the visit, she might be able to bluff him into offering more. But if her blind guess missed its mark, he would know she was lying. And that would definitely put the kibosh on questions two and three.

"I'm not asking out of idle curiosity, Mr. Sheridan," she responded as sweetly as possible. "Are you aware of the threats that have been made against my father's staff?"

As she delivered a brief summary, she tried to judge from his expression how much of the story he already knew. It was a difficult task. Evidently, Impassiveness 201 was a class Sheridan had aced at law school.

"So you see," she concluded, "I think it's important that you share the identity of Mrs. Murchison's biological heir with the Avalon PD. It could be very important to their investigation."

Sheridan frowned. "I'm sure that if that's true, the police department would have contacted me personally. In any event, I would have to tell them the same thing I'm going to tell you. I have no idea who Mrs. Murchison's primary beneficiary is."

Leigh gnashed her teeth. This was not going well. "Oh?"

"I believe I made that clear at the will reading," Sheridan offered peevishly. He then launched into a statement he appeared to have long-since memorized. "The identity of the beneficiary was intentionally concealed by Mrs. Murchison. At such time as that individual provides 'sufficient and compelling' proof of his or her identity, then

I am, in the presence of certain named witnesses, to open a sealed document that is currently being maintained under lock and key. It is my understanding that that document will settle the matter. If, however, sufficient proof of a biological heir is not presented within five years of the date the will is probated, the document is to be destroyed."

The lawyer then leaned back, drumming his fingers impatiently on the desktop. "Any more questions?"

Leigh's smile was now openly saccharine. She had a hard time liking people who charged by the hour to cop an attitude. "Just two. What happens if Mrs. Murchison's body is never recovered?"

"Then her beneficiaries could either wait seven years for a certificate of death to be issued, or take the matter to court," Sheridan answered. "Either way, the process will not be rapid."

"I see," she responded. "And what if Lilah Murchison got off that plane before it ever left the gate, and was now back in town sneaking around and spying on the fallout?"

Sheridan's colossally bored eyes suddenly piqued with interest. "You have evidence of that?"

Obviously not. She considered telling him

the truth, but decided against it. No one un-familiar with Jared's gifts could be expected to take his story seriously. "Enough to take to the police," she hedged. She *would* take it to a county detective — tonight, hopefully. "We have reason to believe she's been back at the mansion, as recently as last night."

The lawyer looked at her another moment, then shrugged. "It would certainly make my job easier." He rose to dismiss them, and his mouth curled into something that was probably as close to a smile as his face ever got. "If the old girl does turn up," he said as he shook Randall's hand, "you tell her I'm raising my fees."

13

Leigh paused on the sidewalk along California Avenue to covet another homeowner's stand of Dutch tulips. There had been tulips at her house, too — until Bambi's evil twin had chomped them all off at ground level. Pittsburgh's spoiled suburban deer had the size of ponies, the appetites of goats, and the unmitigated gall of cockroaches. Once they mastered crossing roads and avoiding the color orange after Thanksgiving, the state would be theirs.

A footstep crunched behind her, and she looked over her shoulder expecting to see a more hurried pedestrian she could politely let pass. But there was no one in sight.

Unconcerned, she began once more walking toward the clinic. It was only eight blocks or so from the attorney's office to her car, so she had let her father drive back alone, feeling she needed both the exercise and the time to think.

Sheridan had offered precious little new information, but at least she did have a better handle on the situation with the will. Mrs. Murchison had gone to great lengths to do one of two things: offer a real biological child the opportunity to choose between anonymity and riches, or drive Dean to distraction. Either way, Lilah had led her adopted son to believe she would die soon — probably in an effort to control him. Could she possibly see surviving a fatal plane crash as a fortuitous opportunity to test the true devotion of her nearest and dearest?

If so, she had undoubtedly been disappointed. And when would the game end? The woman couldn't go sneaking in and out of her house forever. Even if the entrances were well concealed with shrubbery, Nikki lived in the house too, and despite her dedication to the job, Leigh doubted the forthright personal assistant would comply indefinitely with such nonsense.

Another footstep crunched, and this time Leigh saw a flash of olive green dodge behind a brick garden wall.

Don't panic. A kid is just toying with your mind, she told herself. *A kid in army fatigues.*

She took a deep breath and continued. It was broad daylight on a late April afternoon. She could see at least three other people out within a few hundred yards or so. What could happen?

She kept walking at a normal pace, and though she didn't hear any more footsteps, the little hairs on the back of her neck seemed quite certain she was still being followed. Creepy, yes, she assured herself. But not dangerous.

At the turnoff to the clinic, she decided to try a little maneuver of her own. As soon as she was no longer visible around the corner, she hustled in between two parked cars and crouched low. If somebody was following her, they were about to make a mistake.

She had to wait only a few seconds before her pursuer slinked hesitantly around the corner and looked down the street in confusion.

Leigh sighed out loud. She should have known. There were only three things in the world that shade of green. Militia gear, bathroom fixtures in trailers, and a thirty-year-old polyester skort set worn by Adith Rhodis.

"I'm here!" Leigh shouted, standing up. "Where did you think I was going?"

The septuagenarian looked appropriately sheepish. "Oh . . . um, hi, honey! Where're you headed?"

Leigh approached her with a stern expression. "If that's all you wanted to know, why didn't you just ask me? I could know karate, you know."

Adith smirked. "But you don't, do you?"

"That's beside the point. Why are you following me?"

The older woman shuffled her feet. "I wanted to know where you were going."

Leigh waited.

"Oh, all right!" Adith spluttered. Her eyes brimmed with defiance, but after a few seconds, she had morphed into the picture of innocence. "I've been calling your place all day. I even left one of those messages, and you haven't answered it."

"I have a job —"

"I called there too. They said you were out and they didn't expect you till tomorrow, so finally I went down to the clinic to ask your daddy where you were and they told me you'd both gone to see the lawyer fellow."

Adith took a breath, and Leigh cut in. "What was so important you had to track me down right away? Did something happen?"

"That's what I want to ask you!" Adith said with frustration. "You're supposed to keep me updated. The girls are getting restless, you know."

Leigh's eyebrows rose. She didn't know who "the girls" were, but if the rest of them were as relentless as Adith, she was in trouble. In Avalon, the street value on Lilah Murchison's dirt was higher than heroin.

"I followed you to the lawyer's," Adith continued, a hand planted on each well-padded hip. "And when your daddy drove off without you, I thought maybe you found out who the real heir was and you were going to pay them a visit. So I figured, since you don't seem to want to tell me anything, I'd just follow you and see for myself." She straightened her back and smoothed out the skort. "So sue me."

Leigh couldn't help but smile. "I haven't been avoiding you on purpose," she said apologetically. "It's just been a very busy day. At lunch, I —"

"Uh-huh," Adith said impatiently, grabbing her by the arm and steering her down the street. "Just get to the good stuff, OK, honey? Time's wasting."

Gray clouds muscled their way across the river, the ominous tone of the thunder that rumbled down from them being surpassed only by the grumbling of Leigh's own stomach. She had been dishing a judiciously edited script of her adventures to Adith in the parking lot of the Koslow Animal Clinic for a full half hour, and both her watch and her blood sugar told her it was time to head

205

home to Warren's promised Mexican tamale bake.

She had to choose her words carefully; as much as she could use Adith's local insight into the whole situation with Peggy's family, she didn't want Dean's true parentage to get out that way. Little as she thought of the man, it hardly seemed fair for "the girls" to know before he did. So she had edited out the whole interlude with Becky, choosing to make what she had learned about the baby switch sound like pure conjecture.

"So anyway," she summarized, "if Lilah Murchison wasn't actually on that plane, the whole inheritance issue is moot. But I do believe that Lilah gave birth to a stillborn in seventy-seven, and that Peggy Linney helped her quickly locate an adoptable baby. I guess Lilah felt she needed a baby to keep her marriage intact, and that that pregnancy would be her last chance."

Adith's prunelike face was twisted into a coarse frown. "Well, that may be, but it doesn't tell us if there's still a missing millionaire, does it? And it doesn't tell you who's threatening your daddy's people, either."

Leigh's stomach moaned, expressing her mind's thoughts. "No, I guess it doesn't."

Adith continued frowning. "I don't buy

206

it," she said finally.

"Buy what?"

"The stillborn thing."

Leigh stared at her. "Why not?"

"Too convenient."

Leigh exhaled. She was entirely too weak from hunger to draw inferences. "What do you mean exactly?"

Adith's mouth screwed up tight as she thought. "Lilah claims to have another baby out there. But the girls don't see how she could have had one any time after she came straggling back to town without her first husband. Some people get fatter as they age; Lilah got skinnier. I don't know if she went anorexic after the car crash that killed him or what, but she lost weight. And ever since then she's been too skinny to cover up a goose egg — much less a baby. So she either had the baby way, way back" — she leaned closer for effect — "or the baby she had twenty-five years ago *wasn't* stillborn."

Leigh blinked. "Why switch them at all, then?" Adith *tsk tsked* and stretched a bony hand out to pat Leigh's back. "Honey, honey. I know you think women now are liberated and all that, but Albert was of the old school. I'll bet you anything that old coot had his heart set on a son."

A weight settled in Leigh's midsection.

"Give up her own baby girl and raise a stranger's child . . . just to make her husband happy?" Her hand moved reflexively to her waistline again, and this time she didn't bother to pull it back. The mere thought of trading off one baby for another made her nauseous. A lot of things made her nauseous. "I can't believe that," she said weakly.

Adith patted her back again. "You didn't know Lilah Murchison, honey," she said softly. "*I* did."

The tamales sat steaming on Leigh's plate, melted cheese and hot sauce running in tempting rivulets down either side.

She couldn't begin to touch them.

Warren watched her worriedly. "I didn't think you'd ever meet a tamale you didn't like. Should I take this personally?"

"No," she said sadly. "I'm sorry. They look wonderful. It's just . . . I don't feel all that well."

Her husband's eyes widened just a bit before he turned his face away.

Leigh watched him with a sigh. *Oh, no. Now he'll think . . .*

"I had some old leftovers at the clinic earlier," she said quickly. After their two previous pregnancy disappointments, they had an unspoken agreement: she didn't obsess over symptoms, and he didn't ask. She knew her waffling appetite problems stemmed purely from her head, and she was loath to raise false hopes.

In the last hour, she had thought of little else besides Adith Rhodis's theory. It made an awful lot of sense; even more knowing everything that Adith hadn't. Peggy Linney could easily have held her granddaughter's baby as an insurance policy for Lilah. If Lilah had a son, fine. If she didn't, maybe Becky would. The odds were three-to-one in their favor. As for Peggy telling Becky that the adoptive mother had had a stillborn, that made sense too. The less the girl knew about who was adopting her baby and why, the less likely she would be to resurface as a blackmail risk later.

The twosome had covered their bases well. Becky's family lived in Brentwood, on the other side of the burg. Lilah Murchison's reputation, however lurid, would not have stretched so far. Even if Becky did learn, years later, that her grandmother's employer had a son about the same age as her firstborn would be, that knowledge alone would be unlikely to set off any alarm bells. Particularly since no one else had any reason to believe that Dean was adopted.

The only thing Leigh couldn't imagine was what the two women had done with Lilah's baby girl. Couldn't they have kept both infants and claimed they were twins? At the very least, she would think Lilah would want to know exactly where the baby was going, and would want to keep tabs on her. Maybe even keep her close? A girl just Dean's age . . .

She scooted her chair back from the table abruptly. "Is Maura coming over tonight?"

Warren shook his head. "I called, but she's on duty till eleven."

Leigh gazed back at her tamale and thought hard. She needed info on local families, and she needed it now. Who else could she ask? Maura's mother, the ultimate source on Avaloners, had been beyond answering questions for a while now. There was Adith . . . but any suspicions admitted to her would be broadcast across the North Boros by "the girls" in a matter of minutes, and this was a delicate matter. Her father knew people with pets, but the kind of information she needed, his brain simply didn't store.

"Are you going to tell me what's going on now," her husband asked pleasantly, digging into his tamales, "or am I going to have to go on a cooking strike?"

"You couldn't be so cruel," she returned absently. "I'll explain everything in just —" A bald, jolly head popped suddenly into her mind. Its lips were moving.

Of course. She got up and walked to the phone, pulling out the white pages. In seconds she had her man.

"Vestal? Hello, it's Leigh Koslow. Sorry to call you at home, but —"

He responded as she had expected — as though it were a privilege to be bothered.

"I'm looking into some things for my father," she explained vaguely, knowing she could get away with it, "and I thought maybe you could help me figure something out."

"Delighted."

Leigh smiled. She just might have to purchase one of those prepaid burial plans someday. "You know Jared Loomis, who works at the clinic?"

"Fine boy."

"Yes, he is. I know that he has a sister and two brothers; it's kind of a delicate question to ask the family, but — I was wondering if it was common knowledge whether any of those children were adopted."

An odd, snuffling sound piped through the phone wire. She would guess it was either a muffled snicker or a sob, and the latter seemed unlikely. Vestal reserved his voluminous tears exclusively for the funerals of people who would appreciate it.

"I'm sorry," he said after a bit. "Didn't mean to be disrespectful of Wanda — God rest her soul. She died in ninety-eight. Cancer, I believe. But my, my, what a question. No, Miss Koslow, I sincerely doubt Wanda Loomis would have ever adopted so much as a kitten. The woman was what they call perpetually pregnant. Six kids and more miscarriages than anyone could count."

"*Six* kids?"

"Oh, yes. The oldest two are long gone. The other boys, Bill and Red, are born troublemakers. Spend as much time in the county lockup as home. Then there's Jared, whom you know, and the girl, Nikki. Now, she's a bright one. Had to be tough, too, growing up in that mob."

Leigh could imagine. "Did they — all have the same father?"

The muffled sound came again. "Um, well . . ." Vestal began when he recovered, "I doubt that. Loomis is Wanda's maiden name. She never married anybody."

"I see," Leigh responded. It wasn't the information she was expecting, but she wasn't finished yet. "One more question. Wanda

Loomis — do you happen to know of any connection, however thin, between her and Lilah Murchison?"

"Oh, of course," he answered immediately, as if anyone with half a brain should know the same. "The Loomises and the Beemishes were thick as thieves once upon a time. I believe maybe Wanda's mother and Lilah's mother were cousins. But as I'm sure you know, the late high-and-mighty Ms. Murchison — God rest her soul — wouldn't have a thing to do with the likes of Wanda. You can imagine we were all pretty surprised when Lilah took on Wanda's daughter as staff. Not the charitable type, that woman. But it seems to have worked out."

Leigh thanked the funeral director profusely and hung up with a smile. Warren leaned back in one of the real chairs he had dragged in from the living room. "You've got fifteen seconds to start talking," he informed her. "If not, the tamales go to Mao Tse."

"You wouldn't dare." She sat down quickly and snatched up her fork. "I'm starving."

14

"Do you think Nikki knows?" Warren asked, leaning close to the windshield of the blue Beetle. It was pouring buckets, and the trip from the North Hills down to Ben Avon seemed to be taking an eternity.

"It seems like she would have to in order to claim the inheritance," Leigh reasoned. "Unless Lilah left her a sealed envelope or something. But my instincts say Nikki doesn't have a clue. She just doesn't act like she knows. She doesn't even act likes she cares."

Warren queued the Beetle in a line of cars stuck at an unilluminated stoplight. "But you think Dean knows."

"He must. I don't know if Lilah told him or if he figured it out, but he must know. And I think he's trying to threaten Nikki out of claiming the inheritance."

"Why through the clinic, though? Why not contact her directly?"

Leigh had been thinking about that. "Well, first of all, I don't think Dean planned any of this. He's more the waving-his-hands-around-screaming type." She was *not* going to think about the incident in

214

the Chuckwagon again. She had mercifully left that part out of her explanation to Warren, for his own good. Not that he was the type to go punching anybody out — but woe unto Dean if he ever needed paperwork from the county.

"It's his wife Rochelle who's the schemer," she continued. "My guess is that they're not sure if Nikki knows yet or not, and if not, they don't want to tip her off prematurely. Or anybody else, for that matter. But they can preemptively threaten her — and by implication, Jared — through the clinic without anyone knowing their exact target."

Warren was quiet for a moment as he steered carefully through the intersection. The wind was blowing hard against the Beetle, and the lifeless stoplights swayed violently over their heads. "I wish we could get hold of Mo," he said finally. "Don't you think you should at least tell someone at the Avalon PD?"

"I can, but they won't care," Leigh insisted. "Dean Murchison is already suspect number one for the threats; but as Maura said, they can't charge him because they don't have any evidence. All I could provide at this point is more motive."

Warren did not appear appeased. "I'm

just not sure confronting Nikki about this now is the way to go."

"If all goes well, I won't have to," she responded brightly. "All I want to do now is tell her about Jared seeing Mrs. Wiggs. She should be able to tell if there are any other signs of Mrs. Murchison roaming around the place. And if there are, the whole inheritance thing is moot, and Rochelle's reign of terror is over."

Warren threw her a skeptical look. "And then you'll trot off merrily home and leave the whole mother-daughter reunion thing to follow its natural course with no interference."

"Sure," she agreed. Then she considered. "Well, probably."

A bolt of lightning split the sky, and she looked anxiously out the window. They had reached Ben Avon — finally. She directed Warren to the Murchison mansion, then around the side to the driveway. The zigzagging maze that passed for Lilah's front walk might be fine in the daytime, but at night in the middle of a thunderstorm, she would take her chances on a more accessible route.

Warren pulled into the awkwardly angled drive, and they made their way slowly toward the garage. "I'm surprised she doesn't have a gate," he commented.

"Physical barriers are a Sewickley Heights kind of thing," she said philosophically, referring to an even ritzier borough farther downstream. "People like Lilah prefer to keep out the riffraff with good, old-fashioned psychological intimidation. More sporting, you know."

He threw her a skeptical look, but said nothing. A second later, they lurched forward as he slammed on the brakes. "Who is that?" he exclaimed, looking at the bright-yellow hooded raincoat bobbing around a few yards in front of the fender. "It looks like a kid. Came out of nowhere."

Leigh rolled down her window, and the hood turned in her direction. "Nikki?" she called. "Is that you? It's me, Leigh! Can we come in for a minute?"

The hood made its way around to the passenger side of the car, and Nikki Loomis's wet face appeared. "Are you nuts?" She rolled her eyes. "Never mind. Yeah, whatever. Park in front of the garage and come to the porch." She uttered an expletive, pulled the yellow slicker tighter over her head, and marched off toward the house.

Refusing her husband's offer of his umbrella, Leigh made the sprint from the garage to the back door in record time, but was still soaked. The glass-encased sun-

217

room was nicely furnished, but since the carpeting was AstroTurf, she didn't feel too bad about dripping on it. "I know you weren't expecting us, Nikki," she began breathlessly, "but I had to see you right away. There's news about Mrs. Murchison. Have you talked to Jared today?"

Looking confused, Nikki shook her head slowly. "I teach aerobics at the Y on Tuesdays. Is Jared OK?"

"He's fine," Leigh said quickly.

"He didn't hear those rumors, did he?" she asked with alarm. "I got an earful of that at the Y already. Everybody thinks Lilah faked her own death now."

Leigh took a deep breath. News couldn't travel that fast — even in the North Boros. Sure, the whole clinic staff had heard Jared's story, and the communicative powers of Mrs. Rhodis and "the girls" should not be underestimated. But still. "Why do they think that?" she asked.

Nikki shrugged. "I guess just because her body wasn't found. You know people. Everything's a TV movie."

Warren walked in through the porch door, turned around to shake out his umbrella, then leaned it carefully against the doorjamb. He was almost perfectly dry. "Nikki," Leigh said, "this is my husband, Warren —"

"Warren Harmon, County Council, District Two," he said in his best politician's voice, extending a practiced hand. "Delighted to meet you. I've met your brother — wonderful guy. My father-in-law thinks the world of him."

"You mean Jared," Nikki said with a rare smile. "Thanks." She turned back to Leigh, and the smile disappeared. "Now, why are you here? And don't ask to come in again. I'm still trying to fix all those pictures up on the third floor your old-lady friend rearranged."

Leigh cringed. "Sorry. But this is important. Jared thinks he saw Mrs. Wiggs last night."

A well-timed bolt of lightning accentuated the blanching of Nikki's small face. "He what?" she croaked.

"He told me he saw Mrs. Wiggs last night. On the third floor, sleeping on the windowsill. He was certain Mrs. Murchison was alive too, though he said he hadn't seen her." She was going to ask Nikki how reliable she thought her brother's observations were, but the look on the younger woman's face made that clear.

"I'm always out Monday nights," Nikki answered numbly, turning toward the house with her key outstretched. "Ms. Lilah

219

knows that." She inserted the key into the heavy back door, opened it, and began punching some buttons on a security panel around the corner. Rain was still beating heavily on the glass roof of the sun-porch, and Leigh, following close behind, had to strain to understand Nikki's mumbling.

"I'm always out on Tuesday afternoons, too. I teach at the Y and then I go out to eat with Leslie and them — I'm almost never back before seven." She was staring at the security console, the puzzled look on her face deepening. "This isn't right."

Warren followed the women into the house and closed the door behind them. The loud hammering of the rain ceased, leaving an eerie quiet.

"What isn't right, Nikki?" Leigh asked.

The stillness was interrupted by a rumble of thunder. "It's off," she said simply. "Somebody turned it off." She exhaled loudly, then slammed her back against the wall with a thump. *Damn her.*

Warren suddenly turned his eyes toward the ceiling. "Wait. I heard something."

Leigh listened, and she heard it too. A low moaning, almost a sobbing. This time it didn't sound like a Siamese. It sounded like a man.

"Jared!" Nikki shouted, bolting forward.

Leigh leaped after her, careful to avoid her husband's would-be restraining clutches. The three raced up the back stairs of the kitchen and emerged, one by one, in the upstairs hall.

Jared sat hunched on his knees in the middle of the corridor, swaying slowly backward and forward. His face was buried in his hands, and he appeared to be half crying, half hiccuping from too many lost breaths. He made a noise that seemed as though it was intended to be words, but came out only as a garbled moan.

Nikki was with him on the floor in a flash. "Jared," she said soothingly, pulling his hands down. "What happened? Are you all right? Are you hurt?"

The young man looked at his sister for a long moment, and his breathing gradually steadied. "Nikki's at the Y on Tuesdays," he said calmly.

"Yes," she answered. "But I'm back now. You cleaned the cages?"

He thought a moment. "I was cleaning the cages in the basement, Nikki."

"You were cleaning the cages in the basement and something happened?" she coaxed.

"I heard the doorbell," he replied more evenly, and adjusted himself to sit in a more comfortable position. One of several Siamese prowling the hall strolled up, approached his arm, and rubbed against it gently. "I heard the doorbell, but I didn't open the door, Nikki. I don't open Mrs. Murchison's door."

"No, that's right, you don't," she confirmed quickly. "Then what happened?"

"Mrs. Murchison opened the door herself."

Nikki took a deep breath. "Did you see her come in?"

Jared shook his head. "She was already in, Nikki. She opened the door."

Leigh stepped forward. "Jared, do you mean that Mrs. Murchison opened the door for somebody *else* to come in?"

He nodded.

Warren stepped around the women and began looking down the hall, cell phone in hand. Siamese were everywhere, but they were all strangely silent. Leigh squatted down on the floor next to Nikki and Jared. "Did you hear Mrs. Murchison and the other person talking?"

Another loud crack of thunder shook the air, and the women both started. Jared didn't seem to notice. "I heard the doorbell ring," he repeated. "I heard Mrs. Murchison open the door and shut it."

He seemed to have no more to say. The friendly Siamese hopped onto his lap, shamelessly nudging his arms for a stroke. He obliged.

"What happened after that, Jared?" Nikki urged. "Something must have happened. Why did you come up here?"

The man's eyes misted over. "I heard Mrs. Murchison scream, Nikki."

Leigh heard the familiar sound of Warren's cell phone beeping from down the hallway as he dialed the phone. Then he was talking to someone, but she couldn't make out the words.

"Mrs. Murchison screamed," Nikki said tensely. "And you came up to see what was wrong?"

Jared's face was stricken. "I'm not supposed to bother Mrs. Murchison, Nikki."

"No, of course not," she agreed. "But you were worried about her, so you came upstairs."

"She stopped screaming."

"That was when you came upstairs?"

He didn't respond immediately. "When something's around your neck tight you can't breathe, Nikki. People got to breathe, Nikki. Animals too. Everything's got to breathe, Nikki."

Leigh's pounding heart seemed to stop in

mid beat. She rose.

"That's right, Jared," Nikki answered. "Everything's got to breathe."

"She couldn't breathe, Nikki."

Leigh continued down the hall in the direction of Warren's voice. She found him standing at the doorway of a bedroom on the left side of the hall, and he quickly put out a hand to stop her.

"Who couldn't breathe, Jared?" Nikki was asking.

Leigh looked over her husband's outstretched arm and into the bedroom. Not five feet in front of her, a woman's body lay on the floor, legs and arms sprawled, neck reddened, open eyes bulging. On one side of her blond head lay a heap of thin leather that looked like a whip. On the other lay a particularly ancient Siamese cat.

Jared's trembling voice drifted down the hallway. "Mrs. Murchison couldn't breathe, Nikki."

15

"If that cop so much as looks at Jared funny, I swear to God I'll pound him," Nikki fumed, pacing the hallway outside the Murchison kitchen. Leigh had practically pushed the female fireball out after she had begun to accost the perfectly polite Ben Avon police officer with her biceps-flexing routine. "Those cops'll look at him like he's some sort of animal and they'll arrest him on the spot. I know they will."

"No, they won't," Leigh assured, projecting more confidence than she felt.

"Do you have any idea what would happen to Jared in the county jail?" Nikki practically screamed. "Any idea?"

In truth, Leigh knew much more about the Allegheny County Jail than she cared to relay. "It won't happen, Nikki," she continued. "Jared was just an innocent bystander, and the detectives will realize that when they get here."

Nikki stopped pacing and leaned back against a wall of cabinets. "He pulled that whip away from her neck. His prints are going to be all over it."

"That's perfectly explainable. Any detective worth his or her salt knows that just because a person is first on the scene doesn't make him the murderer." Leigh tried to get the words out without thinking unkind thoughts about Maura's detective boyfriend, but it was tough. "Maybe we can help them figure out who their real suspects should be," she suggested. "Have you ever seen that whip before?"

Nikki shook her head. "Of course not! Mrs. Murchison would never keep anything like that lying around."

"All right. There's something. Whoever killed her brought it with them. And if someone came over here to kill her, they must have known that she wasn't already dead."

The younger woman sighed. "But everybody already *suspected* she was alive. Rumors were flying all over the place."

Leigh took a deep breath. "OK. But only two people we know of stood to benefit from her death — at least monetarily. The mystery heir . . . and Dean."

Nikki seemed to think a moment, then shook her head. "I still don't believe there is a mystery heir. I told you, Ms. Lilah liked to jerk people around. Why do you think she didn't come forward after the airplane crash? She had to know it went down and

226

that everyone thought she was on it." She muttered a series of extremely unkind words. "Screwing around with other people's minds was what Lilah Murchison did best, believe me."

"So then Dean must have done it."

"No!" Nikki protested angrily.

Leigh's eyebrows rose. "Why not?"

Nikki made an unintelligible sound of frustration and bounced back off the wall. "Because Dean's a moron, that's why. And a crybaby. He's not the sort that goes around strangling people, least of all his mother. He talked a big game, but I'm telling you he was scared to death of her."

"What about Rochelle?"

"She can be a schemer, but —" Nikki shook her head. "I just can't see it. Why would they kill Ms. Lilah now? Jeez, once he knew she was alive, Dean would have been better off to make nice and try to get her to change her will again. Even if they got away with killing her, as things stand now they'd have to wait a whole five years for the money."

Leigh debated with herself. She could swear Nikki really didn't believe Mrs. Murchison had another child. Much less . . . "Nikki," she began before she could talk herself out of it, "why are you so sure that

Mrs. Murchison doesn't have another heir? Because I've got to tell you, I think she does."

The other end of the hallway filled with the form of a large man, and a familiar face looked them both over. He seemed puzzled for a moment, then smiled ever so slightly. "Hello. Detective George Hollandsworth, here. Allegheny County, Homicide." He pointed a notebook toward Leigh. "You're Bess Cogley's niece, aren't you?"

She smiled too, also ever so slightly. Whenever she got referred to as Bess Cogley's niece, it made her nervous. She had met Hollandsworth over a year before, when he had investigated an incident near her aunt's house in Franklin Park. Why he should remember her aunt was something no one who knew the woman would have to wonder.

"Um, yes. Leigh Koslow. Nice to see you again."

"Quite," he said pleasantly. "I understand you're married now, to a County Councilman."

Leigh nodded mutely. Evidently, the incident in Franklin Park had not been the last he had seen of her hopelessly flirtatious Aunt Bess. Interesting.

The detective turned toward Nikki with

his hand extended, but the younger woman stood perfectly still, staring daggers at him. When her tiny fists started to twitch, Leigh decided to intervene. "Why don't we all go into the kitchen?" she said smoothly, waving Hollandsworth ahead while planting herself between him and Nikki. "I'm sure you have questions for all of us."

And that he did — though when he proposed questioning them one at a time in the adjoining family room. starting with Jared, Nikki's fists immediately went back into action. "I stay with my brother," she snarled. Jared was still sitting quietly at the table next to Warren, his head down. It was the same position he had been in since the police arrived, and he hadn't said another word.

"He's mentally challenged, sir," the Ben Avon officer explained. "He hasn't responded to any of our questions."

"My brother was born with Down's Syndrome," Nikki said. "You have to ask him questions in a certain way, or he won't answer you. It doesn't mean he doesn't know the answers. He knows a hell of lot more than most people."

Hollandsworth sized up Nikki with a tired look, then nodded. "All right. Stay as you are, then, if he's comfortable. How about I ask the questions, and you translate as necessary? Just translate — no answering for him."

Seeming a little more content, Nikki nodded. Jared relaxed again as she sat beside him, and when the questions came from her, he answered easily. They moved quickly through the business of establishing why he was in the house and what he was doing, but when they reached the part where the doorbell had rung, the young man got increasingly nervous.

"And how long was it between the time the doorbell rang and when you heard the scream?" Hollandsworth asked, his eyes moving back and forth between brother and sister as he scribbled on his pad.

"He can't —" Nikki began, but then she got an idea. "Jared," she asked, "whose cage were you cleaning when the doorbell rang?"

"Mr. Moto's, Nikki. It was very messy, Nikki."

"And whose cage were you cleaning when you heard the scream?"

Jared thought about it. "Dr. Goldfinger, Nikki. Almost done with Dr. Goldfinger."

Nikki looked up at Hollandsworth. "He always cleans left to right, top to bottom. Those cages are right next to each other, so I'd say five to ten minutes, max."

The detective looked impressed. "And

after he heard the scream, did he hear anyone leave? A door slamming?"

Nikki bit her lip. "Jared, the person that Mrs. Murchison let inside the house — when they left, did you hear the door slam?"

He seemed to shiver. "I heard a door slam, Nikki."

"What were you doing when you heard the door slam?" Hollandsworth asked for himself.

"I was taking off the thing, Nikki," Jared said softly. "The thing around her neck."

His sister exhaled with a shudder. "The person was still in the house, then," she said out loud, her eyes wide. "They saw Jared with her."

"Did you ever see the other person, Jared?" Hollandsworth asked.

Jared simply shook his head.

"Why *did* you go upstairs?" Nikki asked, cutting off the detective's next question. "Did you go up right after you heard the scream?"

Jared began to rock back and forth in his chair, obviously agitated. "I heard the scream; then I got Dr. Goldfinger's food and water, Nikki. I'm not supposed to bother Mrs. Murchison. I got the food and water for Dr. Goldfinger and I — I wanted to know why Mrs. Murchison was screaming, Nikki. I shouldn't have bothered her. I don't bother Mrs. Murchison."

"You did good, Jared," Nikki broke in firmly. "You did everything just right." She stood up and walked over to Hollandsworth's chair. "He's had enough for now, do you hear me?" she whispered intently. "He feels guilty because he went against my instructions by going upstairs when Mrs. Murchison was home. He also feels guilty because another part of him thinks that if he'd gone upstairs as soon as he heard the scream, she might still be breathing. But none of this is his fault, and I won't let *anyone* make him think it is. Understand?"

Hollandsworth, who had the good sense to show no reaction at all to Nikki's display of bravado, offered a solemn nod. "I think Jared can take a break while I interview the rest of you. Just one more thing, though. How does he normally get through Mrs. Murchison's security system to come in and clean?"

"He has his own code," Nikki answered. "Any time he goes in or out, he uses his key and punches in his code. That keeps the system on in case anybody tries to open any of the doors while he's working inside."

"What if he forgets and opens a door to leave without punching in his code first?"

Hollandsworth asked.

"Jared never forgets his routine," Nikki said defensively. "The alarm didn't go off tonight because Mrs. Murchison turned it off herself. She always turned it off completely when she came home; she was too lazy to learn how to manage the settings."

Leigh wondered if Hollandsworth had taken note of the personal assistant's distinct lack of empathy for her murdered employer. Whether Lilah had been killed in a plane crash four days before or strangled to death a matter of hours ago seemed of little consequence to Nikki. The only thing that appeared to matter was protecting her brother.

"I'd like to interview you privately now, Ms. Loomis," the detective said emotionlessly, rising and pointing toward the door to the family room. "Shall we?"

Nikki hesitated, throwing a nervous look at her brother. "It's all right," Leigh said, moving over to take Nikki's empty chair. "Jared will be fine. We'll stay with him."

Somewhat appeased, the younger woman stepped out with the detective. Jared perked up as soon as Leigh began chitchatting with him about his work at the clinic, but she was only half listening to his answers. Nikki's reaction to Mrs. Murchison's murder was nothing less than callous, but her devotion to her brother was endless. Could she have no feeling at all for a woman she knew to be her biological mother?

Maybe Leigh was wrong, but she didn't think so.

"I hope to hell you've got something good to eat," Maura Polanski announced when Leigh opened her front door at 6:45 the next morning.

Leigh blinked back some cobwebs and squinted. "Did I invite you over?" she asked sleepily.

Maura chuckled as she walked inside. "What do you think?"

"Um . . . I think not."

"Ten points." Maura looked around the house as she strode purposefully toward the kitchen. "Where's Harmon?"

"Are you kidding me?" Leigh responded with a yawn. "You've got to get here earlier than this to catch the world's most conscientious politician. Time is taxpayer money, you know."

"Damn." Maura removed a bagel from the refrigerator and popped it into the toaster. "How is he?" she asked more seriously. "OK?"

Clearly, the detective had already heard

all about last night's adventure. "He took it like a trouper," Leigh answered, feeling a renewed sense of guilt. When you had karma as lousy as hers, you eventually got used to stumbling over dead people. But for Warren, it had been a first. And the fact that he had been involved at all was — of course — her fault.

Maura poured herself the last cup of coffee, and began to make a fresh pot. "You know," she said philosophically, "I was all set to come over here and ream you out."

"Does that mean —"

"I'm not done talking yet," the detective said sternly, delivering her best glare. "I was going to come over and ream you out for sticking your nose where it doesn't belong *yet again,* but then I thought to myself: Polanski, you're going to get an ulcer. So why fight it? I thought maybe marrying Harmon would keep you in line, but now I see that you, my friend, attract crime like garbage attracts bees."

Leigh's brow furrowed. "Lovely analogy. Thanks."

"Anytime." The bagel popped up, and Maura began slathering it with a huge knifeful of margarine. "So, here we go. As of this morning, the Avalon PD is turning over the case of the threats against the Koslow

Animal Clinic to me, to investigate any possible connection to the murder of Lilah Murchison. Since I warned you approximately" — she glanced at the thick black plastic watch on her wrist — "eighteen hours ago to back off the case and stay the hell away from Dean and Rochelle Murchison, I'm assuming you've now talked to both of them and about three other suspects, plus you've got some new crackpot theory about who Murchison's other kid is. Am I right?"

Leigh sat down at the table and folded her arms defensively. "No, you're not. For your information, I interviewed Dean and Rochelle Murchison exactly nineteen hours ago. And my theory is not crackpot. I'm ninety-five percent certain I know exactly who the real heir is."

The detective threw her a long, hard look, and cursed under her breath. "I was kidding, Koslow."

Leigh tried not to smile. "Oh."

Maura exhaled loudly as she popped another bagel into the toaster, brought the first to the table, and took out her notebook. "Now, start with nineteen hours ago," she said with a scowl, her round baby face a disturbing shade of red. "I want it short, to the point, and complete. Because if I find out later that it's not —"

"Yeah, yeah, I know," Leigh said with a wave of dismissal. "The disemboweling thing."

Maura narrowed her pretty blue eyes. "You'd better believe it."

Leigh sat idly in her Cavalier, her eyes glued on the Civic parked in front of her. Between the endless replays of Lilah Murchison's twisted body that had kept her up most of the night and the extra crack-of-dawn police grilling, her brain was fried.

Nothing about Lilah Murchison's murder made any sense to her, but — she dutifully kept telling herself — it didn't have to. Because both good and common sense dictated that now was the time for her to wash her hands of the whole ugly mess. Trying to figure out who was pestering her dad's staff was one thing, but bumping into a murderer in the night was another. And with Maura on the case, the threats at the clinic were sure to get the attention they deserved. Her assistance in the matter was no longer needed — nor, as the detective had made so abundantly clear — wanted.

Furthermore, after hearing all Leigh had to say, Maura herself did not seem in the least bit confused. According to the detective, it was blatantly obvious that Dean and Rochelle were the prime suspects in both the threats and the murder.

It seemed blatantly obvious to Leigh, too. But it also seemed dead wrong.

She sat for almost ten minutes, waiting for some reasonable explanation to pop into her head for why she gave a damn if Dean and Rochelle were falsely accused of anything. None did. Maybe it was some primitive sense of justice, or maybe it was just an ego thing. Either way, it didn't justify the mental energy she had already put into the puzzle, much less the waste of any more.

Yet here she was. She should be getting out of the car now, making her monthly visit to Maura's ailing mother and then trooping off to make up some of the time she'd lost at Hook. Instead she was memorizing the shape of a rust patch on the back of somebody's Honda.

Maybe it was Nikki who was bothering her. Jared's valiant defender Nikki, who might be the heir to millions and not realize it. Leigh had wanted to say something to her last night, but to say that the woman was otherwise occupied would be the understatement of the year. How would she find out now? Would Maura talk to her? The detective had not been exactly forthcoming with her plans.

It's not your problem, Koslow.

On that note, she forced herself to hop out of the Cavalier and walk double time toward the azalea-flanked entrance to Maplewood Eldercare. Visiting Maura's mother would help her regroup. Mary Polanski, for all her renowned ability to retain local trivia, had always been a master at minding her own business.

The fact that she had recently confessed to hating Lilah Murchison's guts was irrelevant.

16

The Alzheimer's wing of Maplewood Eldercare was about as pleasant as such an institution could be. Mary Polanski's room was in the blue hall, which was fitting given the number of pictures of her policewoman daughter and late police chief husband plastered from floor to ceiling on the wall opposite her bed. Leigh wondered how much Mary saw of them, however, given that the sprightly sixty-something woman was up and on the move every time Leigh came to visit.

Mary had ceased to recognize her or Warren many months ago but seemed to enjoy their company regardless and often entertained them with absorbing ramblings from her past. Today, Leigh found her walking in large circles around the lobby fountain and waterfall, which was conveniently flanked by a padded walkway and handrail. "Hello, Mrs. Polanski," she said pleasantly, extending her hand. "I'm your daughter Maura's friend, Leigh."

Mary's light gray eyes looked at her critically, but she merely offered a nod and kept walking. Leigh walked with her, and it was only a moment before Mary began talking. "Do you know Ed?"

Leigh nodded emphatically. "Chief Edward Polanski, oh yes. Best police chief Avalon ever had."

Mary smiled broadly. "I think he's cute."

The conversation continued in like vein for another few minutes, with Mary circling the fountain at a good clip, shifting back and forth in time between her childhood and Maura's. As always, Leigh learned an interesting tidbit; this one, which involved a certain detective, her aunt's brassiere, and a tube of orange lipstick, was definitely a keeper.

But there was more she wanted to know. Her guilt-o-meter was riding high at the prospect of pumping a friend's mother for nebby information, but, she told herself repeatedly, if Mary didn't want to answer a question, she wouldn't — Alzheimer's or not. And in any event, whatever reason Mary had for hating Lilah was unlikely to affect the issues at hand. Leigh was asking — she rationalized — out of simple, innocent curiosity.

She took a deep breath. "Mary," she began casually, "do you remember Lilah Murchison?" She tried to catch the older woman's eye, but Mary kept her head down, plowing around the fountain in earnest. Leigh decided to try again. "I think her maiden name was Lilah Beemish. I understand that Lilah Beemish and Wanda Loomis were second cousins. Do you remember either of them?"

Mary Polanski stopped suddenly, straightened, and looked down at Leigh over her long, beaklike nose. Like her daughter and her late husband, she was over six feet tall and could definitely get one's attention when she wanted to. "It's none of my business what they do, is it?" she asked sharply.

"I suppose not," Leigh said quickly, disturbed by the uncharacteristic animosity. "I just wondered if you knew them. Wanda's daughter and son are very nice people. Her son Jared —"

"How can that woman call herself a mother?" Mary interrupted.

Leigh swallowed. "You mean Wanda?"

"Lilah Beemish doesn't care about anybody but herself. She's despicable."

Mary's tone was growing agitated, and Leigh's guilt-o-meter teetered into the red zone. "Oh, I'd have to agree with you there," she said soothingly, encouraging the older woman to resume walking.

"To do that to a *baby!*"

The word stopped Leigh in her tracks again. How would Mary know anything about a baby? Had Maura said something? Possibly. But things happening in the present almost never penetrated Mary's mind anymore. "Do what to a baby?" she whispered.

"Despicable. Absolutely despicable."

Another resident stumbled into their path and grabbed Leigh's arm. "Do you have a cigarette?" he begged.

"Now, Mr. Travis," an aide said evenly, intervening, "let's not bother our guests about that." She steered the man away from the fountain, and Mary Polanski decided to leave it as well. Ignoring everyone else completely, she began a determined march up the blue hall.

Leigh caught up with her. "Mary, what was that you were saying about a baby?"

The older woman didn't stop walking, but she did smile. "Maura's my baby. Want to see her pictures?"

Leigh's heart had settled somewhere down in her stomach. "No, thank you. Not this morning. I'm afraid I have to be at work soon." She gave the older woman's arm a light squeeze. "You take care of yourself. All right?"

Mary continued walking, taking no notice

whatever of her guest's departure, and Leigh began wandering just as aimlessly in the other direction, eventually ending up at her car. She put the key in the ignition, but didn't turn it, preferring to reacquaint herself with the rust spot.

To do that to a baby. What could Mary possibly be referring to? If Leigh didn't know better, she would assume that Mrs. Polanski knew all about Lilah's self-serving disposal of her own baby girl. But that was ridiculous. Mary might have had the inside track on Avalon residents, but by the seventies Lilah was already a rich Ben Avon socialite. Mary Polanski, on other hand, was vintage blue-collar — a stay-at-home policeman's wife raising a rambunctious little girl. There was no reason for the women to have any connection, and certainly no reason for anyone to know about the baby switch except for Peggy, Wanda, and whatever doctor they had bribed into signing the birth certificates.

But that's OK, Leigh stressed to herself, letting out a long, tired breath. Because it wasn't her problem anymore.

Even after a large cup of McDonald's coffee, the pile of work on her desk at Hook, Inc. was too frightening to contemplate.

"Well, well," kidded her office mate, designer Alice Humboldt, who was in the midst of opening a steaming bag of microwaved popcorn when Leigh walked in. "I should have known the mere aroma of melting fat would make you reappear. Wish I'd made some yesterday — I got tired of listening to your phone ring."

"My phone rang a lot?" Leigh asked, grabbing a handful of hot kernels. "That's odd." Business at Hook was pretty decent, given that the firm was less than two years old. But it was their account manager and would-be motivational speaker Jeff Hulsey who got the calls. The only people who ever called her were relatives and clients who didn't like her ideas. Clients who liked her ideas called Jeff Hulsey.

She looked curiously at the illuminated voice-mail light on her phone.

"Been ringing all morning too," Alice added, tilting up the popcorn bag to direct a stream of kernels into her mouth.

Leigh smiled at her coworker. Alice was impatient, brusque, and lived on high-fat food. There was nothing better than working with someone who shared all your own vices — only worse.

"One of them had to be your mom," Alice announced, flicking greasy white

245

crumbs off her desktop.

Leigh's eyebrows rose. "How do you know?"

"Something about the ring," the other woman said thoughtfully, leaning back in her chair. "It conveyed a certain 'motherly' tone."

"You mean guilt-inducing angst?"

Alice tapped her nose. "Bingo."

Leigh groaned. It was inevitable that news of Lilah's murder would spread quickly in the North Boros, regardless of whether or not it got top billing in the Pittsburgh news. Her and Warren's names would probably not make the cut for the latter, but locally, no minutiae would go unspoken. Hence, hiding the details from her mother was not an option. But oh, how she wished it were. Because this time, it would not be Leigh's own role in discovering the body that would get Frances going. It would be the fact that she had dragged the world's most sainted son-in-law along with her.

As if she didn't feel bad enough about that already.

Leigh dialed into her voice mail with a heavy heart. To her surprise, only one of her many theoretical callers had actually left a message. Not to her surprise, that caller was

Frances. "Leigh, dear, aren't you supposed to be at work by eight-thirty? It's nine-thirty in the morning now, and I'm calling to let you know that your father needs your help at the clinic right away. It's important. I'll meet you down there." There was a pause, as if Frances was readying to hang up, then a shuffling noise as she retrieved the phone. "Oh! And bring your lunch. Something light, I hope."

Leigh replaced her own phone without taking a breath. Frances was on *her* way to the clinic? Frances was demanding her daughter play hooky from a paying job? This could not be good.

When she could breathe again, she rose and headed for the door.

"Hey!" Alice demanded. "Where're you going? Is something wrong?"

"The clinic," Leigh answered numbly. "And definitely."

The Koslow Animal Clinic's tiny parking lot was full as usual, but Leigh quickly found on-street parking a block up. She noticed as she walked in that the number of cars parked there seemed small — terribly small, in fact, for a Wednesday morning, when the full staff usually ran a dual appointment and surgery schedule.

The staff. Leigh's eyes widened as she looked over her shoulder and noted the lack of familiar cars. Where was Nora's beat-up VW van? Jeanine's annoying little Geo? The only cars she recognized were her dad's wagon and her mother's Taurus.

Her steps quickened. *And Maura Polanski's Escort.* She arrived at the back door at a jog.

"Thank goodness!" Nancy exclaimed, grabbing her immediately by the arm as she entered the treatment room. "Can you get these stitches out? The doctors are both busy and the client has been waiting and waiting —" She struggled to put the wriggling young beagle in her arms down on the exam table.

"Where is everybody?" Leigh asked, plucking a pair of suture scissors from the instrument rack.

Nancy exhaled in frustration. "They walked out."

Leigh's eyes widened. "What do you mean, 'walked out'?" She showed Nancy how to get a firm grip on the squiggling dog, then snipped out the spay sutures.

"They just went home." She paused. "We got another threat this morning, by regular mail. At the same time, everybody found out that Lilah Murchison had been murdered, and they all got really scared."

"Everybody?"

"No, not everybody. Nora's really sick, I think; she didn't even come in. But the others came and left. Marcia and Michelle — even Jeanine. We're missing Jared too, but not because of the threat. I think he's being questioned by the police again."

Leigh's stomach did a painful flip-flop. Jared, being questioned again? He must be a wreck. And another threat? Wasn't enough enough?

"I'm working the desk, and your mother is helping your father in the surgery," Nancy continued, holding the slaphappy beagle at arm's length to keep it from licking her face. "But Dr. McCoy has a full schedule, and we've got nobody to help in the rooms. We really need you, Leigh, if you can spare the time. I don't know what else we can do."

She disappeared around the corner toward the reception area, and with like speed, Maura appeared through the door to the surgery. "Koslow," she said cheerfully. "You come to help out?"

She nodded. "A new threat?"

Maura reached into a shirt pocket and pulled out a sealed plastic bag. Leigh grabbed a corner and tilted it up to the light.

Inside was an ordinary postcard, the kind one could buy in any local drugstore. It showed a man relaxing in a folding chair in the middle of a roadway, his fishing line cast in the depths of a large rain-filled pothole. The caption read "Springtime in Pittsburgh." On the reverse was the address of the clinic and four words in plain block letters. ANYONE TALKS — EVERYONE DIES.

"Mailed yesterday," Maura elaborated. "Looks like our threatener is still feeling threatened."

Leigh let go of the bag. "Nancy said Jared is being questioned again. What's that all about?"

The detective shook her head and shrugged. "I need to talk to Hollandsworth again; see where's he at. But I have a feeling both these cases will be wrapped up pretty soon."

"Have you talked to Nikki?"

"Not yet. I've got another case going to hell this morning." She threw Leigh a stern look. "But I'll get to it. What I said earlier still goes. You keep your mouth *shut*. Got it?"

Leigh nodded. It must not have been a convincing enough nod, however, because Maura responded to it with a distinctly evil eye. "What?" Leigh defended. How could one lie with a nod?

"You know what." The detective began walking toward the door.

"Wait," Leigh called. "Did you tell your mother anything about a baby? When you were talking about Lilah Murchison?"

Maura stopped and turned. "No. Why?"

Leigh explained.

"Interesting," the detective commented, her eyes flickering. "Very interesting."

"Maura, I really don't think —"

"Gotta go, Koslow."

With a brisk wave, the detective was gone.

"Leigh? You back here?" Dr. McCoy, her father's associate, poked her head around the corner. With all these well-timed entrances and exits, Leigh was beginning to feel like she had walked into a stage play. "I need to draw blood in room two. Can you come?"

"Sure," she answered mechanically, following the veterinarian. At this point she wished she were in the middle of a stage play. At least then there would be an intermission.

"Just squirt this in her mouth three times a day," she explained, holding out the bottle of pink liquid to the woman with the black-and-white cat. "Get it as far back in her mouth as you can, otherwise she'll just spit it out."

And she'll probably spit it out anyway, she thought to herself. It was the fourth batch of medicine she had doled out for Dr. McCoy, in addition to the ten veins she had held off, the three heartworm and two feline leukemia tests she had run, the dozen or so vaccines she had drawn up, and the hundred or so toenails she had trimmed. She was beginning to remember why she had gone into advertising. It was easier on the feet.

Thankfully, the associate veterinarian was now with the last patient of the morning, and after ascertaining that her help would not be needed with the ear recheck, Leigh retired to the basement bathroom for a few minutes of solitude. It was on her exit that she realized from whom the loud caterwauling she had been listening to all morning had come.

"Number One Son!" she exclaimed, rubbing the Siamese's elongated nose through the bars of his cage. "You're looking awfully chipper for having had major surgery just —" She thought a moment. It had been less than forty-eight hours since her father had performed that surgery. Only the day before yesterday. It seemed more like a week.

The key. The memory washed over her

with the same stupifying clarity with which one realizes, in the classic nightmare, that they have arrived at school wearing only their underwear. How could she have forgotten about the key? Dean and Rochelle Murchison had been so desperate to retrieve it that they had hired Ricky Rhodis to steal the cat from the clinic. But right after Randall had recovered it, the package with the doll had arrived and everything had turned to chaos. Leigh's plan had been to show the key to everyone in the clinic, to watch and see if anyone's eyes lit up. . . .

She had gotten sidetracked. But the game wasn't over. She left Number One Son's cage and walked quickly to the basement supply closet. It was highly irregular of her, and she would probably still get in trouble with her father over it, but she hadn't left the key in the surgery as she should have. Instead, she had pocketed and stashed it. She knew that her father would simply give it back to Nikki, and since Nikki claimed to have no idea what lock the key fit, Leigh knew that route would be a dead end. No — she had had other plans. She had been certain, once upon a time, that the key held the secret they were all being threatened over.

Did it still? She moved a small stool to the rear of the closet, stepped on it, and reached for the ancient plastic flowerpot that was crammed into the back corner of the top shelf. She pulled the pot down into her arms and smiled. There was the key all right — just as smelly and disgusting as ever. She carried it, pot and all, to the sink in the kennel room and began to rinse. After a little dishwashing liquid, the stench of the attached cloth was almost tolerable.

If Dean and Rochelle were so anxious to get this back — she thought to herself as she cleaned — why did they give up so easily? There hadn't been any more break-ins at the clinic. Nor did Dean or Rochelle simply present themselves at the door saying that they had dropped their key in Lilah's living room. As long as Ricky Rhodis kept his mouth shut, there would have been no reason they couldn't — as far as they knew, no one had yet connected them to Ricky, or Ricky to the cat. And Ricky's silence was assured with the promise of inheritance money. At least until . . .

Until the will was read.

The wheels in Leigh's overcrowded brain began to turn again. When Dean and Rochelle contracted Ricky Rhodis's services, the plane had not yet crashed. Since the plane crash was due to pilot error and the pilot had gone down with the plane, she was hard-pressed to assume it was anything but a horrible accident. Therefore, it stood to reason that Dean and Rochelle, whether they thought Lilah had a long life ahead of her or not, at least expected her to return from New York and pick up Number One Son.

And they did *not* want her to know about the key.

Leigh tried drying the object with some of the cheap, brown paper towels her father insisted on buying, which were only slightly more absorbent than the stainless steel exam tables. She finally gave up and used a cloth towel.

Once Lilah was believed dead, her theory continued, the key had not mattered so much anymore.

She leaned against the sink and twirled the tiny key in her palms. The timeline here was important. Nikki said that Dean had had a falling out with his mother shortly before she left town. He and Rochelle then came over to the mansion when Nikki was there alone — presumably either to get the key or to bring the key and use it to open something in the house. But they got careless, and Number One Son had been right at their heels.

They needed the key back, or they needed

to keep Lilah from realizing it had been out where the cat could get it. Had Dean known yet that he was out of the will? Had Lilah been taunting him about it? Or did he only know that he was on shaky ground with her and feared that if she knew about the key, it might be the last straw?

Leigh clutched the metal tightly. Her money was on the last one. Once Lilah was presumed dead, keeping the key from her was no longer an issue. Maybe what they were trying to do with the key was no longer an issue either. Because after Saturday night, they had known exactly where they stood.

Because they had found out by then what was in the will. A smile spread slowly across her face. She would bet her mother's best feather duster on it. This key had something to do with Lilah Murchison's last testament. It probably fit a locked briefcase or some sort of chest that contained her important papers. Dean and Rochelle had wanted a peek — to find out for sure if they were in or out. But they couldn't let Lilah know they had been snooping, because they still had to mind their p's and q's.

She pictured them again at the will reading, jumping up and down with glee when the lawyer had said "one and only blood heir." They had thought, quite obviously, that that meant Dean. And what was it that Dean had said as he jumped? She remembered he had seemed pleasantly surprised. As if up until that point, he had not been at all sure of being included.

Her legs began to feel a little wobbly. Dean didn't know who the real heir was either, she thought to herself tenuously. That explained his and Rochelle's behavior when they had met at the diner. They had assumed the heir was real, but they didn't have a clue. They had probably been hoping to get some information from her.

Her legs began to feel a lot wobbly. If everything she was thinking was true, then Maura was definitely on the wrong track. Dean and Rochelle really didn't have anything to do with the threats. The threats had started Saturday — before the will reading, before they even knew another heir existed.

Maybe the gruesome twosome *was* responsible for Lilah's murder — maybe it was a crime of passion brought on by the humiliation her will had put Dean through.

But any way she looked at it, she couldn't see the two of them as the force behind the threats to the staff. Which meant that someone else was.

Which meant that she was back to square one, because someone else was still out there.

17

Leigh returned to her father's office, opened his desk drawer, and rummaged until she found the key to his file cabinet. He would not be pleased if he caught her, but she would take that risk. Having the run of the place as a child offered her certain advantages. Adults routinely allow children to witness things they wouldn't let other adults witness, assuming they aren't paying attention. But inquisitive children notice things, and Leigh was one inquisitive child.

She found the key just where she knew she would, in an old coin purse stuffed behind stacks of outdated business cards. Randall, thankfully, was a creature of longstanding habit.

The rusted metal file cabinet was older than she was, and probably for at least as long as she had been alive, her father had kept his confidential files in the locked bottom drawer. She inserted the key and, after jiggling the lock interminably, managed to coax the drawer open.

GILMORE MARCIA. Leigh pulled out the file and flipped to the relevant records quickly. DOB: 11-20-79. Her brow furrowed. Hysterical-screaming Marcia was only twenty-two. And if hysterical-screaming Marcia was only twenty-two, hysterical-screaming Michelle probably was also.

Did it matter? She was already ninety-five percent certain that the missing heir was indeed Nikki Loomis; the birthdates were just a double-check. What she didn't know was who at the clinic knew all about it, and how. What she also didn't know, and what was currently making her heart beat like a jackhammer, was what second *who* was trying to make the first *who* keep their mouth shut.

If she ruled out Dean and Rochelle, who was left? The only theory that even halfway made sense — and she hated to admit it — was the idiotic thing she had come up with to rattle the couple when they had met at the Chuckwagon. What if the true villain wasn't someone in the will at all, but a would-be "heir imposter"? Someone who knew about the baby switch, knew who the real heir was, and knew — even before the will reading — that an unnamed heir would inherit?

It made a sick kind of sense, because as soon as news got out that Lilah Murchison's plane had crashed, the scare tactics had begun. But was this person trying to threaten Nikki through Jared, or was he or she trying to threaten someone else who knew who she was?

The room had started to revolve a bit, and Leigh sat back and forced herself to take a deep breath. HOLMES, MICHELLE. DOB: 6-10-79. Naturally, the girls had been classmates. Both of their parents' addresses were in Avalon. She flipped through the rest of the folder, but there was little else to help her. Michelle was allergic to shellfish and raspberries; Marcia had had her appendix out last year. Nothing.

GARRETT, JEANINE. Leigh chuckled. Her father had never been a zealous keeper of alphabetical order. DOB: 3-31-58. The queen bee was forty-four. She would have been nineteen when the babies were born. But, Leigh noted with a sigh, she appeared to have only moved to Pittsburgh in 1988. Furthermore, being perfect, she had no allergies.

Leigh replaced the file and moved on. LOOMIS, JARED. DOB: 4-24-1976. So — Jared was about to turn twenty-six. He and Nikki had been born close together. Not so close, however, that Wanda couldn't pass both off as her own. Maybe she was a heavy woman who never lost much weight after

Jared was born. Maybe she could simply show up with another baby eleven months later, tell people it was hers, and not have a head nod.

"Leigh Eleanor Koslow!"

Leaping up from a squatting position is tough for anyone over thirty, and being no athlete, Leigh proceeded to topple over sideways, smash her thigh on the corner of the file cabinet, and scatter Jared's confidential papers in a wide arc over the concrete floor.

"What in heaven's name are you doing in your father's files?" Frances's screeches were far worse on Leigh's head than the file cabinet had been on her thigh, and both the room and her mother's disapproving, blue-hair-framed face were weaving about precariously.

"Calm down, Mom," Leigh croaked, trying to catch her breath. "You about gave me a coronary."

"I may give you more than that if you don't explain yourself," Frances retorted waspishly, straightening her shoulders. "Now, *what were* you doing?"

"Looking something up for Dad, of course," she answered easily. She had long since learned the skill of telling her mother technical truths that were also practical falsehoods. Unfortunately, Frances had long since learned the skill of knowing when her daughter was doing it. Her eyes narrowed.

Leigh replaced the scattered papers and shut the file drawer. "I didn't find it anyway," she finished, rubbing the dust off her hands and rising. "Am I needed upstairs again?"

Her mother's features softened a bit. "No, the rush seems to be over for now. I'm going to start on the cages. They didn't get thoroughly cleaned this morning and Jared still isn't back yet. Did you bring a lunch?"

Leigh shook her head. She had been counting on talking Alice into walking half a block to their favorite North Side grill for cheese sandwiches with pickles. Now it was looking like a Wendy's double with everything. And maybe some chili.

"Well, I brought a salad," Frances offered. "You can have half."

Leigh replaced her father's key in its hiding place, then felt a sudden wave of warmth. The clinic basement seemed awfully muggy for April. "How's Dad?" she asked, hoping to distract both from the salad and her health in general.

"Your father is disappointed in his staff," Frances offered critically. "Which reminds me . . . before Jeanine left in a fit of hysteria, she told me to make sure that if you came, you didn't get anywhere *near* the x-ray machine." She crossed her arms and fixed her daughter with a classic, chin-down stare. "You mind telling me what that's all about?"

Oh, no. Not Frances. Not now. If she ever saw that wretched little snitch Jeanine again, so help her —

"Leigh," Frances repeated irritably. "What exactly did you *do* to the x-ray machine?"

She let out her breath with a whoosh of relief. "Nothing, Mom," she answered honestly. "You know Jeanine — she just likes to do all the radiographs herself. It's a status thing."

Frances looked skeptical again. "Indeed. Well, why don't you help yourself to that salad? Nancy has rescheduled most of the afternoon's appointments, so you should get back to work at Hook. Thanks for pitching in. I know your father appreciates it."

"No problem." Leigh studied her mother's face curiously. She was clearly annoyed about the employee walkout, but she didn't seem half as agitated as she undoubtedly would be if she knew that Leigh and Warren had been the ones to discover Lilah

Murchison's body. Ergo, she didn't know.

Major kudos to Randall; he must have kept his wife cloistered in the surgery all morning. Leigh rose again and patted the key that lay in her hip pocket. "I do have a lot to do today. And thanks for the salad, but I think I'll grab something on the way."

Muttering something about fried foods and cellulite, Frances turned and began a visual inspection of the kennel room. Leigh trotted up the stairs with haste. Jared was a darned good kennel cleaner, but there was only one Frances Koslow, and Leigh knew that staying in that basement one more minute carried significant risk of recruitment. There were at least five types of household dirt that only Frances Koslow could see — God only knew what she could find in the basement of an animal clinic.

The upstairs was eerily silent, and Leigh wandered into the recovery room to find her father and Dr. McCoy talking in low tones beside one of the cages.

"It's amazing she's lived this long," the associate veterinarian was saying. Leigh realized suddenly that she hadn't even considered Dr. McCoy, who was nearing fifty, on her suspect list. But then she might as well not have. Not only was the levelheaded veterinarian every bit as uninterested in life outside of work as Dr. Koslow, but she commuted in every day from the East Hills and didn't know squat about the North Boros.

Leigh pressed forward and peeked in at the slight form lying peacefully on a heating blanket in one of the smaller cages, one back leg connected to an IV bag. It was Mrs. Wiggs.

The ancient cat had seemed a little lethargic last night when she had been separated from her mistress's body; Nikki must have brought her in first thing this morning. "What's wrong with her?" Leigh asked quietly.

"She's in end-stage kidney failure, I'm afraid," her father answered. "But it comes as no surprise, given her age. Mrs. Murchison had known for weeks that it was only a matter of time."

Leigh confessed surprise. "But what about all that sneaking around she did after the plane crash? I can't believe she would drag the cat along for all that, if she knew how sick it was."

Randall looked at her thoughtfully. "If you ask me, Mrs. Wiggs probably saved Mrs. Murchison's life. At least temporarily," he added ruefully. "The cat's got hematomas on all four legs — it's obvious she's been on IV fluids somewhere else. I bet Mrs. Murchison got off that plane at the last minute because the cat took a turn for the worse, and she wanted to get her to the nearest animal clinic."

And when the cat was released, she brought it home to die, Leigh thought. Sometime in between Lilah must have heard about the crash and decided to capitalize on it. Sick pet or no, she would have to be aware of the plane going down — her hostess was missing and presumed dead, for heaven's sake. Perhaps she had found the opportunity to see how Dean really felt about her too tempting to pass up. Or perhaps, upon realizing that the secrets of her will might already have come out, she was none too anxious to face the music.

Leigh left the vets and walked toward the reception area. She needed another crack at those personnel files, but even if she succeeded in sneaking past Frances to get there, she would never get back out without having to scrape, scrub, or dust something first.

Nancy. Leigh had been wanting to question her again ever since finding out that her mother had worked for Lilah Murchison, but she hadn't gotten the chance. Could her mother — or by extension Nancy herself —

know something about the baby switch? She poked her head around the doorway to the reception area and was pleased to find the business manager sitting alone, chomping carrot sticks while typing at her keyboard.

If Nancy did know something, it was ironic that she was the only employee besides Dr. McCoy who had *not* bailed out that morning. Pulling up a stool with a smile, Leigh thanked her for just that.

"Your father is a wonderful man to work for," Nancy responded modestly. "Of course I wouldn't walk out on him."

There was a moment of silence, and Leigh considered her strategy. She didn't want to frighten away the last of her father's staff, but if it was common knowledge that the late Mrs. Johnson had worked for Mrs. Murchison, it could be Nancy herself who the threats were targeting. Had her mother been working for Lilah in 1977?

"I wondered if I could ask you a question," she began gently. "Exactly how old were you when your mother started working for Mrs. Murchison?"

The business manager's eyebrows arched as she cracked another carrot stick. "I was five or so, I guess," she answered. "Why?"

Leigh tried to hide her disappointment as the math played out in her head. No way was Nancy more than thirty years old. That meant that her mother wouldn't have come on the scene until the early eighties — several years after Dean was born. But the housekeeper could still have known something. She or even Nancy herself could have discovered something later. . . .

Leigh's hand felt for the key in her pocket, and a hopeful thought formed in her brain. *Children can be very observant.* "I thought maybe you could help me with a puzzle," she explained. "Did you spend any time at the mansion when you were little?"

"Actually, we started off living in the basement," Nancy answered. "I suppose at that point it was prestigious to have one's staff live in. But —" She halted for a moment. When she continued, her tone was stiff. "I guess I already told you about our problems with Mrs. Linney. The woman did not take kindly to sharing the same roof with black people. So my mother and I moved into the garage apartment of one of Mrs. Murchison's friends, and my mother worked there part-time as well."

Leigh remained silent, in hopes that Nancy would keep talking. The business manager wasn't ordinarily the chatty type, but she seemed to enjoy reminiscing about her mother — at least when she wasn't remembering Peggy Linney. "I used to go to the mansion every day after school," Nancy continued, her tone sentimental again. "Mrs. Murchison was quite tolerant about letting me run around the place. I wasn't the best-mannered thing, despite my mother's efforts."

Leigh had to smile. It was difficult to imagine smart, even-tempered Nancy as a hellion grade-schooler, but one never knew. An amusing thought crossed her mind. "Did you and Dean ever play together?"

The business manager's face flooded instantly with embarrassment. "I suppose we did."

Leigh laughed. It wasn't something she would relish admitting either. "So, you snooped around the house together, did you?" she asked with a grin.

Nancy hid a smile. "I plead the fifth."

Leigh pulled the key from her pocket and held it out on a palm. The other woman looked at her strangely and shrugged. "What's that?"

"I was hoping you might know," Leigh said. "Nikki Loomis doesn't recognize it. She denies knowing all the mansion's contents, and I believe her. But no self-respecting *child* could possibly resist peeking into drawers and cubbyholes, and this looks pretty old. It's a key, and it used to be on some sort of woven chain —"

"An oriental pattern," Nancy said wistfully, her eyes widening. "Oh, my God. I do recognize it."

18

"Is this what Number One Son swallowed?" Nancy asked incredulously, taking the key in her hand for a closer look.

Leigh nodded. She had always suspected that the overachieving business manager was not fully plugged into the clinic grapevine. For one thing, Nancy kept her nose down and her mind on her job; for another, most of the staff openly resented her status with the proprietor.

"I knew that Dr. Koslow did surgery on the cat," she continued, "but I never heard what he found."

Leigh quickly explained the link to the break-in, and Nancy's eyes sparked with understanding. "All your father told me was that he dropped the charges against Ricky Rhodis because Dean had tricked the boy into thinking he was saving the cat somehow."

She leaned back in her chair and clutched the key tightly in a hand. "But he really wanted *this*. Didn't he?"

Leigh nodded again. "What is it?"

Nancy's brown eyes held a glint of mischief, giving a glimpse of the child she had been not all that long ago. "It's the key to what Dean always called his mother's 'treasure box.' It didn't have any treasure really, it was just a curiosity. A pretty metal box, about so big." She gestured to form an object a little bigger than a shoe box. "It was hand painted with scenes of green hills and rivers and people fishing — Dean used to say it was Chinese."

She smiled ruefully at the ancient memory. "Which, if you know Dean, will not surprise you, because he always knew *everything*. I was like a little-sister substitute — more accurately, a warm body to impress his great wisdom upon." She laughed a little. "As my mother used to say, 'have mercy.' "

Leigh grinned. "What did Mrs. Murchison keep in the box?"

Nancy's eyes narrowed in concentration. "Not much, as I recall. There were papers in the bottom, but that was boring to us, of course. She had black-and-white photographs of some cats — pets from her childhood, I think. No jewelry or anything like that. I'm sure the only reason Dean found it so fascinating was that Mrs. Murchison always kept it locked with a key." She opened her hand and gazed at her palm. "This key. And the really intriguing thing was — she hid both the key and the box in different places."

Leigh's eyebrows rose with interest. "Where?"

"The key was in one of her jewelry boxes. Dean had watched her enough to know what it was, and he used to sneak it out now and then and open the box just for fun. He would take me along and we would pretend we were on some grand, top-secret expedition. We always hoped that maybe next time, there *would* be real treasure."

"And the box," Leigh coaxed, trying not to sound too eager, "where did she keep that?"

"Oh, I'm not sure where it would be now," the other woman answered, as if a disclaimer were required. "But when I was little she kept it in the bottom shelf of the linen closet, off the second-floor hallway. It was under some sheets or blankets that weren't used very much."

She held out the key and Leigh pocketed it again, thinking hard. So far, every word Nancy was saying only confirmed her previous theory. If Dean and Rochelle had expected that Mrs. Murchison would not return from New York, they would have had no need to fuss with retrieving the key. They could simply acquire the box's contents by

274

lifting it from the mansion and smashing it with a sledgehammer. Clearly, it was Mrs. Murchison's wrath they had feared when hiring Ricky Rhodis. They wanted to check out the contents of the box without Mrs. Murchison ever finding out.

And Leigh was pretty sure she knew why.

"Nancy," she said quickly, fearing that the clinic's afternoon clientele would show up at any moment, "I don't know how much of this you're aware of, but . . ." She offered a brief summary of the events before the plane crash, including the facts that Mrs. Murchison had recently changed her will and that she and Dean — according to Nikki — had had some sort of row immediately before the New York trip.

"So tell me," Leigh asked, "what would you guess that Dean was looking for?"

Nancy shrugged, but it was a purposeful gesture. "I can't tell you exactly what kind of papers used to be in the box, if that's what you're asking. Much less what she might keep in it now. But from what you've told me, I would guess the same thing you already think. That Dean wanted a peek at her new will."

Leigh smiled broadly and rose. "Thanks, Nancy."

"No! Wait," the other woman said earnestly, rising also. The anxiety that had faded from her voice as she talked about her childhood was now back in full force. "I'm not sure why you think this is related to the threats. I mean — you don't suspect Dean of those, do you?"

She looked genuinely concerned, and Leigh paused. "You don't?"

Nancy shook her head. "No." She glanced around the clinic furtively for a moment, then stepped closer. "Not that I want to be known around here as a protector for Dean Murchison — but, Leigh, I did know him very well once. And I know that he's not a cruel person." She paused a moment as if considering whether to say more. Finally, she exhaled sadly. "He used to cry every time one of the cats killed a sparrow. He gave them all funerals in the backyard."

She paused once again, fidgeting with a pen over her ear. "I'm not saying the man's a saint," she continued finally, her voice low, "but if the police are thinking for one moment that he would kill his own mother — they're just plain wrong."

Leigh's eyes met Nancy's levelly. She was pleased that her own gut instincts about Dean seemed to be on target. But there was more to the story. "What about Rochelle?"

she asked quietly.

The business manager shook her head. "I don't know anything about her. But I refuse to believe Dean would ever involve himself in anything — well, *violent*."

Leigh regarded her closely. "Did you tell the police that?"

Nancy immediately turned away and returned to her desk chair. "I know this may not make sense to you," she said, her voice resolute, "but unless absolutely necessary, I would rather the police didn't know anything about my history with Dean."

"But why not?" Leigh protested, following her. "It could help them rule him out as a suspect, so they could concentrate on finding the real killer — or extortionist — or both."

Nancy's gaze fixed on the blank computer monitor in front of her. "I'm hoping Dean will be cleared on his own," she answered. "But if I say anything to the police —" She broke off. "Well, it might not be smart, that's all."

Leigh thought she was beginning to understand. She pulled over the second desk stool and sat, putting herself and the other woman back at eye level. "You think the threats are directed at you, don't you? You think someone suspects you know something because of your history, and that if you cooperate with the police at all, they'll think you squealed. You're afraid that someone here at the clinic may get hurt because of you."

Nancy's dark eyes bored into Leigh's. "But I *don't* know anything," she said vehemently, her voice rising. "I don't know who Mrs. Murchison's other child is — if there even is one, I don't know who's making the threats, and I don't know who could have killed her." Looking suddenly embarrassed, she turned away again. "I'm sorry, but I *don't*," she finished softly.

The clinic door opened wide, and three small children filed in noisily, followed by their harried-looking mother and a boisterous chocolate Labrador retriever. Nancy jumped at the interruption, then shuffled some items on the desktop to regroup. "Hello, Mrs. Castellani. Just have a seat. Dr. Koslow will be right with you."

Leigh rose again and slipped quietly out of the reception area before she could be re-recruited. She had officially exceeded her quota of toenail clippings for the day.

And the key in her pocket might as well have been a hot coal.

"Going somewhere? Besides Hook, I

mean." Warren leaned against the side of her Cavalier, his fingers drumming steadily on the hood.

"Well, hello," she answered, trying hard not to appear disconcerted. He looked darned appealing standing there with his tie loosened and his sunglasses on. Very unpolitical. But she couldn't afford to be distracted.

Or waylaid. "What are you doing here? I thought you were busy at lunch."

"I changed my plans," he said, straightening. "Mo called me this morning and filled me in on the latest. She said you might still be here. How about a grilled-cheese sandwich?"

Leigh's eyebrows rose. It was that mind-reading thing again. But this time it went both ways. "Maura told you not to let me out of your sight, didn't she?"

He opened the door of the Cavalier with his spare key, slid behind the wheel, and opened the passenger door for her. "Actually, her exact words were a bit stronger. Something about leg irons."

Leigh got into the car. She *was* starving. But there was no time for grilled cheese. Mrs. Murchison's "treasure box" might contain a copy of the will — but it also might contain something else of interest. Something Dean and Rochelle would not even have been looking for.

"How about Wendy's?" she suggested innocently. "I'm kind of in a rush. Work's piling up."

"Fine," he said agreeably, steering the Cavalier out into the street. "Then afterward I'll drop you off at Hook. I can come back for you around five-thirty."

She crossed her arms over her chest and glared at him impishly. "You *know* that won't work."

He grinned, but kept his eyes on the road. "And *you* know you're not going back to the Murchison house alone."

Leigh stamped her foot impatiently on the mansion's front walk. "Nikki will talk to us," she assured herself more than her husband. "I'm sure she will."

It was several moments before the security guard returned from inside the maze of shrubs. "Yeah, OK," he announced blandly, gesturing them past. "Ring the bell."

"I guess it was a good idea to hire a guard," Leigh admitted as they proceeded. "There have probably been some reporters here, not to mention general busybodies."

Warren, who was not at all pleased to be back at the scene of the crime, didn't answer. He just followed her up the walk with his standard "you owe me for this" look, which Leigh took quite in stride. He was the one person to whom she didn't particularly mind being in debt.

"I'm just going to see if she'll show me what's in the box," she stated again. "Maura would want to know if Dean had access to a copy of his mother's will before the plane crash, right? And we need to know if he and Rochelle had time on Friday to sneak a peek before Number One Son ate the key. If not, I think the evidence really points against them — at least for the threats. Just let me do the talking, OK?"

He looked at her sternly. "My orders from Maura are to keep you from saying *anything* to Nikki Loomis about your theory that she's the real heir."

"I won't!" she protested, and a guilty feeling immediately brewed up in her chest. She didn't make a habit of lying to her husband, and try as she might to justify the claim as a white lie, she knew full well that it was patently untrue. "Unless absolutely necessary," she amended.

He wheeled around toward her and opened his mouth to speak, but as luck would have it, Nikki chose that moment to push open the front door. "Come on in,"

281

she said gruffly, turning back inside.

Leigh followed her quickly, avoiding Warren's gaze. They stopped in the foyer, which was dark, cat filled, and loud. And for the first time at the mansion, she noted the distinct aroma of cat litter wafting through the air. "Is Jared all right?" she asked with concern.

Nikki crossed her arms over her chest. Her eyes had huge bags underneath and she was sporting wrinkles Leigh hadn't noticed before. "He's a wreck," she answered. "Seven o'clock in the morning those blasted detectives were back here wanting to take him to the station. Kept him there for hours saying the same things over and over. *Then* they made us take the freaking bus back home!"

The woman looked ready to kill something, and Leigh took a reflexive step backward. "I'm sorry," she offered genuinely. "I thought they were going to go easy on him. They don't really think —"

If a person's ears could steam, Nikki's would have. "They *wouldn't* think it if it weren't for that son of a —" The stream of vulgarity that issued from the younger woman's mouth included several adjectives Leigh had never heard before. All were applied to Dean Murchison.

"You wouldn't believe what he told them! They picked him and Rochelle up too, early this morning, and grilled them over good. So Dean goes and starts saying all sorts of complete crapola about how his mother was *scared* of Jared, how she was worried about him becoming violent — he even said she was worried about Jared attacking her in her bed!"

"That's ridiculous," Leigh agreed. It was ridiculous. It also smacked loudly of more husband coaching on the part of dear, devious Rochelle, who was undoubtedly smart enough to fear being blamed for the murder herself.

"Well, those idiot detectives didn't seem to think so!" Nikki railed. "They wanted to know about any violent incidents in Jared's past — any fascination with whips or torture —" Her voice wavered, and she took a deep breath and swallowed. When she spoke again her voice was controlled but simmering. "My brother doesn't have a violent bone in his body. Not one. He's big, yes, but he has no idea what kind of power that could give him. His mind doesn't even work that way. He could never intentionally hurt anybody."

"The police will see that," Leigh said calmly. "They'll know exactly what Dean and Rochelle are trying to do."

"The detectives are idiots!" Nikki yelled, her eyes flashing fire. "If it weren't for this broad with the hair, we would never have gotten out of there. She told that Hollandsworth guy to lay off Jared, and damned if he didn't listen to her. If she hadn't, I swear they would have arrested him then and there."

Leigh and Warren exchanged glances.

"Um . . . what kind of hair did 'the broad' have?" Leigh asked tentatively.

Nikki looked at her as if she had gone mad. "Red. And it was all piled up on her head like in the sixties or something."

Kudos to Aunt Bess, Leigh thought with a smile. The woman could always be counted on when the cavalry wasn't available. What she was doing interfering in her paramour's work on the middle of a Wednesday morning was an open question, but, given her gene pool, not a particularly surprising one.

"I'm sure they were just doing the good cop/bad cop routine or something," Leigh assured. "They have nothing to charge Jared with. They were probably testing him out for themselves, to see if they could get a rise out of him —"

"A rise?" Nikki shrieked again.

Leigh noted that of the half-dozen cats that had been prowling around the foyer when they arrived, only one remained. Odds were, it was deaf.

"A rise," Nikki repeated, smacking a fist into a palm. "Do you have any idea what *hell* my older brothers put Jared through? They beat him up every chance they got. Treated him like a damned punching bag! And Jared never fought back — *never*. He would just huddle up and take it. If I hadn't been there to protect him, I hate to think what might have happened!"

Leigh's eyes widened as she looked at the tiny woman, who, compared to Jared, gave new meaning to the phrase *little* sister. "But how did you —"

Nikki offered an evil smile. "Let's just say I wrote the book on fighting dirty. If Bill and Red ever have kids, it'll be a miracle."

Warren, who had to that point been standing close by Leigh's side, shrank back a step.

"Nikki? Are you up there, Nikki?" Jared's voice traveled from the direction of the kitchen, and his sister quickly turned toward it.

"Just a minute!" she called back. Then she turned to her guests. "Grab a seat somewhere."

As soon as the other woman had disappeared down the hall, Leigh poked her husband soundly in the ribs. *"Wuss."*

"Hey!" he protested, rubbing his side. "You didn't marry me because I was macho."

"Why did I marry you, then?"

"Free financial advice for Hook."

"Oh. Right."

Nikki returned almost immediately, and she appeared to have rethought the sitting idea. "I'm taking Jared to the clinic as soon as he finishes here," she announced. "The sooner he gets back to his normal routine, the better."

She eyed them critically then, as if realizing she had not been offered an explanation for their presence. "So, what do you need?" she asked sharply.

Leigh pulled the key out of her pants pocket. "Remember this?"

"Yeah," Nikki responded, unimpressed. "What about it?"

"We think it unlocks a decorative box of Mrs. Murchison's. Something hand painted with scenes from the Orient."

Nikki still looked unimpressed. "Yeah, so? I've never seen anything like that."

"She kept it hidden," Leigh continued. "Dean has known about it since he was a kid. She kept it on the bottom shelf of the linen closet on the second floor."

Nikki's eyes widened. She took the key from Leigh's hand, and a devilish smile spread slowly across her face. "So. Dean wanted something of Ms. Lilah's, did he?"

She turned from her guests without ceremony and started up the stairs at a jog. Careful to avoid catching her husband's eye, Leigh followed. He *might* have made a grab at her arm as she went, but the whoosh of air behind her right elbow, she reasoned, could just as easily have been a draft.

Leigh kept pace with her hostess up the flight and down the corridor, stopping outside a dark paneled door. Nikki flung it open to reveal a closet with two opposing walls of wide, relatively shallow wooden cabinets. She dropped to her knees and flipped the tiny metal latch that held the bottom compartment shut tight.

Leigh had seen such "Pittsburgh closets" before; with all the ash that used to float around during the days of big steel, one's linens had to be protected from "the gray factor." She could still remember the smoky skies from her own childhood, but for the last two decades, the burgh's air had been almost squeaky-clean.

"Which side?" Nikki asked, hauling out

piles of linens into a tangled jumble on the floor. "And by the way, how do you know all this?"

"I guess the other side," Leigh answered, noting that the first compartment contained nothing but yellowed sheets and a few odd place mats. "And Nancy Johnson told me. She used to roam around the place when she was a child and her mother worked here."

Nikki paused for a split-second only. "Nancy? Oh, yeah. I guess I knew that." She had the mirror-image compartment half emptied when a gleeful smile lit her face. Leaning farther into the deep cabinet, she pulled out a shallow, gold-gilded oriental chest, its gleaming black sides beautifully decorated with pastoral scenes.

"That's it," Leigh whispered breathlessly. She threw a quick look over her shoulder to see if Warren had followed her up the stairs. Oddly, it appeared he had not.

"I've got one word for you, Dean old boy," Nikki chortled, taking the chest into her lap. She inserted the key into the tiny golden lock, and it fit perfectly.

"*Gotcha.*"

19

Nikki pulled, and the lid of the chest creaked open on its stiff metal hinges. She gave the contents only the most cursory of glances before diving in and pulling things out.

"Wait!" Leigh begged, kneeling down to collect the stray sheets of paper the other woman was strewing across the closet floor. "Some of this might be important!"

"The only thing that's important," Nikki growled, "is putting nails in Dean Murchison's coffin. Him and that witch of a wife of his. They killed Ms. Lilah — I'd bet my life on it!"

Leigh paused a moment. "But you said you didn't think Dean would kill his own mother."

"Well, I changed my mind," she railed. "The two of them killed her and now they want Jared to take the fall while they walk off with all her money. And I say — over *somebody's* dead body!"

The phrase sent a little chill down Leigh's spine. Partly because she was standing not a dozen feet from where Mrs. Murchison had, only last night, had the life choked out of her — and partly because she had no doubt that Nikki meant every word she was saying.

"This is garbage!" the woman raged, emptying out the last of the papers. "The latest will in here is from nineteen eighty-two. The rest of this crap looks like she's had it in here since she was a kid. Cat pictures, stories about cats. Who the hell cares?"

Leigh sifted hastily through the piles of paper. Nikki was right. It looked as if Lilah hadn't put anything in the box in more than a decade. It also looked as if the box had once served as her personal memento trove — full of the kind of things everyone has that they don't want anyone else to see, yet can't quite part with either.

"When did Albert Murchison die?" Leigh asked, poring over one of the wills.

"I don't know," Nikki answered gruffly. "Sometime when Dean was a kid."

"This was the last will she needed to hide from him then," Leigh muttered. Whether Lilah and Albert ever had a joint will, or whether Albert only thought they did, Leigh didn't know. But Lilah had been quite insistent in the 1982 will that her cats be generously provided for in the event she should predecease her husband. And the legal document attached, which to Leigh's untrained

290

eyes appeared to be some sort of prenuptial agreement, made that seem quite possible. The fate of the couple's young son, however, was mentioned more as an afterthought. "Well, how do you like that? Dean had to split it with the cats even way back then."

"It doesn't make sense," Nikki said to herself. She had scooted back to lean against the wall of the closet, her eyes fixed on a point somewhere in space. "He and Rochelle *had* to be looking for her latest will."

"I'm sure they were," Leigh said, eager to take advantage of the other woman's quixotic state. Perhaps it would make her talkative. "Dean probably remembered that she kept wills in the box and figured maybe she would have a copy here. But she didn't, because after Albert died she had no need to hide her copies anymore. She probably just left the box there because she had no particular reason to move it. Presumably, her later wills were all similar anyway — providing for both Dean and the cats. It was only recently that she decided to cut him out altogether." She cleared her throat. "And admit to the world that he wasn't her biological son."

Nikki ceased staring into space and focused on Leigh. "She knew she was going to die," she said self-importantly.

Leigh's pulse quickened. "She did?"

Nikki nodded slowly. "She never admitted it to me, but I knew. I made the doctor appointments; I submitted the insurance papers. I couldn't figure out exactly what was wrong with her — it was all medical mumbo jumbo to me. And she seemed fine, except for a few bad headaches. But she started getting all philosophical on me. Talking about everything in the short term. Met with the new lawyer; didn't breed any more of the cats." She let out a long, heavy breath. "I knew, all right."

Leigh leaned in. "Did Dean know?"

"I think so," Nikki answered shortly, her eyes once again flashing with anger. "I think she told him the night before she left for New York, when they had that huge fight. Jared could hear them yelling all the way out in the garage apartment."

"Did she tell him he wasn't her son?" Leigh asked breathlessly. She didn't think Nikki had any idea how important the timing was. Whoever was responsible for sending the threats to the clinic had known about the missing heir *before* the will was read. Had Dean?

Nikki shook her head again. "I didn't hear

anything like that. All I heard was a bunch of screaming about money. I thought it sounded like she told him he *wasn't* going to be rich and that he needed to get over it and start planning otherwise. She did a lot of bragging about how she had started out with nothing and did just fine." She paused. "He was like — really, *really*, POed."

"Was Rochelle there?" Leigh asked.

"No."

"When Rochelle was in the house on Friday and stole this key — did she have time to get in the box?"

Nikki was thoughtful for a moment. "You mean, could she have actually *found* the real will and then taken it?"

"No," Leigh answered slowly. "I can't believe Mrs. Murchison would let this box sit idle for twenty years and then hide a new will in it. Nor does it make any sense that Rochelle would have stolen twenty years' worth of wills instead of just the top one. But if she did, she would have had to replace everything in this cabinet just perfectly afterward."

Nikki scooted forward and looked at the disheveled piles of linens she had created in her search. "No way," she decided. "She wasn't out of my sight anywhere near long enough to pull that."

Leigh smiled to herself. "Then Number One Son probably swallowed the key before she got a chance."

After a moment's pause, Nikki's face reddened, and she rose with a jerk. "What difference does that make?" she asked angrily. "You'd think Ms. Lilah would have left some clue in this stupid box about who her real kid was, wouldn't you?"

Leigh blinked. "I thought you didn't believe she had another child," she said carefully.

Nikki rolled her eyes. "I didn't. But now I wish she did. I'd love to wave the proof right under Dean's snotty little nose and watch him walk away without a dime. Better yet — get locked up for murder too."

Leigh didn't respond but began neatly compiling the scattered papers and photographs, not one of which featured a human. It was no use trying to convince Nikki that Dean wasn't responsible for the threats, even though she was more sure than ever that his shocked reaction to the news of another heir at the will reading had been genuine. She also seriously doubted that he had killed his mother, but no way was she arguing with Nikki about that.

"Would you mind if I take these papers to Detective Polanski?" she asked, rising with the box in hand. "She's a good friend of mine, and she's on Jared's side, I promise."

"Whatever," Nikki answered. "They're not doing me any good." She looked past Leigh to the mounds of linens behind her. "You forgot something."

Leigh turned around and noted a yellowed paper corner sticking up from behind a fold of sheet. She pulled it out.

"An empty envelope," Nikki announced with a snort. "Now, that's worth keeping."

Leigh held the envelope up to the chandelier in the hall. "It's not empty," she corrected. Without giving herself time to think better of it, she opened the back flap, which pulled up without tearing. It appeared the envelope had never been sealed; rather, the glue had simply stuck a bit with age.

So Lilah could open it and look inside once in a while, she thought to herself. She wondered again, briefly, where on earth Warren was. Why hadn't he followed her upstairs, and why wasn't he stopping her from opening this envelope now? It certainly seemed like the sort of thing he should do.

Oops. Too late. She peered down into the yellowed recesses of the envelope, and her breath caught. It was hair, just as she had suspected when looking at it in the light. But she had feared it was only cat hair.

It wasn't. The soft strands of wavy, dark hair were most definitely human.

"What is it?" Nikki asked, leaning forward. Her eyes widened, as Leigh was sure her own just had. "Get out!" she exclaimed. "You think this could be her real kid's hair?"

Leigh smiled to herself. "Maybe."

Nikki's army cut was too short to judge natural curl, but the color was a perfect match, and it was all Leigh could do to resist holding the swatch up against the other woman's head. One thing she knew for certain. If Nikki Loomis was indeed Lilah's biological child, she had been kept completely in the dark about it. Because if she did know, she would not have wasted a second before pulling the inheritance out from under Dean.

But how on earth had Lilah expected her to find out? There was no letter left with the will; no letter in the memento chest. Could she have left something else that Nikki hadn't found yet?

"I suppose even if it is, it doesn't help much," Nikki said with discouragement, referring to the hair in the envelope. "Baby hair looks different anyway."

Leigh's brow furrowed. Her pregnancy guides didn't cover newborn hair, and her knowledge of babies in general was sketchy. Her cousin Cara's baby had been born with gorgeous strawberry-blond hair and still had gorgeous strawberry-blond hair. But then, her cousin never did anything by the book.

"Oh?" she asked encouragingly.

"Sure," Nikki answered. "And it usually falls out and comes back in another color. You know how blond Jared is? Well, Wanda said when he was born, his hair was jet-black."

Leigh seized the opportunity. "Wanda?"

"My mother," Nikki said offhandedly. "We always called her Wanda."

Leigh took the plunge. "She was related to Mrs. Murchison somehow, wasn't she?"

Surprisingly, Nikki rolled her eyes again. "They were distant cousins or something. Who cares?"

Hearing what were probably Warren's footsteps coming up the stairs, Leigh started talking quickly. "Oh, I just wondered if you knew Mrs. Murchison before — I mean, before you got this job. . . ."

It was a risky maneuver, and Leigh acknowledged that she was only half sorry Warren was on his way. Predictably, Nikki's face took on a tomatolike hue, and her hands clenched tight. "You want to know how I got this job?" she said. "Well, you and everybody else in the nosey little burgh! And *yes*, my mother had something to do with it. *Are you happy now?*"

Leigh attempted an apology, but got cut off.

"For your information, my mother, who did practically nothing else for me and Jared her *whole miserable life*, found out when I was just eighteen that she was dying of ovarian cancer. She was worried about what would happen to us, as she *damned well* should have been. So she went on her knees to her rich, nasty relative and begged her to give me and Jared any kind of job that would set us up anywhere but in that god-awful apartment with Bill and Red. And if you think Ms. Lilah did it just because she felt sorry for her, you didn't know Ms. Lilah!

"She interviewed me like I'd come straight off the street. She wasn't even *half* serious about the whole thing. So I told her *exactly* where she could cram this stupid job of hers, and she smiled that evil smile of hers and told me I was hired. Of course, once she saw how much Jared and I liked her cats — and how good he was at cleaning things — she changed her tune.

"So," she finished, her voice still rising, "while we may have *got* these jobs because of Wanda's deathbed guilt attack, you'd better believe we've kept them by *working our stinking butts off!*"

Leigh swallowed. Such a tirade was, she had learned through her long association with Maura Polanski, best left uncommented on. Warren, who had at least an equal amount of experience with irate females, had stopped a few paces short of Nikki down the hall, and was waiting politely until she stopped screaming.

When Nikki noticed him, she took a breath. "And where have *you* been?" she asked suspiciously.

He offered a disarming smile. "I heard Jared calling for you after you had gone up the stairs."

Nikki's eyes sparked with alarm, and she started to move down the hall. "Is he all right?"

Warren stopped her with an extended arm. "He's fine now. He wanted to clean out the litter boxes on the first floor, but he was a little nervous about coming up from the basement. So I carried them down for him."

Nikki's flushed face developed a bit of a glow. She smiled back. "Thanks."

Leigh threw her husband — who would not touch Mao Tse's litter box with a ten-foot pole — a warm glance. He could be so sweet. It was one of the benefits of marrying a reformed geek.

His eyes moved to the box in Leigh's arms. "So," he said, "what have you two been up to?"

His tone was pleasant enough, but the look he gave Leigh indicated that the ice under her feet was thinning.

"Nothing," Nikki said brusquely. "Can't find squat to put Dean away. But you'd better believe I won't give up."

The doorbell rang, and Nikki let out an anguished groan. "I told that guard to tell everyone to go away!" she ranted as she started down the stairs.

Warren turned quickly to Leigh. "*Did you* —"

"No!" she said defensively, clutching the chest a bit closer. "I didn't say a word. But I did get this box open, and it might have something in it that Maura will find useful."

He appeared only minimally appeased. "Let's get out of here before you do something else I'll regret. My credibility with Mo as your keeper is falling lower and lower —"

"*You damned well better let me in!*"

Leigh and Warren both headed toward the sound of the shriek, whose source Leigh could easily guess. From the top of the stairs they could see Nikki in the foyer, standing her ground with her hands on her hips. Framed in the doorway was a frothing Rochelle, complete with neon-green midriff shirt, hot-red spandex bike shorts, and three-inch-high yellow sandals. The security guard stood to one side of the door, looking from one woman to the other uncertainly.

"You've got a lot of nerve coming here," Nikki responded coolly.

"*I've* got nerve!" Rochelle shrieked again, her heavy shoes clunking on the tiles as she stepped forward. Leigh felt shivers up her arms as two Siamese leaped up the stairs and brushed by her leg; others scattered radially in all directions. She put out a foot, but Warren's arms quickly grabbed hers.

"Stay out of it!" he whispered. "The guard's there."

"*I've* got nerve!" Rochelle continued mercilessly. "Am *I* the one who's trying to bilk poor Dean out of all his money? Am *I* the one who was so upset on finding out his mother wasn't really dead, I killed her anyway? Well? Am I? *Am I?*"

Nikki's eyes narrowed. "Probably."

Rochelle let out a short, piercing scream, but stayed where she was — which might have had something to do with the fact that the security guard had pulled out both his cell phone and his nightstick. "You and that idiot brother of yours are *not* going to get away with it," she continued, her tone deepening. "We don't care if you are Lilah's daughter. We'll fight you every step of the way. And if we lose anyhow, we'll slit both your throats. *Got it?*"

"That's enough!" the security guard interrupted in a thin, nasal voice. He struggled to dial his cell phone. "You'll have to leave now, miss."

Nikki had remained still as a statue, except for the heavy breaths that wracked her thin chest. "*What* did you say?" she asked, her voice deadly calm.

"Oh, come off it," Rochelle snapped, taking a small step backward in deference to the nightstick. "Who else could the woman's real kid be? *You're* the one Lilah paid a fortune to sit around and do nothing all day. *You're* the one she set up to live in this huge old house forever. *You're* the one whose brother gets to hang out over the garage for free. She gave you everything, you wench — and it wasn't because you're so damn good at rubbing her corns!"

For a moment, Nikki didn't speak. The security guard put an arm in front of Rochelle to push her back out the door, but before he had touched her, Nikki waved him away. She took a step closer to Rochelle, biceps bulging. "I don't know where you came up with that crock of bull, you moron, but you're dead wrong. I'm not Lilah Murchison's missing brat. But somebody else out there is, and now that you've killed Ms. Lilah, that person's way to the money is free and clear. *Real smart.*"

The security guard was looking distinctly uncomfortable. Perhaps union unrest was more his forte — but two pint-size females on the verge of a catfight appeared not to be his idea of a good time. He stepped in between the two women and began backing up toward the door, pushing a resisting Rochelle one step at a time.

"I didn't kill her, and you know it!" Rochelle hissed over the guard's shoulder. "You can't protect that *retard* forever!"

Leigh winced.

Nikki sprung.

The next few moments involved flying fur — literally — as Nikki vaulted over the guard's shoulder and landed soundly on a screeching Rochelle. All three fell to the tile floor in a heap, scattering dust balls of cat hair in every direction.

"Nobody . . . calls . . . my brother . . . that!" Nikki bellowed between breaths. She struggled to a sitting position on top of Rochelle's prone middle, pinning her arms with one hand and jerking her head by the hair with the other.

Rochelle's hard heels banged on the floor as she flailed. "Get off me!"

"Say you're sorry!"

The security guard sat on the floor a few paces away, rubbing his head. He had taken a worse tumble than the other two, and apparently did not feel obliged to intercede again — perhaps because the person signing his checks was on top.

Warren groaned. "Oh, for the love of —" He moved swiftly around Leigh and headed down the stairs, but his intervention, thankfully, did not prove necessary. Just as Rochelle spat out a panicked apology, Nikki's small body lifted straight up into the air.

"No, no, Nikki," Jared admonished firmly. He had both hands around her waist, keeping her squirming feet a good eighteen inches off the ground. "No fighting, Nikki. You promised me no fighting, Nikki."

His sister growled but gradually stopped squirming. "All right. All right!" she conceded at last. "I'm finished. Put me down, Jared."

He did.

"Now you!" ordered the security guard,

pointing a skinny finger at a still-angry, but considerably chastened, Rochelle. "Get out. Now! If you don't, I'll have you arrested for trespassing. Do you understand?"

Rochelle opened her lips — which were a shiny lavender today — but closed them again without saying anything. She rose to her feet, threw Nikki a malignant glance, pivoted awkwardly on her square heels, and walked out the door.

"Are you all right, ma'am?" the security guard asked Nikki tentatively, keeping his distance. He was still rubbing his head.

"I'm peachy," she snapped, feeling the long pink streaks across her cheek, compliments of Rochelle's polka-dotted tips. Her voice softened a bit. "Sorry about tackling you like that," she said to the guard. "Nothing personal."

He threw her a skeptical look, then followed Rochelle silently out the door.

"We were just going, too," Warren announced, taking a firm grip of Leigh's hand as she joined him at the bottom of the stairs. Jared had already started back to the basement, and only the three of them remained in the foyer.

Nikki shook her head in disgust, her arms folded tightly across her chest. "Do you *believe* that? Me, Lilah Murchison's kid. Of all the stupid —"

"But how can you really be sure?" Leigh interrupted quickly, careful to keep her tone in check. She was bigger than Rochelle, but she didn't have any fingernails, either. "I mean, there's a *chance*, isn't there?"

"No," Nikki answered. "I *do* have a birth certificate. It says that I am proudly and officially the child of Wanda Loomis and a man both she and the state refer to as 'unknown.' There, are you happy? Sheesh!"

Birth certificates can be faked, Leigh thought, resisting the urge to make the statement out loud. "Listen, Nikki," she said instead, ignoring the paralyzing squeeze Warren was delivering to her hand. "Yesterday I found proof that Lilah Murchison gave birth to another child when everyone *thought* she was pregnant with Dean. She adopted him, and gave her own baby away."

Nikki stared at her blankly. "Say what?"

"I think she gave her own baby away because it was a girl, and her husband desperately wanted a boy. This house, her social standing — everything she had except her cash was tied up in her marriage, and she had to preserve it at all costs. I think the baby she had was you, and that she gave you

306

to one of her only available relatives, Wanda Loomis, to raise."

The other woman's blank look gave way to a slowly spreading, sarcastic smile. "Oh, please," she said with a laugh. "Is that why you keep coming over here and bugging me?"

Leigh didn't answer.

"Well, forget it. For one thing, Wanda Loomis barely raised the brats she had. She wouldn't take in so much as a gnat unless it came with a checking account, and I can assure you there was no money to spare in the Loomis house at any time during my so-called childhood. Secondly, if I was Ms. Lilah's daughter, don't you think she would have told me? You'd better believe if I *did* know, I'd be in Tahiti right now sunning my butt on the sand."

She took a breath. "And even *besides* all that — I'm only twenty-three! Dean is twenty-five." She threw Leigh a withering look. "Got any other bright ideas?"

"No," Warren said loudly, moving Leigh bodily toward the door. "We've got to get back to work now. Thanks for your hospitality, Ms. Loomis."

He opened the door himself, but found he couldn't go through it. Few people could, with Maura Polanski's two-hundred-plus pounds filling the space.

"I should have known," the detective said heavily, glaring at Leigh. "Murder at the Murchison house — you're here. A catfight at the Murchison house — you're here. Why do I carry a pager, anyway? It would save time if I just followed you around."

"Jared's not talking to you," Nikki said to Maura icily. "We were just leaving."

"I don't want to talk to Jared," Maura answered calmly, stepping inside. She introduced herself. "I want to talk to you. And I'm not here to talk about Mrs. Murchison's murder — just some issues about her estate."

Nikki groaned. "You think I'm her kid, too? Get in line."

"We'll catch up with you later, Maura," Leigh piped up, hastening her way out. "I'll call you in an hour or two. OK?"

Warren followed, but received another elbow in the ribs on the way. "You're fired," Maura growled.

"Hey!" he defended. "You know what I'm up against."

"Yeah," the detective tossed back with a smirk, "but I'm not the one who married her."

Pretending to ignore the exchange, Leigh headed for the car. They could make fun of her all they wanted. She still had the oriental chest under one arm, and neither one of them had noticed.

20

"What *is* it with you?" Leigh's office mate, Alice, complained. "You've had your monitor on that same page for almost an hour, and you haven't typed a word. Furthermore, your disgusted sighs every ten seconds are driving me loco. Why don't you just go home? I hear Saturdays in the office are great for concentrating."

"I don't have a car," Leigh lamented. "My smart-aleck, do-gooder of a husband stranded me here until five-thirty." Her eyes narrowed. "And confiscated my box besides."

Alice threw her a pathetic look. "I don't have a clue what you're talking about. But I *will* float you cab fare if it'll get you the hell out of here."

"Thanks," Leigh said. "But I do need to work. Maybe some more caffeine . . ." She started to get up, but her head swam a little, and she sat back down. Perhaps she had had enough caffeine after all.

She knew, logically, that Warren was right. There was no reason for her to continue to obsess over the threats to the clinic and their almost certain link to Lilah

Murchison's murder. Maura was on it, and the detective was perfectly capable of ferreting the matter out eventually, even if she was busy with other cases. Leigh should never have taken the box out of the Murchison house, and it needed to go either back there or to Maura ASAP.

But she still couldn't stop thinking about it. She had been so sure that Nikki was the one. Furthermore, she had also almost convinced herself that Rochelle was behind the threats — that she had found a copy of the will before the reading and that she too had guessed who Nikki was. But the untouched box, and the women's little tiff, had shot that theory all to heck.

Rochelle might be on the shrewd side, but she obviously lacked the subtlety necessary for an elaborate, anonymous extortion campaign. Subtle people didn't generally confront their nemeses at the scene of a murder and threaten (in front of at least one known witness) to slit her throat.

No. Dean and Rochelle were responsible for Ricky Rhodis's brush with the law, but that was about it. They probably genuinely believed that Nikki and/or Jared had killed Mrs. Murchison.

Someone else was the real heir. And someone else knew the whole story —

without needing to attend the will reading. If Mary Polanski knew about the baby switch, who else might? And why would they have been let in on the secret in the first place?

Alice made an exasperated noise, and Leigh felt a sticky-note pad bounce off the back of her head. "I mean it, you," Alice warned. "One more sigh, and I'll —"

"Mail call," their young receptionist twittered pleasantly, dropping a small stack of mail on Alice's desk, and an even smaller one on Leigh's. "I like that postcard," she said approvingly, pointing to the top of Leigh's stack with a fake nail. "It's so true."

She turned to leave, and Leigh picked up the card. It was addressed to her in plain printed letters, but the part where a message should be was blank. She turned it over curiously, and her blood ran cold.

Springtime in Pittsburgh.

She sat perfectly still for a moment, just looking at it. It could be a coincidence, perhaps. You could get such cards anywhere. But the lettering was familiar. And the two cards had arrived the same day.

It was odd that there was no message. But maybe the sender figured he or she didn't need one.

She swallowed.

"You *are* here! Praise the Lord!"

Leigh looked up into the flushed face of Adith Rhodis, and her brain tried to shift gears. The older woman was dressed in a navy blue polyester skirt, which ended a good three inches above the rim of her knee-high stockings, and a matching polyester top and cardigan, which had probably not been buttoned since the Carter administration.

"I've been trying to catch up with you all day, honey! To think that Lilah Murchison really *was* alive all along, but now she's dead anyway, and you were actually there when it happened — not that you called me, of course, but that's OK — and now every-body's wondering what's going on and you didn't answer your phone here, then they said you were at the clinic, but then they said you'd come back here, except you hadn't, and —" She took a much-needed breath. "I've got something important to tell you!"

Leigh dropped the card like a hot potato. She couldn't think about it now. Why should she? Evidently, someone thought she was being a snoop. But whoever it was could rest easy, because they were going to get exactly what they wanted. From now on, she was keeping to her resolution of the morning. She was leaving everything to the police.

At least to all outward appearances.

She looked eagerly into Adith's gleaming eyes. "What?"

"Excuse me, ma'am," Alice said to the older woman, standing up, "but did you, by any chance, come here in a car?"

Adith looked at her oddly. "Well, sure, honey."

"Excellent," Alice exclaimed, plopping back down in her seat. "Leigh — *go get in it.*"

The ancient sedan rattled like a peddler's cart as Adith weaved fearlessly in and out of the North Side traffic. "I'm afraid I made a mistake the other day," she said regretfully. "I told the girls what I told you and they all told me I was crazy. Course, I never claimed to have known Albert all that well. I just figured he was like a lot of old fuddy-duddies his age. Sexist and all. And I still think I could have been onto something, but that Lois, she's just always so blasted smug about everything, like the time when she told everybody her cousin had had a thing going with Elvis —"

"Mrs. Rhodis," Leigh cut in as politely as possible, "what exactly are we talking about?"

"Oh, sorry," she apologized, narrowly avoiding the rear fender of a white Cadillac, whose blue-haired driver appeared equally competent. "I mean why Ms. Lilah would have switched those babies. The girls — they seem pretty sure that Albert would have doted on a baby daughter just as much as he would have on a son. I guess he had a sister he was pretty close to once, and they just couldn't see him dumping his wife on account of her not having a boy."

Leigh sat back a little, though she kept a tight hold of the handgrip on her door. "Really?"

"So they say," Adith continued. "And I'll tell you what we all agreed. There's only one good reason why Ms. Lilah would give up her own flesh and blood for somebody's else's baby."

Leigh waited. Adith never gave anything away without a suitably dramatic pause.

"There must have been something wrong with it."

She stared at the older woman for a moment, digesting the thought. *Something wrong with it.*

"You got to remember that Lilah was at least forty when she had the baby," Adith went on. "So it wouldn't be too surprising, right?"

Leigh's mind traveled back to the conversation she had had with Dean's biological mother, Becky. She had said that her grandmother had actually encouraged her to keep her baby — right up until the week before it was born. Which would not coincidentally be the week that Lilah's baby was born. The week when a desperate Lilah enlisted Peggy's aid in a hastily hatched scheme.

"So we were thinking maybe the baby was deformed or something," Adith said.

Leigh's stomach had already settled deep into her shoes. *Of course.* She had been so focused on finding a female heir, she had overlooked the obvious. It was Jared, not Nikki, who was the same age as Dean. It was Jared, not Nikki, who had inspired a job offer from Lilah. It was Jared, unlike Nikki, who was blond and blue-eyed, even though the hair he had been born with was black. And it was Jared who formed the link to the Koslow Animal Clinic. *He* was Lilah Murchison's true heir — and it was this fact that someone wanted so desperately to conceal.

"If the baby was in real bad shape," Adith prattled grimly, running a yellow light without blinking, "I bet she put it in an institution. Not everybody kept babies like that back then, you know."

Leigh was only half listening. Did Maura suspect Jared already? She might. Did Nikki know? She couldn't. She was probably Jared's legal guardian already, and if she had so much as an inkling she could and would have gone straight to the lawyer's office to stake her brother's claim — and no creepy little threats would have swayed her, either.

But if neither Nikki nor Jared knew, how did Ms. Lilah expect them to find out? And how were they to prove his identity as the will stipulated?

There was still a missing piece.

"Mrs. Rhodis?" Leigh asked tentatively. She was far too distracted now to pay much attention to the older woman's driving, which, if the object that had just grazed her side-view mirror was indeed a mailbox, was a good thing. "You knew Mary Polanski, didn't you?"

"Of course!" Adith piped up quickly. "Sharpest woman alive. Pity about — well, you know."

"Yes," Leigh agreed. "What I want to ask you is, how well do you think she knew Lilah Murchison?"

Adith's brow furrowed. "When?"

"In the late seventies, when the baby was born."

The older woman quickly shook her head. "Oh, I'm sure Lilah wouldn't have given a woman like Mary the time of day then. She was already a socialite. *La-di-da!*" She made a loopy gesture with her left hand, which resulted in the car swerving wildly over the center line. Gesture over, she swung the car back — and overshot onto the curb.

Leigh took a deep breath. Fortunately, the clinic was only a few blocks away, or she would be forced to ask for a barf bag. "So, you don't think Mary would know any of her secrets? I mean, about the baby? Could Lilah have called Mary and asked for her help in secretly getting it into an institution, or anything like that?"

"Lord, no!" Adith insisted. "Nobody would ever tell Mary anything that was even halfway shady — she was married to the chief of police, for heaven's sake. And everyone knew she wouldn't tell a lie. She'd be the *last* person Lilah would tell anything."

"I see," Leigh answered, but she was lying. She didn't see — not at all. How could Mary have known about the baby?

It was time for one more visit to Maplewood.

"That's Warren's car there," Leigh directed, pointing Adith toward the blue Beetle that was parked at the curb. The sedan missed clipping it by no more than ten inches.

"Are you sure there's nothing else we can do to help?" the older woman asked as Leigh got out. "Should I talk to the detectives myself, you think?"

"I'll tell Maura Polanski everything you told me as soon as I see her," Leigh promised, happy to have her feet back on the nice, safe cobblestones. "Thanks for the lift."

Adith was none too eager to end their conversation, but Leigh was eager enough for both of them. As soon as her ex-chauffeur was out of sight, she hoofed it down the street and into the clinic, making a beeline for the phone in the treatment room.

Unfortunately, Detective Polanski was unavailable. Leigh cursed under her breath, then left a rambling message on the detective's voice mail. She even, she was proud to say, confessed about the postcard and the oriental chest — though the latter, she still had plans for. If she knew her hardworking husband, the chest was probably still sitting on the front seat of her Cavalier in a particular downtown parking garage. And there it would stay until Warren knocked off for the day. Unless, of course, she got to it first.

Which she fully planned to do, just as soon as she had resolved the Mary issue. She would then have the rest of the afternoon to peruse the box at her leisure, and when Maura caught up with her that evening, she could happily turn it over — like the good little citizen she was.

She wanted to talk to Nancy again, but gave up after waiting five minutes for her to get off the phone with an obviously panicked bird owner. Whether Nikki or Jared was the real heir was immaterial to Nancy's situation — she might very well still be the person for whom the threats were intended. Whoever wanted to keep Jared's parentage a secret knew a lot, and it would be no stretch to assume they knew about Nancy's past as well.

And if the person who was sending the threats was the same person who killed Mrs. Murchison, and possibly Peggy Linney . . .

She shook the thought from her head. Whether Nancy knew something or not, she had every reason to look over her shoulder.

And so do you.

Leigh's teeth clenched as she attempted to placate her little voice of reason. It was true that anyone who knew the identity of Mrs. Murchison's real heir could be in danger, including her. But it was also true that once that secret got out, the threat to everyone would be over for good. And thanks to her, the police — as of ten minutes ago or whenever Maura picked up her voice mail — were already in the loop.

No one could possibly fault her for going on an innocent visit to a nursing home.

Mary Polanski was sitting this time, which was unusual. She was reposing calmly in an armchair in the small lobby outside her room, where another woman and a much older man sat ignoring a soap opera on a large-screen TV. She smiled as Leigh approached.

"Hello, Sally," she said pleasantly.

"Hello, Mary," Leigh answered pleasantly back. She pulled up another armchair and sat down. They ran through their usual topics of conversation; the chief, Maura, and a new favorite — the evils of war. Mary's chatterbox was in fine form.

"I never liked Lilah Beemish," Leigh said finally, keeping her voice sympathetic. "It was so awful what she did to that baby."

Mary's gray eyes turned intent, just as they had earlier that morning. "Yes," she said gravely. "It was."

Leigh took a deep breath and prayed that the direct approach was a good one. "Now tell me, how exactly was it that you came to know about it?"

For a long moment, Mary didn't answer. Her eyes darted rapidly back and forth in their sockets, and Leigh had the helpless feeling that the older woman's memories were playing before her like a movie on a screen — a screen no one else could see.

"Do you remember?" she breathed. "Where were you when you found out about the baby?"

"On the wall," Mary answered solemnly. "Sitting on the wall. You used to see a lot of things from the wall."

Leigh was lost already. "What wall?"

"She didn't want it; couldn't deal with it. Set it all up before — so neat and tidy. Would have just aborted it if she could. Instead she figured she'd get a little something for herself, too."

Mary was quiet for a moment again, and Leigh jumped in, afraid of losing the thread. "Did Lilah tell you this herself?"

The answer was a long time in coming as Mary's eyes continued to flicker. "I heard her. I saw everything through the window. She had to tell me."

Leigh's puzzlement increased. Mary Polanski, roaming around Ben Avon peeping in windows? It didn't make any sense. She decided to backtrack for security. "She gave the baby away?"

" 'Gave' isn't the word I'd use," Mary said critically. "It was illegal what she did. Illegal and immoral."

Leigh's eyes widened. "Illegal?"

"Cherry Coke!" Mary spat out suddenly. "Walked right into Meister's and got a Coke. Like nothing had happened."

"I'll take a Coke!" the older man on the couch nearby said loudly. "That sounds good."

"I like Coke, too," Mary answered, smiling.

Blast Coke! Leigh thought irritably. It took so little to get Mary derailed.

"Edward is a Pepsi man," Mary continued lightly. "Most people can't tell the difference, but he can. Never liked anything else. Though he does enjoy a Dr Pepper now and then."

Leigh cursed silently. She changed the subject back to babies, and then to Lilah, trying to steer Mary gently back on topic. But it was not to be. Her mind was on her husband, and everything not associated, she simply ignored.

After a while, Mary announced that she was tired and rose to walk toward her room. Leigh followed, eyeing the phone by her bedside. Did the residents get charged by the call? No matter. She could always reimburse Maura later. The detective would want to know what her mother had said as soon as possible. Leigh hoped she might also understand it — because Leigh herself had no clue.

She called Maura's number, and was again forced to leave a message. Relaying every detail of Mary's story would be important, because although the references to "the wall" and Meister's meant nothing to Leigh, they very well might to a lifetime Avaloner like Maura. Leigh finished the call and said good-bye, and Mary waved in kind. The woman had not shown the least spark of interest as Leigh had repeated her story into the phone, which was a bit distressing. How much of the time had Mary actually been talking about Lilah Murchison? Had her mind drifted somewhere in the middle?

Leigh contemplated the situation as she drove Warren's Beetle back downtown. There was not a doubt in her mind that Jared was Lilah Murchison's son. It explained perfectly well the shallow socialite's reluctance to acknowledge her child until after her death. But why had she never told Nikki? Was she afraid of being bilked out of her money early? Being prosecuted for an illegal adoption? Child abandonment? Mary had said that what she did was illegal. But there were always statutes of limitations . . . except, of course, for murder.

She shuddered as she pulled into the parking garage, and tried again to shake off the creepy feeling that kept making her arm hairs stand on end. Lilah Murchison had been murdered, and her killer was still out there. Maybe Lilah had sent the threats to the clinic herself, and maybe she had been murdered by someone who had no connection at all to the whole mystery-heir thing. But Leigh's instincts told her that the clinic's prankster and Lilah's murderer were one and the same — even if a few things still didn't add up.

She spotted the Cavalier and parked the Beetle a few lengths behind it in the through lane, hoping no attendants were attending at the moment. She moved quickly to switch the cars, then, after leaving Warren a suitably dutiful message about how she was helping the oriental chest along on its journey to the authorities, drove off in the Cavalier and headed for home.

It was the anonymity of the threats that still bothered her. Who exactly was the target? Nancy, because she might remember something from her childhood? Randall Koslow, because Mrs. Murchison might have confided something to him over the years? Jared, to keep him quiet? Nikki, because threatening her at her own workplace would draw too much suspicion to Jared? Or somebody else, with a link she hadn't uncovered yet?

Perhaps the answer was all of the above. Perhaps the best way to threaten anyone who might know about Jared was to threaten anyone who had anything to do with him.

But to what end? How could the perpetrator have a prayer of inheriting Mrs. Murchison's money through a scam, when anyone claiming to be the heir would immediately be a suspect for not only the threats, but also murder one?

By the time she pulled into the sanctuary of her own suburban garage, her jaws were sore from grinding. She still couldn't answer any of those questions. But if she was lucky, the chest in the backseat just might.

21

After an uncharacteristically paranoid check of doors, windows, and phone messages, Leigh pushed a few boxes to the side and settled down on the floor of the family room, a delighted Mao Tse purring loudly in her lap. Mao, who did not appreciate sharing her master with anything besides a can of tuna, and who had been doing her "I'm so neglected" sulk all week, was clearly counting the early return as a personal victory. The cat had sniffed the oriental chest in front of them perfunctorily, then ignored it. Why the mingled scents of two dozen Siamese did not interest her when she went nuts over Warren's dirty socks was puzzling. But pondering the olfactory fetishes of a Persian was a task for another day.

Right now, Leigh was determined to have one more go at figuring out who could be behind the threats — and most probably Lilah Murchison's murder. It was perfectly safe, she assured herself, to think about the matter in the privacy of her own home. Had someone warned her off snooping? They had. Had she done anything suspicious since then? She had not. One trip to the clinic, one to her husband's parking garage, and one to an assisted-living facility were all perfectly ordinary. Granted, she had made the trips in three separate cars, but that just made it all the less likely that anyone had tracked her movements in the first place.

The ornate key remained nestled in the chest's lock, and she turned it and lifted the lid. There was no need to treat the contents with kid gloves, she told herself, since they had been thoroughly picked over and trampled already. She would sort everything into nice neat piles, then set it all safely aside until Maura came to retrieve it. She had done the detective a favor, actually — if Maura was out working another case for the county, she would probably rather pick up the box at the house than downtown anyway.

Rationalizations completed, Leigh dug in.

Into one pile went photographs — all of which were of cats. Some were labeled, others not, but from the backgrounds she gathered that most had been taken during Lilah's childhood, in the forties and fifties. The cats, none of which were Siamese, ran the gamut in terms of appearance, but all looked well fed and cared for.

Into another pile went cat-related "literature," a term that Leigh applied purely out of respect for the dead. Poem after dreadful poem, written on scraps and the occasional napkin, all vainly attempting to extol the virtues of bright eyes and soft paws. There were a few stories too, frighteningly anthropomorphic, in which cats invented human-vaporizing guns, dog-enslaving potions, and space travel. These, Leigh graciously assumed, must have been by-products of the grade-school years.

Into the third and last pile went what Leigh believed to be the latest offerings — things Lilah had wanted to conceal from her third husband. Included were the hair swatch; a playbill from an off-color, off-Broadway production (as best Leigh could tell, Lilah had not been in the cast herself, though if rumors about her character were true, she might have been familiar with someone who had); the prenuptial agreement of sorts; and three successive last will and testaments.

The first was written in 1973, evidently not long after Lilah and Albert's marriage. It was short and to the point — if Lilah were to predecease her husband, he was entitled to just enough money to keep him and the house afloat. The rest went in trust to the cats.

The next was written in 1977, soon after Dean's and Jared's births, and Leigh read it over carefully. The cats were still well provided for, but Lilah had decided to leave the lion's share to baby Dean, with a little for Albert on the side. Peggy Linney, interestingly enough, was to receive quite a tidy sum — much more, ironically, than she had been allotted to receive in the most current will.

As Leigh pored over this will a second time, her blood pressure rose. There was not one word about Wanda Loomis, who was presumably raising baby Jared as her own. Not one red cent to a legitimate second cousin — even though such a bequest would probably not even raise an eyebrow. Couldn't Lilah have left at least a little money in trust to make sure her son was adequately provided for? Leigh wasn't sure what Jared's overall health had been like when he was younger, but she knew that children with Down's Syndrome often had special medical needs. Who did Lilah expect would pay for them?

Her blood was close to boiling when she set will number two aside and began to study number three. The cat-money to son-money ratio had increased considerably over five years, perhaps testifying to Lilah's opinion of motherhood. What had not increased, Leigh noted with agitation, was any concern whatsoever for the child she had given away.

Leigh paused a moment and took in a breath. The contents of the box, more than anything else, were giving her a disturbingly clear picture of the kind of woman Lilah Murchison had really been. She did not eat kittens, but no decent person would sneak up behind a six-year-old girl holding a dead mouse in a bag and say "boo" either. Lilah was antisocial. Not a sociopath, perhaps, but a person who didn't like other people. She preferred to devote all her affection to her cats, which, while not a bad sentiment in itself, was not the healthiest way to raise a son.

Perhaps Jared had been better off than Dean after all.

She picked up the 1982 will once more. Lilah had shown some improvement in the generosity category, Leigh noted, even if it didn't extend to family members. Peggy Linney again received a generous bequest, along with a dozen or so other employees. A few of the men's names Leigh thought were familiar — and, remembering Adith Rhodis's gossipy prattle at the will reading, she couldn't help wondering what the men were being rewarded for. But it was the name at the end of the list that stopped her short. The name . . . and the amount.

To my good and faithful housecleaner Hetta Johnson . . . a trust . . . sufficient to provide an annual stipend of approximately $30,000 . . . for the next twenty years . . . or to her heirs should she die before the twenty years has elapsed. . . .

Leigh's breath caught. *Thirty thousand* dollars a year? To a housekeeper? In 1982 dollars? For *twenty* years?

She let her hands fall limply onto Mao Tse's vibrating back. Hetta Johnson. Nancy Johnson's mother. The woman must have provided a service to Lilah Murchison that went far beyond housecleaning. It must have gone far beyond helping to cover up a baby switch, considering the much lesser amount reserved for Peggy Linney. And it must have been a service she was expected to keep on providing.

All of Leigh's previous questions began swirling in her head, and after a few stormy rotations, they settled into almost perfect formation. She ousted a displeased Mao Tse from her lap, packed up the contents of the chest, and slid it behind a handy pile of unpacked boxes.

Grabbing her keys from the kitchen table,

she headed straight for the Cavalier.

She knew now why Lilah Murchison had been unwilling to provide for Jared. She also knew who had — all along — been the sole target of the threats.

Because in 1977, Lilah Murchison had *not* given birth to a baby boy with Down's Syndrome. She had given birth to a half-black baby girl.

The clinic was eerily quiet as Leigh walked in the back entrance, particularly for the afternoon following such a hectic morning. She knew Nancy had rescheduled all but the most urgent appointments, and she imagined that her father was on the phone in the basement, busily attempting to reconstruct a staff for the next morning. The clinic could not continue indefinitely with unskilled help, and she could not continue indefinitely putting off her work at Hook.

But the advertising business could at least wait until tomorrow. Because at the moment, she was on a mission.

She found Nancy sitting in an empty waiting room, reconciling the checks, credit-card receipts, and cash with the computer, as she ordinarily did at the end of every workday. She acknowledged Leigh's entry with only a brief nod, then returned to her task.

Leigh pulled up a stool and sat down next to her. There was no point in pussyfooting. Who knew what the next threat would entail?

"Nancy," she began calmly, but firmly, "I know you think that keeping quiet about who you are is the best thing for everybody, but I think you're wrong. I think you need to tell the police."

Nancy's fingers stopped flipping twenties in mid pile. Her dark eyes caught Leigh's for a moment, then looked away. She rose with a jerk and walked to the front door, pulling on the handle to check the lock. Then she returned to Leigh's side and gestured wordlessly, her hands trembling.

Follow me.

Leigh got up and followed the other woman into the small half bath that doubled as the x-ray-processing room. Nancy shut the door behind them, flipped down the toilet lid, and sat down heavily.

"I know you think this is silly," she said shakily, her voice barely above a whisper. "But I can't trust anyone anymore. I'm afraid all the time that someone is listening to me." Her head sank slowly down into her hands, and for a moment, she was silent.

"How did you figure it out?"

"I saw a will from nineteen eighty-two," Leigh explained. "It seemed odd that Lilah would leave your mother so much money. But there were other things too."

The younger woman's eyes brimmed with moisture. "Like why any woman would give up her own flesh and blood, then adopt another baby?"

Leigh nodded silently.

"Well, now you know." Nancy's voice was still unsteady, and she breathed deeply to regain her composure. After a few seconds, she succeeded. "In a way, I'm relieved," she admitted. "I've never discussed it with anyone before. Except *her*."

There was no need to ask who "her" was. "Hetta didn't tell you?"

Nancy shook her head. "She had promised Mrs. Murchison that she would treat me as if I were her own, and that's exactly what she did, for as long as she lived." Moisture swelled beneath her eyes again, but she removed it with an almost-vicious swipe of her hand. "It was Mrs. Murchison who told me, the day my mother died. I suppose she thought it would help. She was wrong. I loved my mother; she was one of the greatest women I've ever known — or ever will know. I was devastated to find out I wasn't her biological child."

Nancy's hands moved down to hug her middle. She doubled forward on the seat, almost as if her stomach was hurting. Perhaps it was.

"Mrs. Murchison tried to explain why she had given me up. She used phrases like 'another time' and 'the way things were back then.' She said that she had been trying to get pregnant for years, but was having no luck. She was getting old and her husband was older, and time was running out. So she started having affairs — for Albert's sake. Even at sixteen, of course, I knew that was rubbish. The woman clearly had the morals of an alley cat. Eventually she did get pregnant, by a man she hired to paint the house. The ironic part was, for obvious reasons, he was the only one in the lineup she did *not* want to get pregnant by."

She pulled out an attractive, milky-brown arm and looked at it critically for a moment. "It's funny — I always knew that my father must have been white, even though my mother would never confirm it. She refused to talk about my father at all; it was as though my conception were immaculate."

Her eyes suddenly turned hard, and she pulled her arms tight around her again. "All the time I had it backward. My mother was white as a lily, and my father was a man she slept with once whose name she couldn't remember."

Leigh trembled a little herself as she leaned back against the sink. She wished there were something she could do or say, but she knew that there wasn't.

"She moaned about how Albert would have divorced her in a heartbeat, and how there was nothing else she could do," Nancy continued grimly. "She made a big production about how she had trolled the earth for the perfect adoptive mother, and how she had given Hetta a place to live and enough money to stay home with me until I went to school. Then she had brought both of us back into her own house."

Nancy paused.

"And Peggy Linney hit the roof," Leigh whispered.

"Dean was her great-grandson," Nancy answered matter-of-factly. "As far as she was concerned, he was the only child Mrs. Murchison had any business fussing over. She hated that Mrs. Murchison wanted to keep me close. After Albert died, I think she lived in constant fear that Mrs. Murchison would disinherit Dean and acknowledge me. Which I suppose she eventually did," Nancy hedged. "Sort of."

"All the secrecy," Leigh asked, unintentionally holding her breath. "Why? Do you know?"

There was no answer for a moment. "I suppose that might have been for my sake. But I'm not really sure."

The next pause was so long, Leigh thought her lungs would burst.

"She never out-and-out offered to acknowledge me publicly," Nancy said finally. "Almost ten years have passed since the day she told me everything, and not once did she ever admit that she had done anything wrong, much less apologize. What she did do was tell me that she had always been fond of me, and that she would be happy to pay for my education."

Leigh considered. She knew for a fact that Randall Koslow had offered to help Nancy pay for graduate school. But even with the money couched as an employee benefit, Nancy, knowing that she would not work at the clinic after graduating, had flatly refused the offer. Now it was apparent that the manager, who had busted her butt working full-time while getting her business degree, hadn't *had* to work at all. She could have gone straight to Carnegie Mellon, or the Wharton School of Business —

"I didn't want anything from her," Nancy

insisted, as if reading Leigh's mind. "I didn't want anyone to ever know that I was her daughter. And I told her that, in no uncertain terms." Her eyes clouded over. "I suppose I was a bit harsh about it. Well, let's not mince words. I screamed at her. I even tried to strike her. I was sixteen and I was hurt and I was furious. But I went way out of control."

"Of course you did," Leigh defended automatically. She would not let Nancy feel guilty now for what was a perfectly understandable adolescent reaction. What she herself might have done under similar circumstances, she shuddered to think.

"I'm not sure how our relationship might have developed if it hadn't been for that one awful day," Nancy continued. "But what happened was that she would drop by to see me once in a while — maybe every six months. She would ask if I needed anything. I would say no. Then she would leave."

There was another long pause.

"When I heard that she had died in that plane crash, I didn't know what to think. I'd be lying if I said I would miss her. In a way it was a relief. I always worried that someday the truth would come out, and I didn't want it to. All I've wanted to be, since I was six-

339

teen years old, is Hetta Johnson's daughter. With Mrs. Murchison dead and buried, there was no one who could say otherwise."

Leigh swallowed. "You didn't know about the will then, did you?"

Nancy shook her head slowly. "I wasn't notified about the reading . . . officially, I mean. I only heard about the 'mystery heir' business when the staff started talking about it."

Leigh's brow furrowed. She understood that Lilah wanted to offer Nancy the option of preserving her anonymity. But how could Lilah have been sure that her daughter would find out about the will at all? There was certainly a good chance she would, given her current employment and Randall Koslow's involvement in the inheritance. But it was not a sure thing. What if Nancy had suddenly decided to leave the clinic and go to graduate school out of state?

"I was glad, at first, that she set the will up the way she did," Nancy continued. "Not that it was some great act of kindness on her part, you understand. It was just a dangled carrot. 'Here's the money, free and clear. . . . You just have to acknowledge me.' Of course, she had no interest in acknowledging *me*. Not while she was alive to suffer the embarrassment."

Oh. Leigh breathed out in frustration. "I'm sorry, Nancy. I don't know what to say except that the woman was not only evil — she was a complete idiot. And the more I think about it, the more I believe she and Dean were made for each other." She slumped back over the sink and stared idly at the processor. "You're like the daughter every woman dreams of. Hell — my own mother would trade me in for you in a minute."

Nancy laughed, and there was another moment of silence. Then her tone grew serious. "I thought maybe the will could be a good thing because all I had to do — it seemed — was nothing. In five years, Dean would get his money and all would be well. I didn't care in the least if he went through it all in a week. In a way, I've always felt sorry for him. He had plenty of money and opportunity, but he never had a Hetta. He was a dopey, undisciplined kid, and he grew into a complete jerk. Mrs. Murchison shouldn't have been surprised."

Leigh sat up a little. "He doesn't know, then?"

"About me?" Nancy shook her head. "No way. I'm sure he's as confused about these threats as I am."

The threats, Leigh remembered painfully.

As much as she had learned in the last half hour, she was still no closer to finding the perpetrator.

"Nancy," she began hopefully, "you must have some idea who could be threatening you. Someone, somewhere knows who you are. But how could they?"

Nancy shook her head again. "I have no idea. Mrs. Murchison claimed that no one knew the whole story except my mother and Peggy Linney. There was some doctor — who she was probably also sleeping with — whom she paid off to attend the pregnancies and keep his mouth shut. But he died of a heart attack even before she told me all this. Dean's birth mother never knew the whole story. . . . I just can't think of anyone."

"One of those people must have told someone else, then," Leigh thought out loud. Her stomach rolled a little as she faced the fact that Peggy Linney's death had, almost certainly, been unnaturally hastened. Two women murdered to keep the secret safe; Nancy herself repeatedly, and anonymously, threatened to keep her mouth shut.

"I hate to admit it," Leigh muttered ruefully, "but this person has been fiendishly clever. He — or she — has got you too scared even to talk to the police, and they were able to do it without tipping anyone off to your identity." She looked at Nancy. "Did any threats come directly to you? To your apartment?"

She shook her head.

"They wouldn't," Leigh continued to hypothesize. "If anyone found out about that, it would be a dead giveaway." She thought some more, nibbling nervously on her fingernails. "Silencing Peggy Linney was easy. No one suspected a thing. She didn't seem like a threat to spill the beans when I talked to her. . . . In fact, she had every motivation not to, if she wanted Dean to inherit. But I'm sure whoever killed her didn't want to take any chances. Particularly if they found out that she had been meeting secretly with Mrs. Murchison's lawyer."

"But explaining my death would be trickier," Nancy said gravely.

Leigh looked at her sympathetically. It was true. A deceased Nancy, or even a missing Nancy, could lead the police right to the truth. And she was darn lucky that was the case.

"What I've worried about," Nancy said, her voice truly miserable, "was that somebody else at the clinic would get hurt. The threats were clear — it might not be me who paid for my indiscretion. It could be anybody." She swallowed, and her eyes grew moist again. "How was I supposed to handle something like that?"

She was silent for a moment, then wiped her face with a handful of toilet paper and stood up. "All I could do was comply. And I have. But the threats keep coming. And I don't know where it's going to end."

Leigh took a deep breath and faced her. "I'll tell you where it's going to end. It's going to end when the police find out who's behind this. With all the information you've just told me, I'm sure they can figure out the rest. It's the only way."

"No, it's *not*." Nancy protested, her eyes resolute. "This person is watching me twenty-four/seven. I can feel it. One trip to the police station, and they're going to retaliate. I can't have that on my conscience. Don't you understand?"

"But it has to end somewhere," Leigh argued reasonably. "You can't go on walking on eggshells forever. Maybe this person will make their move for the money in a couple of months, maybe not for a couple of years. Maybe they're sitting on a big pile of forged documents right now, waiting for just the right time to come forward as Mrs. Murchison's heir."

"Fine!" Nancy shouted. Then, suddenly

fearing they would be overheard, she dropped her voice low again. "I don't care who gets the money. The sooner the better. Once they have it, they'll leave me alone."

"No, they *won't,*" Leigh insisted heavily. "You'll never stop being a threat to them. Once they've made their claim, you could come forward at any time and put them behind bars for murder one — never mind the money and the fraud. This person has killed twice already. You think they won't take you out too? Years from now, when you least expect it? When the police won't think twice about the connection anymore?"

Nancy turned away and choked back an anguished groan. Leigh hated badgering her like this, but she had to face the facts. "You have tell the police, Nancy," she said. "You have to."

A long moment passed, and still the other woman did not turn to face her. "If I tell them everything, and they still can't figure out who's behind this, then someone else will get hurt."

"You can't think that way."

"I have to think that way," Nancy answered, whirling around. "It's the only thing that matters to me."

"But no one even has to know you've talked to the police," Leigh reasoned. "I'll work it out with Detective Polanski — it can all be concealed. But once the police know that you are the real heir, they'll be on the alert for a phony one. And as soon as this person makes a move for the inheritance, he'll be suspect number one. The game will be over."

Nancy thought for a moment, then shook her head. "What makes you so sure that this person's game is to claim the inheritance for himself? We don't know that. Maybe what this person really wants is for Dean to inherit. I'm not saying Dean or Rochelle are responsible, because I don't believe they are. But maybe this person has plans to bilk them out of their money. God knows it wouldn't be hard.

"Or what about your father and the millions he would control? Perhaps the plan is to get the money by cooking up some elaborate fake cat charity. Or maybe" — she exhaled sharply — "maybe the person just doesn't want me to have it. My point is, we don't know. And if you're wrong, going to the police could backfire."

She faced Leigh squarely. "I've given this a lot of thought already. And the only thing I can do is this: play along. No one else can ever know who I really am."

Leigh plopped back down on the sink.

Regrettably, Nancy had a point. She thought hard, until inspiration dawned. "All right," she said firmly, grabbing Nancy by the arms. "Think about this. The gist of the threats is that you are not to admit that you are Lilah Murchison's daughter. Right? But what if you could refuse the inheritance *without* admitting it?

"I'd have to check with the lawyer," she continued rapidly, "but I bet that you can stake your claim as her heir — confidentially — without any need for your identity to become public. You could refuse all rights to the money, and the will could go straight into probate. You will have kept your part of the bargain, because you will not — at least as far as this person will know — have ever gone to the police. And yet, if the plan was for this person to present himself or herself as the heir, it will be a moot point. If their plan was to steal money from Dean or my dad — let them try. The police will be waiting. And if their only goal was to keep the money away from you — they will have succeeded."

She paused for a much-needed breath. "So they'll have no reason to hurt anybody."

Nancy's eyes brightened, but only for a second. "But how can I know they wouldn't retaliate still?" she argued. "Who's to say this person doesn't already have a screw loose? If they lost the money one way or the other, they could still hurt me — or anyone else — just out of spite."

"If they're acting irrationally," Leigh said, "they could hurt anybody at any time anyway, no matter what you do."

Nancy had no response to that.

"You've got to play it smart," Leigh continued. "And this makes sense."

There was still no response.

"Nancy?" Leigh prompted. "If I set up a discreet meeting with Maura Polanski, will you talk to her?"

The other woman let out her breath with a shudder. "I want to know if it's possible to refuse the inheritance and remain anonymous. Can you ask Mrs. Murchison's lawyer if he'll do that?"

"You really need to talk to the police."

"I want to talk to the lawyer first," Nancy insisted. "But I won't talk to him unless he agrees to keep my name out of it. Can you ask him?"

"If I do, then you'll talk to the police as well?"

"Only if there's no way anyone can possibly find out."

"I understand."

The women exchanged glances. Nancy moved past Leigh and opened the door. "The sooner the better," she whispered over her shoulder, straightening her hair and wiping her eyes again. "I have a bad feeling about this."

22

Leigh flipped through the phone book that was stashed under the counter in the treatment room, located William Sheridan's number, and dialed. She had no time to waste; it was almost five o'clock, and he might very well be on his way out the door already.

"Sheridan," a brusque voice responded.

"Hello, Mr. Sheridan. It's Leigh Koslow," she began, trying her best to sound polite. The grumpy lawyer had never seemed to like her, and this particular request was definitely pushing her luck. "I'm glad you're still in the office —"

"I'm on my way out. Call the office tomorrow morning, please."

"I'm afraid this is urgent," she responded firmly. "I need to ask you a question about the Murchison will. It has to do with the unknown heir —"

"Ms. Koslow," Sheridan said with a sigh, unable — or more likely, unwilling — to conceal his annoyance, "you seem to have misunderstood my role as regards the Murchison estate. I have been paid to clarify issues for the beneficiaries and to determine the legitimacy of any potential claimants. I am not obligated to answer questions from outside parties based solely on curiosity."

Leigh squeezed the phone as hard as she could and counted to five. It was one of many antidetonation techniques she had mastered over the years — an essential skill when growing up with Frances Koslow as a mother. "Mr. Sheridan," she continued, keeping her voice serious, but pleasant, "I have been in contact with Mrs. Murchison's legitimate heir. The questions I need to ask you are on their behalf, not mine. Surely you could wait at your office just a few minutes? I can be there in five."

There was a short pause. "Sorry. I'm on my way to another appointment."

"When do you expect you'll be back, then?" Leigh asked. "Should I wait at your office?"

"I wasn't going back to the office," he practically growled. "My business is in the North Hills."

"Fine — I can meet you up there afterward. Just name a time and place."

There was another pause, punctuated by grumbling. "North Park, then. I'll look for you by the North Carolina Pavilion. But if you're not there, I'm driving on."

"Fabulous. What time?"

"Just wait for me."

The line went dead, and Leigh glared at the receiver. With all due respect to her father, Mrs. Murchison had had an uncanny ability to surround herself with the socially maladjusted.

She hung up and dialed Maura's cell phone, willing the detective to actually pick up this time. Though Maura always had her phone with her, she turned it to voice-mail mode whenever she was working. That was how it had been all afternoon, and that's how it still was. Leigh exhaled in frustration as she waited for the beep. "Maura — it's me again. Listen, the chest is at my house now, and you need to come pick it up."

She looked over her shoulder to see if anyone was listening, but it was too hard to tell. The treatment room was centrally located, and when the clinic was this empty, sound traveled. "I think it will answer several of our questions," she hinted. "I'm on my way now to see Mrs. Murchison's lawyer; then I'll meet you at my house." She checked her watch and gave the time. "If you can't come by, at least call me there, OK?"

After leaving a last brief note on Warren's

voice mail, considerately informing him that she would be late for dinner, she hung up the phone and headed for the Cavalier. *"Just wait for me,"* she repeated with a grumble. She had been feeling pretty good about wrapping up the whole mystery-heir debacle, but the lawyer's poor attitude risked spoiling her mood.

And the rain wasn't helping either. Though she usually enjoyed a good spring thunderstorm, this was one of the uglier, windier ones, and there were places she would rather spend it than sitting in her car in the middle of North Park.

The park was a popular North Hills get-away, replete with paved walking trails, ball fields, playgrounds, Porta Potties, and the ubiquitous "superdeer." But it was no place to weather a storm, and from the moment Leigh arrived at the designated picnic pavilion, she wondered if she was wasting her time. Would the persnickety lawyer even show up? It seemed unlikely. Not if it meant getting his suit wet.

She had just put her hand on the ignition to leave when a gold Town Car appeared through the downpour and pulled into the small graveled lot beside her. She waited a moment, wondering if the driver would make a run for cover under the empty pavilion, but the Town Car's engine remained running. After thirty seconds or so, the horn beeped.

Leigh's jaws clenched. So. *She* was supposed to run out in the rain and come to *his* car, was she?

Her good humor now thoroughly wrecked, she sprinted out of the Cavalier, looked through the window of the ostentatious Town Car to make sure that it was, in fact, Sheridan's, then opened the passenger door and slid in. She smiled evilly as her limbs dripped water on his upholstery.

"You have five minutes, Ms. Koslow," Sheridan said expressionlessly. "What exactly is your question?"

She was in no mood to prolong the interview. "I need to know if Mrs. Murchison's will made any provisions under which the heir could refuse the inheritance and still remain anonymous."

Sheridan looked at her as if she had a screw loose. "Well, of course," he answered irritably. "The heir has the option of not coming forward. That was spelled out quite clearly —"

"No," Leigh interrupted, growing more annoyed. "I mean, can they go through this 'verification' process as the heir, then refuse the money?"

The lawyer's bushy eyebrows conjoined over the bridge of his nose. "Why on earth would anyone want to do that? If the individual doesn't want the money and doesn't want anyone to know their identity, there is no need to do anything."

A loud crack of thunder erupted from the sky. Leigh took a deep breath, stifling her fantasy of shaking the stuffy attorney by his collar. "As you must be aware," she began steadily, "a series of threats has been delivered to my father's clinic — targeted at this individual and threatening retaliation if they come forward. What the heir wishes to do is refuse the money legally to get out from under the extortion, while still preserving his or her anonymity."

At long last, Sheridan seemed intrigued. He reached up a hand and fingered his beard thoughtfully. "And may I ask, Ms. Koslow, what makes you so certain this individual is in fact the heir in question?"

"Mrs. Murchison told them herself before she died," she answered simply.

He offered a patronizing smile. "Indeed?"

"Why would they lie?" she argued. "I already told you, they don't *want* the money."

The lawyer fingered his beard again. "I'm afraid I would have to doubt that as well,

Ms. Koslow. Did it ever occur to you that this individual might just be using you to help garner information?"

Leigh's face grew warm. She hoped it did not look red as well. She would hate for him to mistake her fire-hot wrath for embarrassment. "Did it ever occur to *you* that I might have uncovered proof myself that this individual is indeed Mrs. Murchison's biological child?" she said slowly, struggling to keep her voice down.

He glared at her. "No."

"Well, I have!" she raged, giving up. "Lilah gave birth to another baby when everyone thought she was pregnant with Dean. I have confirmation on that." She was thinking of Becky, Dean's biological mother, but she had no intention of telling Sheridan that. If he was so damn smart, he could gather his own information.

He was silent for a moment, looking at her, and she imagined that his estimation of her had suddenly sprung up a notch. Finally, he spoke. "Your information is correct, Ms. Koslow, but only to a point. Mrs. Murchison did adopt Dean immediately after a legitimate pregnancy."

Leigh waited.

"But the infant she herself gave birth to was stillborn."

The words that had been on their way out of her mouth caught fast. *Stillborn?* Not possible. Even if that was what Becky had always believed. Where was Sheridan getting his information from, anyway? "You said at the will reading," she began, flustered, "that Mrs. Murchison didn't tell you any of the details about Dean's birth."

The lawyer had the nerve to shrug. "I lied, Ms. Koslow. If you remember the tenor of that occasion, you should be able to see why. You should also be able to see that you've been royally had. Whoever has told you that he or she is the legitimate heir, I assure you, if that claim is based on the fact that the individual is the same age as Dean Murchison, it is false."

Rain pounded hard on the Town Car, and Leigh's wet limbs felt cold. Nancy couldn't be lying — she couldn't. She hadn't wanted to admit being the heir in the first place. And what about that shock of baby hair? It all made perfect sense. Could it be possible that Mrs. Murchison had somehow double-crossed Nancy, too?

Leigh looked hard at Sheridan.

"You know who the real heir is, don't you?" she accused. "Lilah Murchison told you. You've known all along."

To her surprise, he shook his head. "That

isn't true. She went to great lengths *not* to tell me."

"Then how do you know that the heir isn't twenty-five years old?" Leigh asked skeptically.

"Because she told me that the other child was born prior to her third marriage," the lawyer responded, his tone growing weary again. He checked his watch. "Your time is up, Ms. Koslow. I trust you will not be imposing further on my good nature."

Leigh took a deep breath and counted to five again. She had accepted a lot of curveballs since this craziness started, but this was one projectile she couldn't quite handle. Either Lilah Murchison had lied to her own lawyer, or Sheridan — for whatever reason — was bluffing. She chose to believe the latter.

"I trust you are not so stupid as to believe everything Mrs. Murchison told *you*," she said carefully, plotting her strategy as she went. "If she was hoping to humiliate her true heir by refusing to acknowledge them, she should have covered her bases a bit better."

She cleared her throat, checking to make sure she had Sheridan's attention. She did.

"For instance, she should have told Peggy Linney to keep her mouth shut about the baby switch. That poor old woman was only too willing to tell me everything."

She watched Sheridan's eyes for signs of panic, but what she saw was closer to hostility.

"Rubbish," he responded flippantly. "Peggy Linney never admitted anything of the kind. You know full well that she insisted she had delivered Dean from Mrs. Murchison herself." He looked at the watch once again. "Now, I have been more than patient with your ramblings, but I really must insist you leave. Don't you have a dinner to prepare, or something?"

A dinner? Enough was enough. This man was toast.

"I'll prepare my dinner right here if you don't lose the attitude and start listening to me!" she railed, eyes blazing. "I've *seen* proof, don't you understand? Lilah Murchison's proof, from her own memento box. I have a hair swatch from the baby she gave away, and it matches this individual perfectly. I have a will, dated nineteen eighty-two, leaving a large sum of money to the woman Lilah paid to raise this individual. And I have —"

"Damnation!" Sheridan cried, a hand flying up to cover his right eye. "These accursed contacts. Where are my glasses —"

He leaned over and began rummaging around under the passenger seat, bumping Leigh's ankles with a roving hand. "Move your feet, blast you!"

Leigh shifted her legs automatically to one side, wishing Lilah Murchison could have chosen a more normal human being for her legal work. Sheridan's attitude was unfathomable; he had to be lying about not knowing who the heir was. Of course he knew. Why *wouldn't* Lilah tell him? He just didn't want Leigh to know.

Which, obviously, she did. The evidence she had just given was real, even if Peggy Linney's confession had not been. But somehow, Sheridan the smug had known that.

Lightning flashed outside, and with it a spike of fear shot through her. How *had* he known what Peggy Linney had or had not told her? He had also visited Peggy on the last day of her life, but he had arrived before Leigh, not after. Yet the way he had just spoken, it was almost as if —

"There!" he said proudly, sitting up straight. There were no glasses either on his face or in his hand.

Almost as if he had been there.

The spike of fear repeated itself, and Leigh looked down sharply to see why she had just felt such a strange sensation on her ankle. It didn't take long to figure out.

He had handcuffed her foot to the car.

23

"What the hell are you doing!" she screamed, jerking her foot up wildly. She fingered the cuffs, but they were latched tight. One ring to her left ankle, the other to the metal underpinnings of her seat. "Are you crazy?"

Sheridan's face was scarlet, and his eyes had lost all traces of equanimity. "*I* am not the crazy one," he shouted back at her. "*I* am not the one who cannot leave well enough alone. *I* am not the one who can take months of careful planning and destroy it with a few days of nosing around in other people's business!"

Leigh stopped pulling at the cuffs. That was pointless. So was opening the car door. For one thing, only half her body would make it out. For another, it was still pouring rain, and not a soul was around to either see or hear half a body sticking out of a Town Car.

She faced the rattled lawyer, and the wheels in her brain began to turn. "You were there, weren't you?" she said calmly, even though her heart was striking her sternum like a mallet. "You were still at Peggy Linney's apartment when I visited her."

The lawyer didn't answer.

"She knew you were there," Leigh continued. "That's why she wouldn't tell me anything."

He still said nothing.

"If she was cooperating with you, why did you have to kill her?"

"Will you *shut up!*" he ranted, little veins popping out like hives on his forehead and neck. "I'm trying to think!"

Leigh stared at him. He was guilty. Guilty of something major. And what she had just so brilliantly succeeded in doing was convincing him that she knew enough to be a threat.

Fabulous.

She decided to backtrack, and quickly. "Look," she placated, keeping her voice as agreeable as possible for one whose leg was shackled, "you don't have to freak out about this. So you and Peggy had words. She got stressed; she had a stroke, a heart attack, whatever. She was going to die anyway. It doesn't matter to me."

The lawyer turned his head toward her slowly. "Well, aren't we bright," he drawled sarcastically.

Stay cool. "Excuse me?"

"It's a nice strategy, Ms. Koslow, but it's too late to play dumb. We both know that *you* know that Nancy Johnson is the legitimate heir."

Leigh shuddered a little. This was bad. "Nancy Johnson? No . . . I was talking about Nikki Loomis —"

"Enough!" he snapped. "It insults us both." He paused a moment, great beads of sweat breaking out around his receding hairline. "How could I have predicted that Mrs. Murchison would leave copies of old wills lying around? She never even asked for a copy of the latest one, convenient as that was. . . ."

He mumbled the last words, then glared at her again. "Miss Johnson has been far too scared to talk. You must have cornered her with some evidence she couldn't refute. So she swore you to secrecy. That's why she sent you to me — she didn't want to confess herself even to an attorney unless she could be certain her name wouldn't get out."

Leigh said nothing, and Sheridan's thin lips curved up slightly. "I judged her well. Some people respond to personal threats; with others, the self-sacrificing types, you have to threaten people they care about. It was unfortunate that Miss Johnson didn't have family to threaten, but I figured that in her case, even the guilt of causing a coworker's death would be too much." His face shone with pride. "I was correct."

His gloating reverie suddenly ceased, and he turned to Leigh with a scowl. "Then there are *other* people. People who are so infernally stupid that no reasonable threats can even begin to penetrate their thick skulls." His beady eyes narrowed at her. "What are you getting out of this, anyway? You barely know these people."

A variety of responses spun through Leigh's mind, most having to do with justice and the triumph of good over evil, but she didn't say any of them. They sounded too much like a *Superfriends* cartoon. Besides, they wouldn't help her now.

She tried another tack. "I'm no vigilante," she informed him defiantly. "Detective Maura Polanski is one of my best friends. I've been helping her. I've been updating her regularly, in fact. *Very regularly.*"

Sheridan threw her another shrewd glance. "Nice try, Ms. Koslow, but I don't believe you. I know your type. You want to be a hero. And heroes work solo."

"Not me. Maura knows all about the chest, and the old wills. She knows everything I know. Nancy refused to talk to her — you're right about that. But I told her myself."

Sheridan started looking more worried,

and Leigh pressed on. She tried not to think about the fact that the small-boned, relatively harmless-looking man sitting next to her might very well have been responsible for two murders already. The upshot was, he was dangerous. And if he thought that getting rid of her would accomplish something, there wasn't a doubt in her mind that he would go for it.

He breathed out angrily. "You're lying. You're lying to save your own skin. You confronted Miss Johnson as soon as you found the will, and then you rushed right out here to see me. I *had* no other appointment, by the way. I just wanted to get you someplace . . . private. Didn't think of that, did you?"

Leigh fought hard to beat back the chill that was creeping viciously up her spine. She could *not* panic. Sheridan was not a big man; in height and weight, they were probably evenly matched. He hadn't pulled a gun on her, or any other weapon, for that matter. He had the upper hand at this point only for two reasons. One: she was in his car in a deserted location in the middle of a downpour. Two: her foot was shackled.

She rallied her strength. This man might have killed twice, but with all due respect to the deceased, they had not been difficult targets. Peggy Linney was practically an invalid. Lilah Murchison might have looked fine, but she was terminally ill. Leigh Eleanor Koslow was neither of those things.

She stole a glance at the handcuff that bound her ankle, and swallowed. It didn't look like the ones she had seen Maura carrying. It was almost . . . decorative. A vision of the leather whip that had been used to strangle Lilah popped unwillingly into her mind. There was a theme here, and if she was going to keep any pretense of a cool head, she had to pretend otherwise.

Who was Sheridan really, and what were his motives? If she was going to do battle with her wits, she would have to know.

She cleared her throat and looked straight at him. "Maura and I," she began, "knew all along that whoever was threatening Nancy had to have inside information. Who knew about the will before it was read? And how could they have known?"

Sheridan smiled broadly. "You obviously didn't think of me, though, did you? People never think of the lawyer. We're rather like invisible servants, skulking around the corner, pretending not to listen." He relaxed a little for a moment. "Of course I knew everything. Mrs. Murchison told me the whole story from the very beginning.

Why wouldn't she? I was her attorney, for heaven's sake. It was all completely confidential."

His grin was positively snide. "It was the perfect setup."

"You must have changed the name of the heir in the envelope, then," Leigh suggested, fishing. She realized now that somehow, some way, Sheridan's motive in all this had to be collecting the money for himself. Her crazy "fake heir" theory had been right all along.

To her surprise, he chuckled. "My foolish Ms. Koslow, you have no idea. I changed *everything*. Additions, deletions, rewordings — by the time Mrs. Murchison signed the final copy, she was too sick of the document to even look at it. She had no idea. She wanted to give Nancy the option of anonymity, yes, but the cloak-and-dagger stuff was all at my suggestion. The sealed envelope, the formal proof of identification — I convinced her to do all of that. For her own protection, of course."

Leigh felt a successive wave of urges to smack the arrogant look off the lawyer's face, but she resisted them all. "I'm guessing then that Mrs. Murchison *did* leave Nancy a personal note, with instructions about how to claim the money, as well as proof of her identity. I'm guessing you never gave it to her."

"You would guess correctly." He seemed to be lost in thought for a moment, then he sat up straighter, his features grim. "And the strategy is still sound. *Provided* that no one ever discovers that Nancy Johnson is Mrs. Murchison's biological child."

He looked at her with a coldness that chilled her limbs. "And with you gone, no one will. I will tell Miss Johnson a frightening story about how you left my office in a mad rush to see someone. . . . Yes, that will do. As long as she stays ignorant of the perpetrator, she'll stay too afraid to come forward, as well. Your 'disappearance' should rattle her nicely."

Leigh fought a rising panic again as Sheridan looked her over, clearly mulling his options. She could only guess what was going through his mind. How exactly could he kill her? Strangulation? A blow to the head? And how could he hide the body? If it was found, would there be anything to implicate him?

He turned the windshield wipers on high and peered out, first at the pavilion area, then at the Cavalier. He smiled.

In the driving rain, the young woman apparently lost control of her car. . . . Or, better yet: A

North Park pedestrian was killed earlier today when she was mysteriously run down from behind by her own vehicle. . . .

No! She pushed the visions forcefully from her mind. No matter what he was thinking, she would *not* be easy either to kill or dispose of, and he was smart enough to know that. He would be in for one hell of a fight — with no guarantee of success. There had to be room for reason.

"Don't be stupid. There's no way you could ever get away with killing me," she said, mustering every ounce of fake self-assurance possible. "I'm not an old woman and I'm not frail, and my disappearance will raise more questions than you could ever imagine."

Sheridan avoided looking at her. She took this as a good sign. "Maura Polanski is probably at the vet clinic right now, interviewing Nancy," she continued. "She knows that I went to meet you. When I don't show up . . . well, have you ever heard the expression 'no-brainer'?"

He clenched his fists on the steering wheel and swung his face back toward her angrily. "And what do you propose as my alternative? Am I supposed to believe that if I let you saunter off back to your car, you will not run and tell the police that I have murdered two people and threatened two more? Not that I'm admitting that, mind you," he tagged on, his legal training resurfacing. "But what do I really have to lose here? What are three murder raps compared to two? I don't believe you've told your detective friend everything you say you have. If I let you go, I lose for certain. If I kill you, I might still lose. But then again, I might not."

He glared at her malevolently. "That's a *no-brainer.*"

Leigh's heart beat faster, and her mind raced furiously. He was right, of course. He had nothing to gain from letting her go, because she *would* turn around immediately and pin his scrawny butt to the wall. It was the right and only thing to do. But then, people like Sheridan didn't understand the meaning of the word "right."

They can't comprehend it.

A coy smile spread over her own face. "All right, Sheridan. You win. The money would never have gone to Dean and my father anyway, would it? You would have gotten it first."

The lawyer's eyebrows arched. He said nothing.

"Of course you would have. So the strategy changes."

Still he said nothing.

"Oh come off it, Sheridan," she derided. "You don't really believe I'm some superhero wanna-be. People like that don't really exist."

His eyes widened with interest, and she surreptitiously took a deep breath, which she sorely needed to maintain her blasé tone. "There are people who uphold the law for a salary, like my friend Maura Polanski. But we both know that people like her never, *ever* get ahead."

She rapped her fingers on the Town Car's armrest. "You're right. I haven't told the detective squat. It's more the other way around. I've been using her to get my own information."

It was not in her best interest to look at the lawyer directly, but if her peripheral vision was accurate, he was eyeing her approvingly. "When I realized Nancy Johnson was the real heir, I was sure I could convince her to refuse the money outright. Then I wouldn't have to wait five whole years for my dad to inherit half of everything."

The lawyer's voice was quiet, but it held a trace of something like glee. "And I thought your father was a sober fellow."

"He is," Leigh said, careful not to sound *too* respectful. "But he's lousy with money.

That's why he hired Nancy Johnson in the first place. I wouldn't have had any trouble getting him to turn over control of the 'feline charities' money to my waiting hands. And I don't think I need to tell you — the felines wouldn't be getting all of it."

She turned to see his face shining with amusement. "Bravo, Ms. Koslow," he offered. "I underestimated you. That simpering face of yours serves you well. Too bad you didn't figure me into the equation earlier, eh?"

Once again, Leigh fought hard not to strike the man. "Oh, I'm not done yet," she returned. "I'm going to make you an offer you can't refuse. You don't have to go down for my murder. You don't have to go down for anyone's murder. You can cash in on that inheritance as planned — with absolutely no interference from me. In fact, I can even lose that pesky little will I found. Just like that." She snapped her fingers.

His cold eyes scrutinized her — hard. "In exchange for what?" he asked, his voice low.

Leigh stared at him just as coldly. "I want half."

For a moment, she thought he might hit her. Then, the diabolical smile returned. "Thirty percent," he said dryly.

She shook her head. Hardball was hardball. If he suspected she was bluffing, she was done for. *"Half."*

Sheridan let out a long, groaning exhale. After a tense moment, he answered, "Fine."

Leigh's heart skipped a beat. Did he believe her? Was he serious? He appeared to be.

"But I'll need some documentation," he insisted.

She looked at him quizzically. "Now, why would I agree to that?"

"Because if I go down," he said menacingly, "I can assure you that you will go down right along with me. In fact, I will claim that you were involved all along. Conspiracy to commit murder sound good? Because that's what you'll be facing if you try to double-cross me." His eyes bored into hers. "I happen to be very good at forgery, Ms. Koslow. You have evidence of that. With your signature on a few blank documents, I can turn your life into a living hell. Do we understand each other?"

She looked back at him levelly, having no intention of signing anything. "Perfectly."

Sheridan stared at her for only a moment, then threw the Town Car into gear and pulled out.

"Hey!" Leigh protested. "My car!"

"Not yet," he said. "I want those papers

signed tonight. I'll bring you back out later."

"No way," she argued. "We'll have to do it tomorrow. My husband and Maura Polanski are both expecting me home. It will look too suspicious."

His eyes narrowed. "Shall we talk about suspicious, Ms. Koslow? I think it's a little *suspicious* that you happened to be the last one to see Peggy Linney alive. It's a little suspicious that you were interested enough in your father's finances to show up at both the will reading and his subsequent 'private' meeting with me. It's even more suspicious that, mere minutes after Lilah Murchison was brutally murdered, you and your husband just *happened* to appear at the mansion. You and your *politician* husband, who I might add has a reputation for generating money in rather novel ways."

Leigh felt as though her blood were circulating through a pressure cooker. "My husband has nothing to do with this," she growled.

"Oh no?" Sheridan said innocently. "The police would probably agree with you on that. Eventually. But I suspect the media might find my side of the story a little more newsworthy. Particularly after I inform them of how the honorable Warren Harmon tried to bribe me for information as to the heir's identity —"

"All right!" Leigh snapped, getting the lawyer's point loud and clear. There was no way he would let her go willingly until he got more leverage. "I'll sign any damn thing you want," she snarled. "Just hurry up — I want to get home."

Surely it wouldn't matter what she signed, she assured herself. If she ran straight to the police afterward, Sheridan would be arrested before the ink was dry.

Or would he? Suddenly her stomach felt like lead. Neither she nor Warren had done a thing they could be prosecuted for, it was true. But for that matter, was there any hard evidence against Sheridan?

If she walked away tonight safe and sound, charges of kidnapping would be a hard sell. And without proof of his involvement in either the threats or the murders, any accusations she made would be her word against his. She didn't have a criminal record per se, but her name had been in the papers a few more times than she would have liked.

Sheridan, on the other hand, was an officer of the court. His record could very well be squeaky-clean. And given so much as an hour in his office, he could undoubtedly destroy all evidence of both his previous and impending fraud. He probably had an alternative "sealed" envelope just waiting — complete with Nancy Johnson's name. How could he be prosecuted then? There would be no visible motive for him to harm Mrs. Murchison. As for Peggy Linney, there was no evidence she had ever been murdered in the first place.

Leigh breathed deeply, trying to steady her nerves. She had two things on her side that Sheridan didn't have: the truth and Maura Polanski. And that wasn't even counting her Aunt Bess, who seemed to have more than a little influence with the county homicide squad. The police would find *some* evidence against Sheridan, she was certain. And in the end, justice would prevail.

But the smart-alecky SOB was right about one thing. It would not take much embellishment on his part for the media to have a field day with Councilman Harmon first.

And retractions never made page one.

Leigh gathered her nerve. She had set up this scheme and she would see it through. It was the only way. When, not if, she managed to get away, she must make absolutely sure that William Sheridan became dog meat. *Fast.*

They both fell silent as the Town Car sidled over rain-soaked roads back into the main part of the park. The storm was letting up, and her spirits rose. She didn't know where he would take her to "sign," but almost anywhere would be safer than the deserted picnic grove they were leaving. And should it begin to look like the whole signing thing was a ploy, she could always grab the wheel and wreck the car.

She reached over and fastened her seat belt.

They were partners now, or so he thought. If he had truly bought her story, perhaps he would let down his guard. There was still a lot she didn't understand, and the police would need specifics.

But she couldn't tip him off, either.

"Are you sure you can get the money?" she asked critically.

His lips pursed with insult. "Of course. That's a stupid question."

"No, it's not," she responded sourly. "I have a lot invested here. I don't want you to screw it up."

His face grew red again. "I assure you I was doing quite well without your interference."

"Oh, really?" she pushed. "The police know that both of us visited Peggy Linney just hours before she died. If you poisoned her, they can still find traces, even though she's been cremated. Did you think of that?"

"Don't be ridiculous," he said. "They can't pull poison from ashes."

"Shows what you know," she bluffed. "You have no idea what they can do with PCR these days. *I* know my forensics. Now, what kind of poison was it? Some are traceable, others aren't. You didn't use a traceable kind, did you?"

She kept her tone as condescending as possible, rather like one child informing another his underwear was on backward. Much to her delight, the younger child bristled nicely.

"I didn't use poison, you idiot!" he fumed. Then he caught himself. "But if I *had* wanted to off the old witch, I would have smothered her with a pillow. I would have called and asked to see her, said hello to a neighbor on the way in, had a nice chat with the woman, then — as far as she knew — left."

Aha. "So you opened and shut the door while her back was turned?" Leigh surmised, feigning admiration. "Pretty good. Then you hid until someone else showed up. Someone who could attest to the fact

379

that you weren't there. Someone like me."

He smirked.

"Then you took off for real, being careful this time that no one saw you."

The smirk widened. "You're a genius," he said facetiously.

"Thank you," she answered. "The only problem is, you didn't need to risk it at all. She didn't tell me a thing."

The smirk disappeared. "I know that, Ms. Koslow. But that doesn't mean she wouldn't have starting yapping if she lived long enough to see Dean lose his money. She was a low risk, granted, but silencing her was a much lower risk, all things considered. One's options have to be weighed."

Leigh was silent for another moment. Sheridan had driven out of the park and onto Perry Highway, one of the North Hills' main corridors. With any luck, he was on his way back to Avalon, and his office.

She smiled a little. He *did* believe her.

"I can't believe you hid there in that dinky little apartment for hours," she continued conversationally. "I'd be bored out of my gourd."

His chest practically puffed with self-regard. "I'm a very patient man, Ms. Koslow. You would do well to exercise that skill yourself. Everything I have achieved so far has been accomplished through consummate patience."

Leigh thought quickly, then gave a rude snort. She needed something to link him to Lilah's murder, and she couldn't help but remember Adith Rhodis's ribald comment at the will reading. Could Sheridan and Lilah have been involved romantically? If so, it could only hurt his case. "Oh, please," she said disdainfully. "Patience had nothing to do with it! Lilah Murchison just happened to pick your firm — the opportunity fell right in your lap."

Sheridan took his eyes off the road just long enough to stare daggers at her. "Nothing *fell into my lap*. I assure you, I had been working for months to get the Murchison account away from Lang and Madia."

She smirked. "Right. A little wine, a little soft music . . ."

The car swerved violently, and Sheridan's face flushed to an odd purple color. The man was a Technicolor marvel. "I'm going to say this one time, and one time only," he began, his tone deadly serious. "I was *not* involved with Lilah Murchison that way. *Ever*. She saw what she wanted to see."

Leigh's eyebrows rose. It was hardly the reaction she had expected. "Fine," she said more amiably, none too anxious to plow into a fire hydrant. Not unless absolutely necessary, anyway.

They moved down Perry Highway at a good clip, then crossed over the interstate toward Avalon. "I knew that Mrs. Murchison was alive after the plane crash," she bragged, still fishing. "*You* didn't know that."

"I had no way of knowing," he huffed. "Speaking of which, how did you? She insisted no one could have known she was alive. She rushed straight from the plane to some veterinary emergency clinic, and after she heard about the crash, she kept out of sight quite intentionally because she wanted to know how her daughter would react. The she-devil had a grand entrance all planned for her memorial service."

The last conversation Leigh had had with Sheridan at his office came flooding back to her, along with a fresh wave of mortification. It was all *her* fault. She was the one who had tipped off the lawyer about Lilah's return. And that very night he had gone to the Murchison mansion. . . .

"She brought the sick cat back to the house with her," she answered dully, feeling nauseous again. "And it didn't hide."

Sheridan swore under his breath. "I

should have known it would be something like that. She was such a fool."

Trying hard not to let her guilt get the best of her now, Leigh baited him further. "Lucky for you she was."

"Pardon?"

"If you hadn't gotten a heads-up from me, you might not have gotten to her before she talked to somebody else," she managed. "And once she found out what you did to her will, it was all over."

"One can't plan for *every* contingency," he said humorlessly. "The woman was supposed to be dead. In any event, Ms. Koslow, it isn't over until it's over. As I told you before, I'm a patient man."

Sheridan's law firm was only a few blocks ahead now, she told herself, and soon she would be free. He would have to unlock the cuff to let her walk inside; he would have no reason to assume she would run. And even if he had been calling her bluff all along, he couldn't possibly kill her in broad daylight in the middle of his driveway.

Of course, once she did run, he would instantly start to cover his tracks. And in the time it might take for Maura to get a warrant, he had a very good chance of succeeding. More nausea rolled up strong. Her only other alternative was to willingly accompany him into his office and hope that he felt confident enough in her *not* to bother destroying any evidence afterward. But how could she be sure of that? If he had even a shred of reservation about their "deal," he could doctor the relevant documents temporarily, just in case. Then there would still be no good evidence against him — but he would have plenty of new, falsified evidence against her. *And* Warren.

A block and a half. She had to run. She had to run straight to the Avalon police station, and she had to have something credible to offer them when she got there. "Well, I'm *not* patient," she groused. "What kind of time frame are we talking about here? When do I get my share?"

"When I say so," he responded flatly.

"Forget that!" she complained. "I need it within a year."

He laughed mirthlessly. "Ms. Koslow, don't insult me. You're in no position to be calling the shots; you are entirely dependent on my plan. And my plan requires several years for the hubbub over the murder and threats to dissipate." He paused a moment. "Besides, my mother has to die."

Leigh stared at him, horrified. "You're going to off your own mother?"

For some reason, he seemed to find that

comment hilarious. "My mother has been in a nursing home for years," he said when his chortles had diminished. "I assure you she'll manage to die without any help from me."

He exhaled dramatically as his office came into sight. "Now, Nancy Johnson is another matter. She may require some assistance."

Leigh's own breaths were coming fast and shallow. She was nauseous as hell, he was talking nonsense, and she had to be ready to bolt. "I thought you said Nancy wouldn't talk," she said weakly.

"Not until the real heir comes forward," he said with a smirk. "Then I suspect she might consider it. But by then, she'll be too dead to consider much of anything. Time will have passed, you see, Ms. Koslow, and time is a patient man's weapon. When the real heir inherits, no one will even think to connect the dots."

"And who is your 'real' heir?" she asked. "His cut had better be coming out of your share and not mine. And you'd better have your ducks in a row. There is such a thing as DNA."

He steered the Town Car into the tiny lane that served as his office's driveway. "Oh, don't worry," he said tonelessly.

"You'll get what's coming to you."

Time is a patient man's weapon.

And in a few years, no one would connect her own death to the Murchison money either.

The car stopped. He switched off the engine and threw her a warning look. "I hope you know that running now is pointless. Anything you *think* I might have said in the last half hour is entirely hearsay, and you have no evidence whatsoever that I brought you here against your will. I met with you at your request, you claimed that your car had broken down, you asked me for a ride to Avalon, and you said you wanted to use my phone. I have no idea why you should do such a thing, unless, of course, it would be to sneak a peek at my files. Which, I might add, can be entirely in order in a matter of minutes. Are we clear, Ms. Koslow?"

Leigh didn't answer. She sat still.

"Well?" he asked again, opening his car door. "Are you coming with me, or aren't you?"

He didn't manage to say anything else. The second his door opened, a pair of strong arms heaved him up, out, and facedown on the hood.

"You have the right to remain silent," Maura began, stealing a quick glance inside the passenger compartment as she quoted.

Leigh breathed out with a smile.

"Anything you say —"

"This is preposterous!" Sheridan ranted, fighting to make eye contact with Leigh through the windshield. "I'm afraid you've made a terrible mistake." His eyes bored into hers with menace. "*Haven't* they, Ms. Koslow?"

Two uniformed officers had appeared with Maura, and one of them opened the passenger door. "No, Mr. Sheridan," Leigh answered, lifting her still-shackled leg into view. "*You* have."

24

"But how did you know he was the one?" Leigh's cousin Cara asked Maura, her eyes widening as she carefully sliced off another bite of pizza with her knife and fork.

It was Friday night, and "pizza fest" was on. Maura and her boyfriend, Detective Frank, lounged comfortably at Leigh's kitchen table, shoveling their own pizza away without a thought to utensils. This was fortunate, since the kitchen was still only half unpacked — a situation Leigh was quick to blame on the fact that she was still behind on her work at Hook.

Cara's arrival had been unexpected, but given that Frank was buying, Leigh was only too happy to invite her to stay. Ordinarily, her cousin would have been miffed at missing the week's excitement, whether she had been enjoying a family vacation at the time or not. But this evening she had dropped by with good news: her little son, Mathias, was going to be a big brother.

Leigh had congratulated her cousin heartily, even though ordinarily she might have felt just the slightest pang of jealousy at her perfect cousin's perfect family acquiring yet another perfect member. But not to-night. Tonight, nothing could get her down. "She knew because I told her," Leigh answered, grinning.

Maura smiled back. "Actually, it was my mother who tipped me off. When I heard the voice mail message from Leigh, I knew something was out of whack." She leaned forward toward the box of sausage and mushroom, then slid three still-connected pieces onto her paper plate.

"Mom said she was 'sitting on the wall,' " she continued. "The only wall I could think of was the old Avalon Elementary School wall, which wraps around the corner of California Avenue and North School. Just about anybody who grew up in Avalon has sat on that wall at one time or another, swinging their feet and watching the traffic go by. But the thing is, the wall's kind of high — it's hardly a typical hangout for women in their forties."

Maura paused to take a gargantuan bite of pizza, and Detective Frank, who ordinarily said next to nothing, continued for her. "There was the Cherry Coke thing, too. Prefab Cherry Coke didn't come out until the eighties. But soda shops used to make their own, with cherry syrup."

Maura agreed with a nod, then swallowed. "I'd never heard of anyplace called Meister's either, so I asked around. Turns out that there was a Meister's Dairy Store on the corner right across from the school wall — back in the fifties."

Cara's eyebrows rose.

"You see," Leigh explained further, "we were stuck on this idea that the mystery heir was born in nineteen seventy-seven, when everyone thought Lilah was pregnant with Dean. And she did give birth to Nancy Johnson that year. But Nancy wasn't her firstborn."

Maura turned to Leigh. "It's taken me a couple trips back to Maplewood," she said, "but I think I've finally pieced together the whole story of what my mom saw."

Leigh nodded encouragingly. "What?"

"She was just a teenager," Maura began, "and so was Lilah Beemish. Mom was sitting on the wall, hoping somebody named Betty would be able to join her for a soda. While she was there, she saw Lilah skulking around a particular house, a house near the corner that all the kids knew they were supposed to stay away from.

"I'm not sure what all else the people who lived there were into, but apparently, they had enough black market connections to broker the sale of a healthy white infant."

Cara drew in a breath. "In the fifties?"

"It happened," Detective Frank said, cutting in. "Sometimes wealthy couples didn't want to wait. Other times, they tried to cover up births that didn't go as planned."

"Just like Lilah herself did — twenty-odd years later," Leigh noted.

Maura continued. "According to my mother, Lilah had quite a scandalous reputation already, even at that age. So Mom figured she was probably involved with somebody at the house. But that worried her. You see, nobody had seen much of Lilah lately, and Mom thought that maybe she'd been sick. And that night in the spring, even though it was warm, she was bundled up like she was about to take a trip.

"Mom waited on the wall a long time, but Betty never showed and Lilah never came out of the house. Finally, she got up the nerve to walk over to the house herself and peek in one of the windows.

"She could hear Lilah moaning as she got closer, and it scared her to death. But when she looked in and saw the man of the house holding a crying newborn, she almost wet her pants. Mom just stood there, watching as his wife helped Lilah pull her clothes back on. Then the man handed Lilah a wad of bills, and she perked right up. She stuffed them in her coat pocket and just walked out the door."

"Good God," Cara breathed.

"It gets worse," Maura replied. "Mom followed her, wondering if she was all right. But Lilah didn't go home. She walked up to the dairy store on the corner, drew one of the bills out of her pocket, and ordered a cherry Coke."

The last bite of Leigh's fourth piece of pepperoni-and-green-pepper went down awkwardly. "Unbelievable," she said with a cough. "You hear about easy births, but for a teenager to take the whole thing that coolly is disturbing."

"What did your mom do then?" Cara asked, her own pizza forgotten. "Did she confront her?"

"Yep," Maura answered between bites. "And I think she would have liked to go to the police afterward, too. But Lilah made that hard for her. She claimed that if her stepfather ever found out she'd had a baby, he would kill her. She also claimed that the father of her baby was somebody named Horace. Mom's story gets a little murky here, but as far as I can tell, Horace was Betty's dad."

Leigh grimaced. "Her own schoolmate's father?"

"Right," Maura answered. "A scandal like that would have destroyed Betty and her family, and Lilah threatened to scream it from the rooftops if Mom said a word. Mom said she was torn, but in the end she figured that whoever the baby had ended up with was bound to be a better parent than Lilah or her alcoholic parents. So she kept her mouth shut."

"For almost fifty years," Leigh noted, impressed. "But it was a good thing she decided to remember it when she did."

"I'll say," Cara agreed, slicing her pizza again. Then she looked back up at Maura. "So you realized that Lilah's firstborn had to be in his or her late forties by now."

Maura nodded. "To be honest, Sheridan was already on my list. There were a few things about his handling of the will that weren't exactly routine. And it was clear that whoever was behind the threats had to have inside information."

She dove in for another bite, and Detective Frank spoke up for her again. "The problem was establishing motive. But once she got a warrant to search Sheridan's office, that became self-evident."

"You had already searched the office before he brought Leigh there, then," Cara surmised.

Maura swallowed. "There was no doubt after that. William Sheridan was Lilah Murchison's biological son. His adoptive mother had informed him of that years ago, but apparently, Lilah herself didn't have a clue. She had never shown any interest in tracking down the baby boy she had sold — which was probably one of the things that irked him.

"My guess is he'd been trying to figure out how to get his hands on Lilah's money for quite a while already. Maybe he even thought about doing it legit — by getting to know her and then acknowledging himself. She and Dean were clearly on the skids anyway.

"But then Lilah found out she was dying," Maura continued, turning to Leigh. "You were right about that, by the way. The autopsy showed she had an inoperable aneurysm. She could have lived a year, or she could have died any day. So she put her affairs in order, which meant making the decision to disinherit Dean and favor Nancy. Sheridan had snagged her business by then, and you can guess how thrilled he was to learn he would be passed over for another bastard child he didn't even know about."

Leigh tried to picture the scene, popping veins and all. "He would have been furious," she declared.

"But he plotted it all out very carefully, still," Maura credited. "I believe his plan was to wait until his mother died, at which point he would claim she had finally told him the truth, or left him a note with her will, or whatever. He could say that he previously had no idea that Lilah was his mother, but that Lilah must have known, which is why she set up the crazy will with his firm in the first place."

Detective Frank clicked his tongue and cocked his head to one side. "You've got to admit — the man wasn't stupid." He smiled at Maura warmly. "But then, he didn't count on the Polanski factor, did he?"

Leigh quickly averted her eyes from the lovebirds, but watching her perceptive cousin grin at her was even worse. She looked at her watch instead.

"What's keeping Harmon?" Maura asked finally. "He'd better not miss two weeks in a row."

"He won't," Leigh answered. "He said he's running a little late, but he'll be here."

"So," Cara said, after a few moments of contented chewing noises all around, "who *will* get the money?"

Maura and Detective Frank both shook their heads. "You're looking at a real legal nightmare there," Maura explained. "The will Sheridan prepared is invalid, so the settlement could take years. But it looks like the last will Mrs. Murchison had with Lang and Madia was almost identical, except that instead of the option of getting everything, Nancy Johnson would get only a small trust put in her late mother's name."

"So if Mrs. Murchison had died back then," Leigh said thoughtfully, "everyone would have gone right on thinking that Dean was her one and only child."

She couldn't help wondering if, now that he knew the whole story, Dean would want to meet his biological mother. Who knew? They might actually have a lot in common. One thing she did know — it would be downright scary if, after all this, Dean and Rochelle did end up as millionaires. Of course, given their combined fiscal acumen, they probably would not be millionaires for long.

"Will there be any trouble getting enough evidence against Sheridan?" Cara probed.

"Lilah's murder won't be an open-and-shut case," Maura said regretfully. "And Peggy Linney's may be a lost cause. But I'm sure the prosecutor can get convictions on the kidnapping, forgery, and extortion charges, at least."

"Don't be so modest," Detective Frank chided. "He'll get murder one. Should have known that buying his grown-up toys online would come back to haunt him."

Maura chuckled. "We owe your friend Jared one, there. If Sheridan had had enough time to get that whip off Lilah's neck, we'd be pretty hard up for physical evidence."

All four jumped as Mao Tse landed solidly in the middle of the table, hissed at Detective Frank, then just as quickly scuttled off. Leigh concealed a grin. The cat had taste.

Cara let out a small laugh. "And what about poor Mrs. Rhodis? Did you explain all this to her yet? I bet she was practically bursting to get in on the action."

Leigh exhaled with a groan. "That woman has called me six times a day, every day, since Sheridan was arrested. 'The girls' want to know every little detail — right down to exactly what the handcuffs looked like. Do you believe that? Like I even want to *think* about Sheridan's idea of leisure time."

Cara grinned. "Now, Leigh, you should be proud. You not only kept her grandson out of jail, but as far as juicy gossip goes, you've put the woman in her glory for years to come."

Leigh returned a sarcastic smile. "Great." She looked at Maura. "Speaking of jail — I assume your friend Hollandsworth won't be pestering Jared or Nikki anymore, especially now that Jared is finally back to his old self again."

Maura's cheeks flamed. "Hollandsworth never pestered Jared. He was quite polite. But that pint-sized sister of his is a flat-out maniac. If it hadn't been for your Aunt Bess, he would have arrested the girl for assaulting a police officer. Not to mention obstruction of justice."

Leigh straightened. "What *is* going on with my Aunt Bess and Hollandsworth? She won't tell me a thing, even now."

Maura's apple cheeks reddened to the max this time, and Detective Frank smiled his trademark crocodile smile. "I believe your Aunt Bess doesn't want to worry you," he said gently. "She's got this crazy idea that you have a hang-up about detective boyfriends at family gatherings."

It was Leigh's turn to flush. "Well," she said uncertainly, "that's just silly now, isn't it?"

The sound of a rising garage door rumbled through the house, and she sprang to her feet. "Warren's here," she said thankfully, moving toward the noise. "I'll be right back."

It was the perfect time to excuse herself, but she had been planning to greet her husband privately in any event. The automatic door was closing again as Warren emerged from his blue Beetle, looking glad to be home.

She stepped out into the garage to meet him, and he wrapped her in a hug that was a little firmer and a little longer than strictly necessary. He had been doing that ever since Maura had called him to pick up a shaken Leigh outside Sheridan's office, and she didn't mind it one bit.

"Gang's all here," she announced as he released her.

"Good," he said cheerfully. "And how are you?"

She smiled at the perfect opening. *"Pregnant."*

The employees of Thorndike Press hope you have enjoyed this Large Print book. All our Thorndike and Wheeler Large Print titles are designed for easy reading, and all our books are made to last. Other Thorndike Press Large Print books are available at your library, through selected bookstores, or directly from us.

For information about titles, please call:

(800) 223-1244

or visit our Web site at:

www.gale.com/thorndike
www.gale.com/wheeler

To share your comments, please write:

Publisher
Thorndike Press
295 Kennedy Memorial Drive
Waterville, ME 04901